The water covered wi formed a b fire which was consuming two small buildings. . . . The fire and the villagers made a great, roaring, incomprehensible noise. . . .

"Fedor! Fedor! Fedor!" cried a plump woman with a missing tooth.

We passed buckets for more than an hour without having any apparent effect. . . . After this, the fire did its work quickly, consuming the shacks and then itself until all that remained was smoldering ash. . . .

An Old Believer with a soot-stained beard pointed at the devastation. "Fedor Yermak," he said.

A young state trooper waded into the black ash bog. He pulled away some charred bits of stuff that wouldn't burn. Tied to a blackened pole with a blackened lock and a blackened chain were the blackened bones of a human being. . . .

Praise for the first Prester John Riordan mystery

THE COLD FRONT
"A riveting chase through a brutal Alaskan landscape, an unusual crime, an appealing hero. . . . Sean Hanlon scores a winner on his first outing."
—Robert Campbell

Available from Pocket Books

Books by Sean Hanlon

The Big Dark
The Cold Front

Published by POCKET BOOKS

Most Pocket Books are available at special quantity
discounts for bulk purchases for sales promotions, pre-
miums or fund raising. Special books or book excerpts
can also be created to fit specific needs.

For details write the office of the Vice President of
Special Markets, Pocket Books, 1230 Avenue of the
Americas, New York, New York 10020.

THE
BIG DARK

SEAN HANLON

POCKET BOOKS

New York   London   Toronto   Sydney   Tokyo

An *Original* Publication of POCKET BOOKS

POCKET BOOKS, a division of Simon & Schuster Inc.
1230 Avenue of the Americas, New York, NY 10020

ISBN: 0-671-65740-2

First Pocket Books printing November 1989

10 9 8 7 6 5 4 3 2 1

POCKET and colophon are trademarks of
Simon & Schuster Inc.

Printed in the U.S.A.

To Allie, Ollie, and Elizabeth

THE
BIG DARK

Chapter 1

I REMEMBER THAT SUMMER AS A CONFUSION OF AROMAS: herring roe and death, halibut and lust, red salmon and the dusty clothes of a dying woman.

It all happened in the shadow of Redoubt Volcano. Everything that happens on the central flatlands of Alaska's Kenai Peninsula happens in the shadow of Redoubt Volcano. It's on your left when you're driving up Thunder Road, and on your right when you're driving down Kalifornsky Beach Road. When you're in Soldotna, Redoubt can pop up almost any place—at the end of a gravel road to nowhere, or behind the phalanx of evergreen trees which protect the Kenai River from the civilization assembling along its banks. Redoubt Volcano last blew up in 1976. Then it covered Kenai, Soldotna and Baranov with a gray and gritty ash that damaged internal combustion engines but boosted the fortunes of celery, tomatoes and other salad ingredients. My friend Michael Gudunov remembers the eruption. Michael lives off the land and knows how to take care of himself. When Redoubt blew he ran around town in a gas mask his great uncle had used in the First World War.

Rachel Morgan and I moved from Anchorage to Baranov because it is one of the few regions of Alaska that has both fish and regular employment. The fish were the important thing. If Baranov had a totem pole, it would have a king salmon on the top, another salmon in the middle and a halibut sucking scum on the bottom. Life in Baranov revolves around different ways of catching fish. Michael and I were sportsmen. We used poles, the Big Beluga's secret

9

salmon jism, and gobs of little red salmon eggs to catch Kenai king salmon one at a time. Rachel was a commercial fisherman. She and her mates used sonar devices to locate schools of every sort of fish and heavy nets to haul them in by the ton.

When Rachel and I were still talking to each other, we would debate which was the more noble way of catching fish. I pled sportsmanship and artistry, while Rachel described commercial fishing as a benefit to society by which millions were fed by the labor of a few. She regarded sportsfishing as the idle vanity of romantic men.

"So you catch a big fish and then get your picture taken and then cover the poor creature with enamel and hang it on the wall. That's a waste of time, money and protein."

My troubles started with fish—Rachel's fish, as a matter of fact: the herring roe. I hope she'll read this and forgive me, although I don't know why she should. It just wasn't fair, even if it was mostly my fault.

We worked hard and had big plans. Rachel fished in the summer. She was the chief cook, slimer and occasional first mate of the *Derring Do*, a fifty-five-foot trawler with Seattle papers. In the winter she taught geography and mathematics at Baranov Elementary School to the children of crusty sourdoughs, oilfield workers, and Kenaitze Indians with Russian names. I edited the news for the *Baranov Beacon*. The sports editor had enscribed our motto on the composing room wall: "If it washes on our shores it must be news." In Baranov, of course, a lot of the news has to do with fish.

We had no children, as Rachel constantly reminded me, and a comfortable life in a fine house on Kalifornsky Beach Road, as I constantly reminded her. We drove late-model vehicles and had saved enough money to buy some stock in the *Beacon*. We would own the paper some day and I'd never have to work again. A newspaper is hell unless you own it. I learned that from Bob Hadley of the *Anchorage Herald*, but that's another story.

We lived out our special dream in our special place above Kalifornsky Beach. If the winters were too dark and too long, the summers were worth it. We took my dog Chena and her horse Natty Bumppo on easy walks along the beach. We watched the sunsets touch the blue sky and the gray water and turn them into red and gold. We saw the persistent tides of Cook Inlet chew away at the steep bluff on which we lived. We walked and talked and made love and didn't work too hard in the shadow of Redoubt Volcano.

It all turned bad after the commercial fishing season started and Boris Yermak was beaten to death with a knout.

Rachel delivered the first bit of bad news while sitting astride Natty Bumppo, a trim brown mare who doesn't like men. They had intercepted me and my big red monster pickup truck as we rolled down the driveway on our way to the *Baranov Beacon*. Natty sweated from her dash up from Kalifornsky Beach. Rachel, as usual, was calm, lovely and a bit of a snot.

"Red called while you were in the shower," she said. Natty poked her head into the cab of my truck and tried to eat my ear. Rachel tugged gently on the reins and Natty sprayed me with a horse laugh, as if to celebrate the bad news I was about to receive.

"And . . ."

"And I'm off to catch some herring roe. My plane leaves for Ketchikan this afternoon, so I've got to finish correcting final exams this morning. Red says the opening starts at six o'clock Thursday morning."

My truck and Rachel's horse grumbled in neutral while we discussed important household matters. Return the videos. Feed the horse. Walk the dog. And don't forget to pay the bills. And for God's sake wash the dishes.

"Last time the sink looked like a biology experiment," she said.

I grunted my replies, as if these things were not important. This was designed to annoy my partner, and guarantee that she would litter the house with reminders illustrated with stickman drawings of me engaged in the various responsible acts which we had discussed: here a stickman Pres eats a salad with low-calorie dressing while a stickwoman Rachel warns him to stay away from the Rig Café; there a stickman Pres changes the oil in a stickwoman Rachel's Subaru; here a stickman this, and there a stickman that. This was one of the treasured rituals of our life together. But no stickman Pres would be portrayed as bravely resisting the enchant-

11

ments of Texas women who, unbeknownst to Rachel, were the real hazard I faced while she was catching herring roe.

Natty Bumppo did an about-face and smacked me with her tail. A few more instructions and a few more grunts and we were on our separate ways—Rachel to the six-hour frenzy of the herring roe opening and me to the insurrection which my sports editor had lately begun to incite against me.

Redoubt Volcano was on my left, hiding behind a cloud of its own making, as I drove toward Baranov. It was a clear, warm day in early June, the best part of the year. The early kings were running and the cold and the dark were gone, but the tourists and the cannery workers had yet to arrive in any great number. Winnebagos already clogged the Sterling Highway on weekends, but weekdays were still pretty quiet. Memorial Day had come and gone. As my big red monster pickup truck crossed the bridge over the Kenai River, I noticed a few tentative fishing poles bobbing along the bank. I wished my own pole were among them.

The office of the *Baranov Beacon* is located at the dusty intersection of the biggest streets in town. One road starts at the airport and heads for Anchorage and is the thoroughfare for the ink, newsprint and cheap labor which is the *Beacon*'s lifeblood. The other road starts out as smooth pavement, but soon becomes a gravel gash in the woods that leads through the Baranov Municipal Golf Course and then on to Soldotna, the town upriver which is the bitter rival for tourist dollars and high school basketball supremacy of Baranov, Kenai and the other small cities of the Kenai Peninsula.

I would have liked to have spent that morning slowly composing my daily editorial and looking out of my office window at the airport and its planes' graceful landings and takeoffs, wondering which one carried Rachel away and quietly hoping that the flying and the fishing and the sliming and the canning which the herring roe required of her would be quickly and safely completed. But two minutes after I sat down, George Morton, my rebellious sports editor, quietly tiptoed into my office and closed the door behind him. These actions ensured that everyone in the tiny newsroom would peep through the glass partition as our pantomine drama unfolded.

George had the makings of a good journalist. If I hadn't

been his boss, I would have encouraged him to quit the *Beacon* and find another newspaper where his talents would be appreciated and exploited more efficiently. He possessed an orderly mind and kept an orderly desk, with a neat stack of newspapers and the *Beacon*'s most valuable Rolodex, in which could be found any telephone number of any consequence on the entire Kenai Peninsula. His one flaw was in failing to see that no amount of agitation could dislodge me from the comfortable rut I had made for myself.

George's constant complaint was that I worked too little and he and my other subordinates worked too much. He was about to make the same complaint again. He shuffled his feet and hemmed and hawed. A small commuter plane lifted off the east–west runway. It could have been Rachel's. We both watched as it made a quick turn and headed south, perhaps to Ketchikan.

"Hey George," I said, "How about those Cubs? They're going to bring a winner to Chicago yet."

He mumbled something that was agreeable in word, though not in tone and then got right to it: "I don't quite know how to say this, Pres. Everybody respects you in the newsroom. We all know about the story you wrote about the Entco pollution and the prize it won and all the rest and everybody thinks you're a great newspaperman." He took a great swallow of air. His tongue was so thick it sounded like a baseball going down. "But I think we've got a problem here. People are starting to talk."

"Starting? I thought they never stopped."

George took one step back and another to the side, as if trying to physically avoid the issue. "You've got a lot of good people in that newsroom." He looked over his shoulder to dramatize his point. Eight of them were looking back at him. "We just wish you were more involved in things. You put Byron in charge and everybody knows he's nuts while Joe breaks his back and nobody seems to notice. What's fair is fair and that isn't fair."

I had long ago learned that the pretense of good humor is the next best thing to good humor itself. There followed a long conversation during which I smiled a lot, nodded in a sincere fashion and jotted down some suggestions which I had no intention of implementing. I finished by hinting that when I left or moved up into the front office, Publisher Jack

13

Wilson's office, George might get my job, which was easily the most underworked and overpaid news job in the entire state of Alaska.

"You're the straw that stirs the drink, George. You are the tie that binds. I appreciate your coming in here. It takes a big man to talk to his boss like you talk to me. I'll think about what you said."

Before he could say anything more, I shook his hand. He looked at it, as if worried a booger had rubbed off and retreated to the newsroom. I watched another airplane land.

George had set me up for the second bit of bad news, which was delivered by Michael Gudunov, my friend who'd worn a gas mask when Redoubt Volcano erupted.

I began to compose an editorial about the need for oil exploration in the Arctic National Wildlife Refuge. Since this was the only real work I had to do that day, it took me a very long time to do it. I wrote the first paragraph as if Jack Wilson were looking over one shoulder. As publisher of the *Beacon,* he was a staunch defender of the oil industry. I wrote the second paragraph as if Rachel were looking over my other shoulder. Rachel was a staunch defender of the environment and a dedicated adversary of oil companies in general and Alaskan oil companies in particular. After about ninety minutes and six delicately-balanced paragraphs, Jack's shade had run out of arguments, leaving me about four paragraphs of balanced punditry shy of that which I needed to fill up the editorial page.

So I decided, at the worst possible moment, to take a walk to the water cooler and think about Jack's next paragraph. When I stepped out of my office, the receptionist announced over the intercom for everyone to hear: "Phone call for Prester John Riordan on line three. Pres, you have a call on line three."

A nervous silence came over the newsroom as I picked up the phone on Byron's desk. Everyone looked at me for a moment and then turned away to fuss with whatever papers were closest at hand. Unsolicited phone calls usually mean work, and are to be avoided at all costs. Greta grabbed her purse and ran out the door.

Michael was on the line. He often called me at work to invite me to go fishing or drinking or both. When Rachel was gone, I'd usually go. But this time he had something else on his mind. "Hey, Shorter-Than-I. You want some news?"

News was about the last thing anybody at the *Beacon* wanted just then, but I couldn't expect Michael to understand that. "Yeah, sure. What have you got?"

"I got a little birdie that told me the troopers found a dead one on the road to Vyg." This was a pronouncable nickname for Vygovskaia Pustyn, an unpronounceable village where the Old Believers lived. "It sounds pretty weird, Short Man. You oughta check it out."

Timing is the mother of luck, be it good or bad. Michael hung up, but I kept the receiver to my ear and nodded sagely so that I could have a moment to think before deciding what to do. Thanks to George, the issue of my "involvement in the newsroom" was on everybody's mind, and everybody was looking at me while pretending to look at their notes or their computers. And, of course, I had nothing much to do but finish that editorial and watch some more light planes drift in and out of town. I'd planned to take a long lunch followed by a longer walk and then return in time to push my people through deadline. After work maybe I'd drink some beer with Michael. On the way home, I'd pick up two chili cheese dogs and a movie to help get my mind off of Texas women. That had been the plan, before George said I should get more involved in the newsroom.

A wise man with no choice becomes enthusiastic about the inevitable. "Holy shit!" I screeched into the dead receiver. "That sounds pretty big. Maybe I should take this one for myself. How far down the road is the body?"

I let the word "body" twirl in the swirl of haste I left behind me. Baranov and its *Beacon* are still small enough for murder to be the cause of considerable excitement.

It was a pleasant drive down Kalifornsky Beach Road. Redoubt vented steam and the snow geese were making their annual visit to the tidal flats, where they refueled for the last leg of their spring migration to their mating grounds on Wrangell Island.

The ride became bumpy when I turned onto the road to Vyg. Cars and trucks had carved deep ruts into the mud left behind by the melting snow. A few days of sunshine had baked the ruts into rock-hard trenches that were a little too close together to comfortably accommodate the wheels of my big red monster pickup truck. The road twisted through deep ravines and past enormous rocks which had been left behind by a retreating glacier. The rocks had served as signs for more than 10,000 years. Lately they pointed to Vyg village in two languages and two alphabets, Russian Cyrillic and our own.

The road to Vyg was exactly the sort of road the people who lived there wanted it to be. The Old Believers had refused offers by the state and the borough to pave the road or smooth it down or grade it with gravel. They wanted the only road to their village to be an almost impassable destroyer of wheels and axles and mufflers so that causal tourists and curiosity seekers would be discouraged from visiting Vygovskaia Pustyn. People who wanted to see what Russian peasants looked like three hundred years ago were advised to turn back and go visit Nikolaevsk instead. Vyg and Nikolaevsk used to be one community, but it split over the issues of power tools and radio. Vyg considered these things to be temptations to sin while Nikolaevsk regarded them as blessings from the Almighty. The men of both villages made fine fishing boats and caught a lot of fish. They sold the fish to brokers for a hard-bargained price and turned the cash to gold. The people of Baranov gossip a lot about Old Believer gold, and wonder where it's hidden: under a tree or in a secret Swiss safety deposit box?

An ambulance and a couple of Alaska State Trooper squad cars were stacked up beside the road about halfway between the main highway and the village. The troopers shuffled through the bushes, poking around and looking at their feet. They had marked the area with bright yellow plastic strips, which lent a festive aspect to what looked like a uniformed Easter egg hunt. Peek-A-Boo Pete directed the activity from atop a rock ground smooth by the action of a glacier.

"Hey Peek," I said. "What's the story?"

The lawman turned to me. His face said it all: horror, fear, anger, nausea and confusion. Plenty of confusion. Peek-A-Boo Pete was a simple man enchanted with his own simple power. He was perfectly suited for police work in an isolated rural community. He'd gotten his name from his habit of hiding behind K-Beach Hamburger Heaven, where he caught up on his sleep and snagged the occasional speeder.

He was aware of his limits and seemed to be very comfortable with them.

"I called up to Anchorage for some reinforcements. Right now, we're just doing what the book says—sifting through the ground over by where the body was. Looking for evidence. You bring your camera?"

I nodded uncertainly. I had as much right taking pictures as Peek had investigating a murder. Neither of us quite knew how to proceed.

"What sort of evidence are you looking for?" I asked.

"We won't know until we find it." At that he turned around and began issuing new instructions. I retrieved my camera and started taking pictures of the troopers in action.

There was a brown smudge of blood where the body had lain before the paramedics had carted it away. They'd left behind an outline made with some lime powder that reminded me of the batter's box at Wrigley Field. The man had perished in the image of the crucified Christ, his legs and feet close together, his arms spread wide to embrace his own death. I took a picture of Peek standing near the spot. Then I took a picture of the spot. A young female trooper poked at the weeds where a lime halo should have gone. I took a picture of her. It looked like she was gardening.

I began to jot down some of the overripe prose which had become the *Beacon*'s trademark since Jack hired me: "His Golgotha was a chilly nook surrounded by trees ready to burst out in summer. But who was his Judas? And who was his Pontius Pilate? Did two Marys from the Ukraine weep for this holy man in peasant garb?"

All I needed were some facts. "Hey Peek," I said. "Was he dressed like an Old Believer? You know. Peasant shirt and Cossack boots?"

Peek said, "Mr. Ivan Smolensk here found the deceased while walking to Vyg, or at least that's what I think he said. Mr. Smolensk is one of those people who don't speak very much English."

Peek-A-Boo Pete pointed at a man of middle age with a full beard and the traditional Russian clothes worn by the Old Believers of Nikolaevsk and Vygovskaia Pustyn: soft leather knee boots, wool trousers and a billowing shirt with a stiff collar buttoned down the side. A bright red belt was tightened around his narrow waist. He had wide cheeks, a narrow chin and brown

17

hair parted down the middle. His eyes were averted from my own, more in anger than in shame.

"Mr. Smolensk here is a resident of the Vyg village. He can't say too much, but I got out of him that the deceased is a Mr. Boris Yermak, also of Vyg village. If I understand what he's trying to say, Mr. Smolensk here ran ten miles all the way up the road to report the incident. We'll take him to Baranov for questions and a formal statement as soon as we secure the area. We'll get the Native priest to translate, I suppose."

I lifted my camera and started shooting. Ivan Smolensk hung down his head, the muscles of his neck twitching with rage. Up close, he looked sullen, angry. Farther away, he looked guilty. Peek wouldn't let me get too close.

I was loading in another roll of film when a trooper yelled, in a tone too jubilant for the occasion: "Captain Roberts! Over here."

We hurried after the voice. I was anxious to see what **had** been discovered before it was surrounded by a bright yellow cordon. The trooper was pointing to an evergreen tree reduced to white splinters stripped of their bark.

Peek looked at the trooper. The trooper looked at Peek. "What's that?" I said. They both looked at me.

Peek bit his lips, but the truth was too horrible to keep to himself. Some secrets rot the soul from the inside out. "The body looked like he was flogged to death with some kind of whip. His clothes were shredded and his back was too. The killer must have tied him to the tree and then stripped away the bark to show him what the whip could do. The killer must have wanted something more than just to kill him, because he peeled him real good. Some of his ribs showed through."

Peek let out a gust of air. I thought it was a sigh, but the female trooper interpreted it as a command. She hustled up and snapped to attention. "Go get Mr. Smolensk and bring him over here."

The flayed tree had a remarkable effect on the Old Believer. He stepped close and leaned over, bracing his broad Slavic shoulders, as if preparing himself for his turn with the whip. His anger was gone, betrayed by hate. He didn't look sullen or guilty any more. He made the sign of the cross and mumbled something in a language I didn't understand. He made another sign of the cross and spat out a word that sounded like he'd spit an iron nail into a tin bucket.

I followed the troopers back to Baranov. We filed past the trailers of the oilfield workers and the cabins of the pioneers, to the ramshackled Old Town where the Kenaitze Indians lived. The archpriest and my friend Michael were discussing an old cast-iron bathtub when our caravan drove into the parking lot of St. Alexander Nevsky Russian Orthodox Church. Michael was the church handyman, because he liked Mrs. Nyuknuvuk's cooking and usually had nothing better to do. One of his jobs as handyman was to help the archpriest battle the tides of Cook Inlet, which were eroding the bluff on which the church and his home were located.

His congregation believed that their church was the oldest standing building in Alaska. They couldn't prove that this was so, but they acted as if it was. It was built by traders in 1794, when Gov. Aleksandr Baranov was the czar of American Russia.

The archpriest nodded his head and Michael slammed his great, blubbery bulk against the bathtub, knocking it over the edge of the bluff. The two men watched as it crashed onto the pile of junk they had deposited on the beach below.

Peek approached Father Nyuknuvuk while two of his troopers stood guard over Ivan Smolensk. "Still at it, Father?" Peek asked.

The archpriest nodded. He and Michael were building a riprap barricade that was supposed to slow the erosion of ground on which the church had stood for almost two hundred years. "We do whatever we can. I don't know if it works, but it makes me feel a little better. What do you need from me?"

Peek explained the situation, nodding every now and then at the sullen Ivan Smolensk. Ivan and the archpriest talked in Russian for a while, until they got to the word that sounded like spitting a nail in a bucket.

Father Nyuknuvuk said, "That's a knout. It's a Russian whip that the boyars used to beat the peasants into submission. This is Old Russia we're talking about, before the Communists came. A knout is strips of leather knotted up and dried in milk. It doesn't sound like much, but it'll skin a man alive, which is a very Russian way to die. The killer was a Russian. I'm pretty sure of that."

Chapter 2

I WROTE THE STORY IN MY HEAD WHILE DRIVING BACK TO the *Beacon*. It was a sad tale about death and faith, with a few details about the Old Believers. They'd come here in 1958 from Oregon. Before that they lived in Brazil, before that in Soviet Russia. They believed in God, work, fish and the internal combustion engine. They scorned Western clothes, modern appliances and the English language as enticements of the Antichrist, but delighted in Fords, Chevys and Subaru pickups with roll bars. They did not trust non-believers, and liked to haggle over the price of fish.

It was after dinnertime when I climbed the stairs to my second-floor office. It would soon be time to put the *Beacon* to bed and dream of Texan women. I wrote my story again, but used a computer this time.

I asked Byron to read it, because he was devoted to correct spelling, proper grammar and bizarre conspiracy theories. He believed the world to be a hostile but logical place. I let him wield power during my many vacations so that Jack would know that if he ever became disenchanted with me his only alternative would be to replace me with a lunatic.

Byron read my story while chewing on a celery stalk. He said, "Okay. I give up. What's a knout?"

"It's a whip they used in Russia before the Reds took over."

This sort of thing appealed to Byron's suspicious nature. "You mean 'whip' as in 'forty lashes with the whip?' "

20

"That's right. That's how the czar kept the peace. His soldiers used to flog criminals with the knout."

"Shouldn't you put something like that in your story? Nobody's going to know what a knout is."

Sometimes Byron was right. That's why conspiracy theorists are so dangerous. "Take care of it for me, will you? I've got to go over the pictures with Ronda."

Ronda was the most important person in my newsroom. She was young and pretty, the mother of three and the wife of none. Fortunately for me, she was not of Texan extraction. Even so, she was the fulcrum of a newsroom love triangle that didn't make any sense. Joe, one of my reporters, loved Ronda, my staff photographer. Ronda loved Byron, and Byron loved dark conspiracies and had a dark and conspiratorial wife, who wrote a column for *Survival Magazine*. No one loved Joe, which was why I was able to get so much work out of him without paying any overtime.

Ronda laid the proof sheet on my desk. It contained two dozen miniature photographs from the place where Boris Yermak was killed. She said, "I think we've got three ways to go: fuzzy, crooked and boring."

I longed for the days of the knout. As staff photographer, Ronda considered it her duty to resent every photograph that she had not taken herself. She regarded the *Beacon*'s policy that reporters should take many of their own photographs as an insult to her profession.

"How would you feel if the pressmen started writing editorials?" she asked.

I would feel relieved, but I didn't tell her this. Instead, I said, "But this is a small paper, Ron. We all have to do our part."

She was right and I was wrong. The proof was all on film. The taped outline of where the body was found looked like a Saturday morning cartoon with technical difficulties. Ivan Smolensk leaned like the Tower of Pisa, while Peek was clear and straight but unexpressive.

"This is our lead story," I said, "and we need some art. What do you suggest?"

"I suggest we hire another photographer and then maybe stop taking a picture every time some politician shakes hands with some businessman."

"I'll think about that. Now what about page one? We're

on deadline here and I really don't have any time to discuss the finer points of photography. Not that I don't want to, but what do you think we should do?"

She threw out the fuzzy cartoon and drew a box around the Old Believer's face. "If we crop it like this and don't run it too big, we can straighten the frame out and maybe it won't look too bad. Run it in a box with the picture of Peek-A-Boo. Then you'll have a picture of a witness looking guilty and a bozo looking competent."

Ronda smiled. Byron stopped typing. George looked up from the rows of baseball statistics neatly arranged on his desk. Quiz time: Does our editor have any scruples?

I have some, but they have nothing to do with news. Still I saw no reason that they should know that, and so I said, "Let's run Peek in a box with a quote in big type. We'll put the guilty-looking picture on file and maybe we can use it some other time."

Ronda disappeared into the darkroom and began the strange, chemical process which produces photographs. George returned to his batting averages. Byron put the finishing touches on my Old Believer story. I edited his story about a conspiracy of silence on the planning and zoning commission. That and a story by Greta on Baranov Girl Scout Troop #563 numbed my brain into submission. It was almost 10 P.M. and the paper had to be done by midnight. It was time to cut the print, smear it with wax and lay it on the page.

The composing room of the *Baranov Beacon* was a breeding ground of discontent. It was where inflamed egos with college degrees and unattainable ambitions nicked their fingers, sweated too much and smeared their hands with ink and wax.

"Fuckin' shit. Goddamn." That was Joe getting to work. Ronda plugged a tape into her ghetto blaster and turned up the volume. Some blue-collar blues by Bob Seger and Bruce Springsteen made the work seem more heroic.

Joe flailed away at the columns of print like one of those knife-throwing cooks in a Japanese restaurant. He wanted to impress Ronda and to save her hands from the corrosive effects of ink and wax. She didn't notice him because she wanted to save Byron from an unhappy life with a crazy wife and needed a man to help raise her three young children.

That Ronda thought Byron and not Joe should be this man
was one of the sad comedies of life.

"Fuckin' shit. Goddamn," Joe said. Bruce sang about a
stolen car and Seger sang about a bottle of wine.

The reader sees the shiny side of a newspaper. That's the
side with boldface headlines and columns of meaningful
gray. To make the shiny side stick to the page, the other
side, the underside, is coated with cheap wax. Then triangle
rulers and Exacto knives are used to trim the print and cut
the photographs down to size. The headlines and the type
and the pictures are all laid out with the shiny side up and
the waxy side down on white sheets covered with blue grids.
When the pages are assembled they are taken to the camera
room where a negative is shot for placement on the printing
press.

Most newspapers pay high school graduates $15 an hour
to do all this stuff. The *Baranov Beacon* paid college graduates $8.50 an hour to do this after they had gathered and
written the stories, taken and processed the photographs.
Bob Seger sang the blue-collar blues.

I said, "You got a bad headline over here, Ronda."

"What's the problem, Pres?"

An Exacto knife whizzed across the room and embedded
itself in the cork board above the wax machine. Ronda was
impressed until she saw that it was Joe who had flung it. Joe
cursed again and buried his face in his hands. A little nubbin
of upside down headline—PLANNERS MUM—had attached
itself to the cuff of his shirt.

I pointed to Ronda's error. "The Iditarod Trial? I think it
should probably be 'Trail'—T-r-a-i-l . . . although it's a trial
too."

Ronda scraped the headline off the page and sat down at
the computer to summon up a corrected version. Joe yanked
his Exacto knife from the cork board and George turned his
lead sports page into a thing of prissy beauty.

There was plenty of work to do, and I didn't want to do
any of it, so I drifted upstairs to slowly, slowly finish the
editorial I'd started that afternoon. Jack's shade still didn't
have anything more to say about drilling for oil in caribou
country, so I recycled some of our standard drivel about
how "Oil is good." Oil is always good at the *Baranov*

Beacon. That's because Baranov is at one end of Thunder Road, which leads to the oil refinery at Nikiski.

I fussed and fiddled with the editorial for an hour or so, until Joe tapped on my door and announced that page one was ready for my inspection and, except for a hole where my editorial would go, the paper was all filled up.

After page one was examined and the hole filled in, I said, "Let's go have a beer."

Joe looked at Ronda. She said no. "I better go home too," Joe added. "I'm supposed to have the bridal section done this week." George, the rebellious sports editor, had no such obligations, and we were on our way.

Unattended Texas women gathered at Baranov Bill's Bar and Grill. Baranov has plenty of Texas women. They are hazardous by-products of the oil industry. The young ones wear tight jeans and loose, sleeveless blouses which promise a flash of bosom to the attentive observer. Their mothers wear red lipstick and red shoes and henna in their hair. Both generations are tough and sexy. They drink hard on Saturday night and pray hard on Sunday morning. Their perfume stuck to my clothes, their beauty to the dark parts of my dreams. The fever got worse whenever Rachel went off on one of her commercial fishing expeditions.

A long-limbed beauty with spike heels and blue jean skin stepped up to the jukebox and leaned over the songs. She punched out twenty numbers in fifteen seconds. Most of them were "Your Cheatin' Heart."

George and I ordered a pitcher of beer and arranged ourselves around a curve in the bar that provided a good view of the jukebox, just in case the woman with the spiked heels and the blue jean skin wanted to play some more Hank Williams. George droned on about sports and working hard while I watched a woman in a cowboy hat dance the Texas Two-Step with a bony man a foot and a half taller than she.

After a while, as I'd expected, the door flew open and the massive girth of Michael Gudunov filled the frame. I tipped my beer glass in his direction and he waddled over to our corner of the bar. He grabbed one glass and two barstools, for it took two stools to support the huge rolls of fat which seemed to shift around his hips like the tides themselves.

Michael is only one of the treasures the Russians left

behind when they sold Alaska to the United States to pay for the Crimean War. There's the blistering onion dome of St. Alexander Nevsky Church and the bits of bullets and rusty tools the soldiers left scattered at the site of old Fort Kenay. The czar's fur traders built a couple of fishing villages, a road, a beach and a school and left behind several dozen Natives named Kalifornsky, because California also used to be a Russian colony.

But the biggest and the greatest and strangest treasure of them all was my friend Michael Gudunov. Michael weighed upward of four hundred pounds, but moved as quietly as a sailing ship in the night. He had the slow, gliding grace which God gives fat men in compensation for their malady. No one knew for sure where he lived or how he supported his gargantuan appetite for American junk food. He was liable to turn up anywhere: throwing scrap metal onto the beach below St. Alexander Nevsky's Church, as he had done that afternoon, or minding the checkout counter at Big Beluga's Bait and Tackle Shop; bossing a crew of college students at the Setnet Cannery or selling black market caribou steaks to the roughneck oilfield workers who lived along Thunder Road. He spent a lot of his time washing other people's laundry and watching his favorite soap opera at the Baranov Wash and Dry.

The sad fact of Michael Gudunov's life was that neither his Native blood nor his Russian Orthodox faith had prepared him for the seductions of American advertising. He no sooner saw a commercial for chips or burgers or Ding Dongs or Häagen-Dazs or Wheat Thins with Cheez Whiz or Froot Loops or Nalley's Chili or salted Nut Logs than he must eat the product and wash it down with an ice-cold can of Diet Coke.

"Hey, how you doing, Shorter-Than-I?" he said while pounding me on the back with a big left hand. He called me this for the obvious reason that I was the only one of his close friends who was Shorter-Than-He.

Short or not, Michael was the stuff of legend. His heart will probably give up soon, but until then the man cannot be destroyed. He carried a leather pouch with chromium-tipped darts which he used to separate cannery workers and other gullible gamblers from their paychecks. They tell the story of an oilfield worker from Nikiski who pulled a gun on

Michael and refused to pay. Some say they screamed and argued, but before the roughneck could pull the trigger, Michael placed a dart between his fifth and sixth ribs. Others say the roughneck shot Michael in the chest, but that the bullet became embedded in fat several inches short of his heart. And *then* Michael split his ribs with a dart.

Or so the stories go. Like another wild tale they tell about the Big Beluga, this story is not to be believed so much as it is to be admired, like a fancy hat or a big red monster pickup truck. I can neither confirm nor deny its accuracy, but I do let Michael call me Shorter-Than-I, which has made him my constant friend and occasional drinking companion.

"So where'd you get the news tip?" I asked once he had settled onto his barstools.

He shrugged his shoulders. One of the barstools groaned. "So let's go fishing tomorrow. The kings are running real good now, so the tourists'll probably start fishing this weekend. I already caught a lunker with a smashed jaw, but I threw him back. The Big Beluga wants to check the Vyg River and see how the rocks got shifted by the freeze."

I considered this proposition while Michael poured himself a beer. The Big Beluga was a part-time fishing guide and a full-time employee of the Kenai Peninsula Borough Public Works Department. He somehow managed to spend more time fishing than repairing potholes. He tells an incredible story about how he'd got his nickname, which I will relate at another time.

"I don't think so, Mike. I've got something else on my mind."

"That's your problem. Too much on your mind. Not enough fishing."

We talked about the murder of Boris Yermak. Michael already knew more than I thanks to his connection with Father Nyuknuvuk. He said Boris and Ivan had fought in the street over a television set. "The cops are using Father Nick to translate the Russian for this Ivan guy. It looks like the Old Believer's gonna take the fall, on account of this television thing, but he still won't wanna talk to Father Nick and he especially doesn't wanna talk to the cops."

"How come?"

Michael looked forlornly at his glass and at the pitcher. Both were empty. I suppose he was broke. He usually was.

"It's some old Russian thing. I don't know too much about it. . . . Hey, George, you wanna throw some darts?"

George wasn't drunk enough to fall for that one yet, but he was getting there. He shook his head and headed for the pool table.

"What old Russian thing?" I asked.

"I don't know for sure, but it's got to do with the Old Belief. The Old Believers think Father Nick is working for the Antichrist. They think that about everybody that isn't one of them. They are crazy people, but very rich. I heard they got a mountain full of gold hidden in the crater of some volcano. When it blows up it'll rain gold dust for a week and then we'll all be rich, but I'm a little short of money right now. Why don't you buy me a beer?"

The second pitcher of beer lured George back to our part of the bar. We talked about sports until the pitcher was gone. I switched to bottled beer. One for me and one for Michael.

"What do you know about the Old Believers?" I asked.

Michael said he didn't know much. They dressed funny, spoke Russian and liked fancy cars. They fished Cook Inlet in brightly-painted boats and never spent a penny on anything, except for fancy cars.

"What about the knout?"

He thought I said, "What about the In-Out?," or pretended to hear me wrong. In any case, he pulled out his darts. "Come on, man. Let's do a game."

The old In-Out is a complicated game requiring unerring aim and considerable mathematical ability. Michael's darts were dwarfed by his girth. Each of his four hundred pounds participated in every throw, starting with a rhythmic two-step, winding into a swivel of the belly and ending with a flick of the fingers. It was as if an elephant was giving birth to mosquitos.

We played for a thousand dollars. This sounds like a lot, but I already owed him more than a million. He let me win a few thousand back, in the hopes that some cowboy bikers from Nikiski could be drawn into a challenge. But the bikers were more interested in pool and Texas women. Michael agreed to give it up on the condition that I buy another pitcher.

He sloshed down two quick glasses and poured himself a third. For a few long minutes, he became very still. I tried to

27

talk, but he ignored me. It was as if my friend was in a trance. Finally, he blinked his eyes and said, "They're nuts."

"Who's that?"

"The Old Believers when they had this big fight about TV. Figure that. How can you fight about something that's as happy as television? Because they're nuts, that's how."

I tried to develop this line of discussion, but the beer was having its effect. My questions were as fuzzy as Michael's answers. Our conversation lost its sense of direction. We talked about TV, sports, Communism and the knout. We used half thoughts and incomplete sentences. Michael challenged George to a game of darts and this time George was drunk enough to accept. I left Baranov Bill's Bar and Grill. On the way home I stopped by the 7-Eleven and picked up two chili cheese dogs and a dirty movie to help me sleep. I think it was *Debbie Does Dallas*, but I never got around to watching it.

Chena was waiting for me when I got home, sleeping on the stairs so that I couldn't get in without waking her. Chena was about 120 years old in dog years. She must have spent at least a hundred of them sleeping. I don't blame her. Her dreams seemed much more exciting than her waking life. In her dreams, she would run and bark and chase after rabbits that in reality had outdistanced her aging legs many years ago.

In her waking hours, she mostly scratched and licked herself, sniffed dead things on the beach and took an occasional leak. But age had not diminished her appetite for chili cheese dogs, although Rachel's constant warnings about cholesterol and worms had diminished their availability. This only made them taste better on the rare occasions that I was able to sneak some into the house. She wolfed down one. I wolfed down the other.

Then we went for a walk. The moonlight bounded off Redoubt Volcano. The sea was a big black nothing that reminded me how lonely I got when Rachel went fishing. The tides made a big, black everything sound as they broke against the land.

Chapter 3

THE NEXT MORNING, IVAN SMOLENSK WAS CHARGED WITH murder in the first degree. A preliminary hearing was held in the Baranov District Court to read the charges. In the gallery were myself, Peek-A-Boo Pete and Father Nyuknuvuk. A stout woman wearing a babushka and a heavy peasant dress attended with equal efficiency to her knitting and seven solemn children. Their father never looked up from the floor. His preliminary bail was set at one million dollars. The judge appointed a Lindy Sue Baker to represent him. She did not attend the hearing, but her name alone made my palms perspire.

After the hearing, I attempted to intercept the archpriest in the lobby, but was myself waylaid by Peek-A-Boo Pete, who proudly informed me that most murders are solved within thirty-six hours of the initial report.

"Nice job, Peek. But you don't really think this Smolensk guy did it, do you?"

"Absolutely." He was well-prepared for the question and recited his answer. "We have a motive and we have certain physical evidence and we have the fact that the suspect refuses to answer our questions or say anything in his own defense."

I asked him about the motive and he said something incoherent about a television set. When I asked him to elaborate, he turned and walked away.

I called after him, "Hey Peek . . . what's the deal on this public defender?" I checked my notebook, as if her name

29

wasn't already tattooed on the dirty part of my brain. "What's her name . . . this Rindy . . ."

"Lindy, short for Belinda. Lindy Sue Baker. Don't know much about her except she's new in town, just up from Outside. Sounds like some more of that Texas twat to me."

That's what I was afraid of.

I stopped by the *Beacon* just long enough to assign a few stories, pound out an editorial and put George in charge of the composing room for the Friday edition. It seemed fitting that he should pay the price for my increased involvement in the gathering of news, which now took me to the Old Town section of Baranov.

The city of Baranov is made of concentric layers, like one of Michael's dart boards or the rings of an old oak tree. The residents of each layer considered themselves superior enough to look down on those who lived in the other layers.

The various layers are distinguished by race, education, religion and housing. On the outskirts are to be found a wide ring of mobile homes and fine, modern houses on two-acre lots in which dwell oilfield workers, government employees and semiprofessional types like Rachel and me. The next layer is older and composed of cabins made of hand-cut birch, prefabricated shops and small office buildings. Here dwell commercial fishermen, merchants and the pioneers who "discovered" Baranov shortly after the Second World War.

At the heart of Baranov, on the bluff which is crumbling into Cook Inlet, is the ancient core of the oak, the bull's-eye of the dartboard. Here dwell Father Nyuknuvuk and his congregation. My friend Michael helps the archpriest with erosion control and occasionally attends services at the old church, as do most of the people of mixed Native and Russian blood. Their Russian ancestors fished, traded furs and built Fort Kenay on the other side of the river. Their Native ancestors fished and hunted and lived in peace for ten thousand years before the Cossacks or the pioneers or the Texans or any other white people "discovered" the place.

Old Town is an artful blend of eyesore and tourist trap. There is a tiny old Orthodox church and a tiny new Orthodox church and a statue of Aleksandr Andreyevich Baranov, the fur trader who founded the Russian American Company. Nearby is a house surrounded by a fence on which are draped fishing nets and setnet buoys. Another house is falling to pieces. A third has totem poles to attract the tourists and malevolent, misspelled signs warning them to keep away. A fourth house sits in the middle of an automobile graveyard and a fifth is about to slide down the bluff and into the sea. This is where Father Nyuknuvuk, his wife Tatiana and their ten raucous children live.

I knocked on the front door, against which rested a splintering advertisement: "Visitors welcume. Enquire inside for a ture of the Historcal St. Alexander Nevsky Russian Orthodox Church."

Mrs. Nyuknuvuk answered the door. She was an attractive redhead from Baltimore with a remarkable tolerance for chaos which she had acquired during the uproar caused by her decision to marry a Native.

"Hello Pres. Come on in."

The entry to the rectory was jammed tight with all manner of things and parts of things. A carburetor with frayed wires and a deflated basketball. Boxes of canned goods and bags of rags. A shoe, a bowl of dog food and the stock and barrel of a military-style rifle that hadn't been fired in years. A dusty old dog slept blissfully amid the commotion of screaming children thanks to the deafness with which the Maker had blessed his golden years.

I screamed some pleasantries at the archpriest's wife, so they could be heard above the steady din. The noise seemed to issue from everywhere at once rather than from any one room or any one group of black- and red-haired children who charged up stairs and blasted through doors. "I'm looking for Father Nick," I said.

Tatiana smiled and said something I couldn't hear. She sat me down on lumpy couch and disappeared into a back room.

The rectory was worn down to that very comfortable condition which immediately preceeds disintegration. The walls and floors were spotless, if a bit crooked, and the few simple pieces of furniture had the smooth, faded pallor which comes from too many bottoms and constant dusting. One corner of the room featured an icon of the Virgin Mary before which were arranged some lit candles that lent a soft glow to the Mother of God. In another corner was an old television set which had been covered with cloth and now functioned as a chess table.

There was soft rustling from behind the couch, but before I could investigate, Tatiana came back into the room and made a motion that I should follow her. When I took my first step, her arm flicked out like a freckled whip and pulled a screaming little girl from behind the couch. She held the child at arm's length until the screams became a giggle.

"Quit screwing around Elizabeth or I'm going to tell your father."

The child answered with a scream of such high pitch and loud volume that her mother dropped her onto the couch, at which point the scream turned into giggles again. The girl bounced up and out into the backyard. We followed her.

They didn't have very much backyard left. The tides had carried most of it away. When it was gone, the tides would go to work on their house, and the onion-domed church that has stood since Russian times. The problem with Baranov is that it is washing into the sea.

To forestall this catastrophe, Father Nyuknuvuk and Michael had planted trees along the bluff and dumped old cars, oil drums, chunks of concrete and other durable junk over the edge to make a buttress of riprap on the beach sixty feet below. At high tide, the water covered the riprap and everything else. At low tide, this buffer looked like Rust-Art mocking America on a grand scale. A Chevy convertible with fins and a Frigidaire, an old kitchen table and a garbage can stuffed with gravel were piled together in no particular order.

God's great tide was winning the battle. Trees the congregation had planted two years ago were already leaning over the deteriorating bluff, dying from the exposure of their roots. Day after day, year after year, the wind and the tide were carrying Baranov away a pebble at a time. In a hundred years or so, Old Town will be gone and the tides will start working on the next layer where the pioneers live.

The great mission of Father Nyuknuvuk's life was to delay the inevitable for as long as possible. His latest recruit was a seedling spruce that had been donated to the cause by the Kalifornsky family and delivered to the rectory in an old wheelbarrow.

"Someone to see you, Nicholas," Tatiana said.

The archpriest looked up from the hole he was digging. A squint darkened his eyes and his mouth tightened into a thin, disapproving line. He was a Native man of middle age with a stringy black beard. His cassock was spotted with dirt and sweat and worn to a rag at the elbows and the knees.

"Good afternoon, Mr. Riordan. Wait where you're at and I'll be with you in a little bit."

The archpriest and his wife wheeled the seedling closer to the bluff and lifted it down to the ground. The dirtbag was poorly attached with splintering twine and leaked black dirt onto the ground. Tatiana scooped up the dirt with her hands and dropped it into the hole they'd dug. After they laid the seedling in, and consecrated it with a brief prayer, the archpriest said, "Fill it up, will you dear? So I can talk to our guest. Now pack it down but not too tight. A tree is alive and needs room to breathe." He turned to me. "God reclaims his own, Mr. Riordan."

All this talk of God was giving me a bellyache. I try to be faithful to the agnosticism which is the journalist's natural creed. "How's that, Father?"

"The church. Give it another fifty years and it will slide down the bluff and be claimed by the sea." He gave me a smile I was not meant to understand. "Of course, it's God's house and God's sea to do with as He pleases. I am just the poor fool stuck between them. I try to do His will, but sometimes it's hard to figure out just what it is He wants me to do. So I plant seedlings that will never grow up and build a wall of junk that will hold back the tide for a little while more in case He decides to change His mind."

Tatiana had finished filling the hole. Her husband inspected the work, and then gave her leave to go shopping at the grocery store. "I saw you at the hearing," he said to me.

"That's why I'm here. I need your help . . . but if now is a bad time . . ."

He grabbed me by the elbow and led me toward the rectory. "No, no. Now is a fine time, but I don't have much to say."

Chapter 4

FATHER NICHOLAS BOBOVICH NYUKNUVUK WAS A POOR man with the responsibilities of a rich one. He was born in Sitka, which had once been the capital of Old Russian Alaska, and educated at the Baltimore College of Christian Orthodoxy, where he became only the third candidate of Native blood to be ordained in the priesthood. There he met and wooed Tatiana, the daughter of Patriarch Philip Ilyich Orlov, the highest ranking clergyman in the Baltimore province. His Holiness was incensed at his daughter's stubborn affection for the interloper and relieved when they moved to Alaska, where the scandal of their marriage would be obscured by distance.

Father Nicholas and Tatiana supported their ten unruly half-breeds on a beggar's income supplemented by the guided tours they gave of Old Town to the visitors who wandered their way. For another dollar, he would unlock the door to St. Alexander Nevsky Russian Orthodox Church and let them look inside. No pictures, please. This commerce earned him the disdain of certain town leaders from the pioneer and petroleum layers of Baranov who dislike Natives and know nothing of the poverty to which a small congregation dooms its spiritual leader.

The archpriest's nose was a monument to godly engineering. It had been scratched and rubbed and picked and poked and broken several times. It had endured almost forty Alaska winters. The constant sniffling and sneezing should have long ago loosened the nose from its moorings, but still it clung to the clergyman's face. It was flat and as big as a small man's fist.

Other features of the archpriest deserved examination. He smelled of fish, like everyone else in Baranov. His stringy beard and sparse mustache were speckled with gray. His tattered cassock was draped over round, tired shoulders. The hem was shredded by having been stepped on time and time again by combat boots of the sort worn by street toughs in the Chicago of my youth. He was short and stout, like most Native men, but his time Outside had given him a hard edge uncommon to his race. His coal-black eyes would glow sometimes, and made him look like a demented prophet when he denounced the sins of Baranov from the pulpit of his church. When not protected by the pulpit, he indulged in many nervous gestures also alien to Native people—hand-wringing and throat-clearing and the like. His voice had a deep resonance which his flock must have found reassuring.

But it was his nose which commanded respect and it was his nose that he rubbed as he directed me to sit down at the kitchen table. The clamor of the house had subsided to a low rumble punctuated by occasional thumps and bangs. "Would you like some tea, Mr. Riordan?"

I nodded. "Yes, Father. If you don't mind." I said this not so much because I wanted refreshment, but because the preparations would give us both a little time to collect our thoughts.

But my thoughts remained uncollected. The archpriest disappeared into a back room and returned moments later pushing a cart on which was set an ornate contraption of regal style and proportion. It most resembled a potbellied stove as might be used by hobbits or elves or some other sort of tiny being. It was about two feet tall and made of well-polished brass. Two sturdy wooden handles protruded from the widest part of the potbelly. There were other knobs and brass attachments of uncertain purpose. Much of the surface had been etched with a great complication of lines and swirls. Carved into that part of the base which faced me were seven letters of the Cyrillic alphabet peculiar to Russians and other Slavic peoples.

"This is a samovar, Mr. Riordan. We use it to brew our tea."

I watched as the archpriest removed one of the knobs and

poured water into the hole it had plugged. From a drawer in the pushcart he retrieved a leather pouch out of which tumbled five small coals. He lit one and dropped it down a chimneylike hole in the top of the samovar. After making sure it burned hot enough, he dropped the other coals in after it.

We waited and talked about nothing of importance. He poured a precisely measured amount of tea into another hole in the samovar. We waited and talked some more. I didn't know where to begin.

"Tell me, Mr. Riordan. Why does this case interest you?"

"Well, it's a little hard to explain, Father. But it's news. Big news. The way he died, in the shape of a cross and all, seems to have religious overtones. And the whip. And the Old Believers are a story in themselves."

"I assure you, Mr. Riordan, that the Old Believers do not want that story told by you or anybody else. All they want is to be left alone. Can you understand that? Why must you newspeople make a circus out of everything? This isn't news. It's a tragedy."

"But it is news, Father. When somebody gets killed in a place like this, everybody wants to know about it."

"Yes, of course. Brutality sells newspapers. People like to read about the misery of others. It makes their own lives seem a little less dreadful. These people should pray more and read less."

The archpriest touched his hand to the swelling middle of the samovar. He seemed disappointed, although I'm not sure whether it was with my news judgment or with the rate of percolation. He looked up at me. I think he could see right through to the back of my head.

"It's not just the way he died, but that's part of it. The Old Believers should be left alone if they want, but not if they start killing each other and especially not by the way he was whipped with a . . . with a . . . what is it you call that thing?"

"A knout, Mr. Riordan."

"That's it. A knout. Tell me more about it."

He explained that the word comes from the Swedish for "knot." Made of leather straps dipped in milk and dried under a hot sun, the result is rock-hard and heavy and can kill a man with just a few strokes. Viking invaders brought this instrument along when they navigated the Russian river system and used it to subjugate the unlettered peasants who lived along its banks. The czars who came to power later used the knout for a similar purpose.

"It was an old family tradition, Mr. Riordan. Peter the Great had his son beaten to death with a knout."

The archpriest touched his hand to the samovar again. This time he was satisfied. He fetched two cups from a cabinet and set them down on paper towels laid out on the kitchen table. He tugged gently on a ring above the spout and deep green tea spilled into the cup. He handed the cup to me. Its handle was broken. The brew was piping hot and smelled of unfamiliar spices.

I asked the archpriest if he thought Ivan Smolensk had killed Boris Yermak, but my question was drowned out by a great commotion coming from the living room. When the noise subsided, I asked the question again.

"No."

"Then why don't he defend himself?"

The archpriest leaned over his cup and took a deep swallow. A brown drop collected on his mustache. "The Old Believers are a curious people, Mr. Riordan. They haven't changed their way of thinking or their style of dress in more than three hundred years. They're sort of like your Amish people in that respect. They distrust some innovations and embrace others. They like cars but not telephones, for instance. They're always on the lookout for the Devil and the Antichrist. They see them under every bed. Right now, they think the General Secretary of the Soviet Communist Party is the Antichrist and for some reason regard me as his agent. Ivan won't talk to me. I tried to explain this to Peek-A-Boo Pete, but he's not the sort of man who can handle more than one idea at a time."

"Who are the Old Believers? What do they believe?"

The archpriest stood up and put his teacup down. He spun around on his heels, as if he wanted to move but didn't know where to go. He started to walk around in ever-widening circles, his hands clasped behind his back and his eyes fastened on the floor. In a singsong voice that was almost a chant, he talked about the Old Believers and what they believed: about the Patriarch Nikon and the reforms he imposed on Orthodox Christians in the year 1659; about

37

their rejection of all things Western, except for the automobile and certain power tools useful in the manufacture of pastel fishing boats; about their struggles with Peter the Great, Czarina Elizabeth, Alexander, Napoleon and dozens of other Antichrists heralding the end of a world that stubbornly refused to end.

"I think it comforts them to have the Devil around. They can understand the Devil and his demons. The Communists confuse them."

The circle he was walking had widened to encompass most of the kitchen. He stepped out into the living room, where there was more room to walk. I followed him.

"They'd set themselves on fire. The soldiers of the czar would come to arrest them for not paying taxes or not saying the proper prayers or not joining the army. The Old Believers would all gather in one room, lock the door and set themselves on fire. Hundreds at a time, sometimes more than a thousand."

He stopped circling the room and came to rest in front of the icon of the Virgin Mary. She had a golden halo and Oriental eyes.

"They're crazy. They set themselves on fire and all the rest because they wanted to make the sign of the cross like this . . ."

He turned to the icon and made the ritual blessing with his first and middle fingers—head to chest, shoulder to shoulder—with broad, confident strokes. "That's how it all started; when the Patriarch Nikon said that everybody should use three fingers to make the sign of the cross."

He made a tripod with his thumb and repeated the blessing. "Like I said, they're crazy. The czar tried to force them to conform to the new way of praying. Peter tried to make the men shave their beards, but they'd rather set themselves on fire. Then he put a tax on beards, but that didn't work either. After that, he let the Cossacks loose and they used the sword and the knout. But Old Believers just prayed harder and set themselves on fire. But that was a long time ago. I don't think it'll help you find out who killed Boris Yermak."

There was a commotion upstairs. The archpriest excused himself and ran up the stairs two at a time. For a moment his voice was added to the general din—something to do

38

with the ownership of a fishing pole—and then for a while the house was still. Three young girls ran into the kitchen and had started yelling about an entirely different topic by the time their father came back downstairs.

The archpriest continued: "They had a problem, because no matter how many Antichrists persecuted them, the world never came to an end. Not yet, anyway. When the Communists took over, they mostly ignored the Old Believers and that was the worst thing of all. The young ones got tired of waiting and the old ones started to die. The few that were left ran away. About thirty years ago they came to Alaska because it's far away from everything and it used to be a Russian place."

The commotion upstairs started up again. Now we had boys screaming on one floor and girls screaming on the other. The archpriest seemed unaffected by the mayhem. I was going to ask him about reports that Ivan Smolensk and Boris Yermak had had a fistfight over a television set, but before I could the front door banged open and Tatiana came in followed by two older girls burdened with bags full of groceries.

Tatiana's arrival was a further stimulus to the general anarchy which governed the house. Hundreds of thousands of children swarmed into the living room to complain about each other. Their complaints grew so shrill that even Father Nick couldn't take it any more.

"Let's take a walk to the bluff," he said. "See how our tree is doing."

The seedling was doing just fine, although it seemed way too small for its assigned task. "Peek said something about a television set."

The archpriest gave me a curious look, almost an accusation.

"They won't talk to me, because I bless myself with three fingers, remember? And I'm an agent of the Antichrist. But as much as I can tell from the questions that the troopers had me ask, Ivan Smolensk purchased a television set a few weeks ago. This was the first one the village ever had, and so the elders had a debate about television sets and Old Belief. Boris is a hard-liner and it seems that he got up in church and said that Ivan and his television set were bringing the Antichrist into the village. They stepped outside and had a big fight. Boris grabbed Ivan by the beard and dragged him up and down the street, but Ivan still wouldn't get rid of his television set, so Boris came to Ivan's house and took a sledgehammer to the TV set. Ivan went to Homer and got a TV repairman. He was hooked on television after just a couple of weeks, just like our friend Michael Gudunov."

The sun dipped behind Redoubt Volcano. Father Nyuknuvuk leaned over the bluff. The evening tide rolled in on gray swells and white foam. Father Nyuknuvuk sighed as the sea got ready to swallow the riprap barricade he and Michael had constructed. "That's why Peek-A-Boo Pete arrested Ivan. I don't think he killed Boris, but I'm not sure I'd blame him if he did. Television is an instrument of the Devil."

We talked about Michael for a while, about how our friend was prostrate before the seductions of American television. Television tormented him with things he couldn't afford, women he couldn't have and calories he didn't need. It was doing the same thing to his body that it was doing to America's mind, turning it soft and killing it young.

"The thing is, to me, in a way, I think Ivan is right. When the Antichrist does get here, he'll be a television star." The archpriest picked up a stick and threw it onto the beach. The tide came in and carried it away.

Chapter 5

I CAME HOME THAT NIGHT TO THE FRAGRANCE OF HERRING roe. Rachel had returned from her fishing frenzy, and we made pungent love in the warm glow of the night. In the morning we ate pancakes sweetened with raw honey and talked about how we'd missed each other so. She discovered evidence of chili cheese dogs in Chena's dish and lectured me about cholesterol and worms.

"Jessica Herman's going to have another baby," she announced while fetching a plastic bag full of frozen herring from the freezer.

This brought up a delicate subject which I was anxious to avoid. I responded with news of my own, describing in detail the brutal murder of Boris Yermak and how Peek-A-Boo Pete had arrested a man whom the archpriest and I believed to be innocent.

But Rachel would not be denied. "That's her fifth child— and her last, I suppose. She's getting past her time."

She punctuated this statement by slamming the frozen fish down on the counter. I organized a second stack of pancakes. She peeled away the plastic bag in which the fish were stored and dumped the lumpy chunk of rock-hard gray into a large cooking pot. This was but the first step in an elaborate process which kept us in herring all year round.

"They run a good ship," she said, while hacking away at a second batch of fish with an ice pick.

"Who's that?" I asked, glad to be off the subject of children. Rachel gave the frozen fish a mighty poke, causing a small herring projectile to fly across the room. Chena woke up long enough to sniff it and decide it wasn't ripe yet. She was snoring again by the time I picked up the fish meat and dropped it into her dish.

"The Old Believers," Rachel said. "They build their own boats and paint them all in bright colors—pastel pink and mauve. They don't harvest herring roe, but I bet we'll see them at the halibut opening."

"When's that?" I asked, glumly anticipating another separation.

She wiped the ice pick clean of smashed fish. "Not until Friday morning, but I'll have to leave for Homer on Wednesday. The state cut back on the harvest, so the skipper wants us all on board right away so we can be all geared up and ready to go when it starts."

She leaned over her cooking pot and poked the contents with the ice pick. "They're very sad in a way."

"The Old Believers?"

She nodded, and turned down the heat. "There's not enough of them. If they marry outside, their culture will be diluted. If they don't, their babies will get weak from all the inbreeding. One way or the other, their days are numbered. They're in trouble. Their gene pool is too small for strong, healthy babies."

She left the herring alone for a moment and stood as close to me as she could without actually standing on top of me. I looked up from my pancakes as she said to me in a tone of such deep melancholy that I had to look away: "People need strong babies if they want to have a future. There is no future for people who die without leaving children behind."

I didn't know what to say or how to say it, so I glanced at my watch and jumped up from my chair. "Oh jeez, I'm late for work." We kissed the air as I ran out the door.

Jennifer Wilson, the *Beacon*'s business manager, intercepted me on the stairs leading up to the newsroom. Her father had a serious problem he wanted to discuss over a threesome of golf. Sometimes I suspected that Jack created problems just so we could discuss them over golf.

"What sort of problem?" I asked.

Her smile was a disturbing combination of secret information and smeared lipstick. "He didn't say. But Jim Bohannon is your third. That ring a bell?"

I shrugged my shoulders as if it didn't, and went looking for Byron Schiller, who covered the Borough Planning Commission in addition to his other duties.

My city editor knew in the very marrow of his bones that something was afoot. He didn't know just what it was, but he knew that it was something. Byron was a refined, articulate man. He was well-versed in classical music and possessed an unshakable conviction that our freedom, our prosperity, our very lives were threatened by a dark conspiracy of international scope. Like most conspiracy buffs, he had an insufficient appreciation of the role of confusion in world affairs and a long list of likely suspects: the Rockefellers, the Masons, liberal Democrats and the Queen of England. Their instruments were fluoride, the World Bank, AIDS, marijuana and the Islamic Revolution. Their goals were world domination and commercial zoning along the banks of the Kenai River.

The proof that human society was about to explode into smithereens was in his inability to hang onto a job. He started at the *Los Angeles Post* as a young reporter of great promise. Over the next fifteen years, he worked his way down to the *Baranov Beacon*, where his ability to spell made him an indispensable part of my newsroom.

The *Beacon* was his revenge and Baranov was his hiding place. His basement was stocked full of canned goods, bottled water and ammunition. He had a burly wife who terrorized him and their six children, whom they were attempting to educate in classical music and literature in case the Forces of Evil triumphed and Baranov, Alaska became the last bastion of Western civilization.

I found Byron brewing himself some tea in the staff lounge. He used special waster from a tin plastic canteen he always carried and stirred with the blade of his Swiss Army knife because the plastic spoons which Jack provided for his employees had been manufactured by the forces of darkness. Byron was a tall man with sad eyes and thinning hair, and very much kinder than his opinions would indicate.

I suggested we talk over coffee and tea. I ate some company doughnuts. Byron ate a handful of something he kept in his suit coat pocket. The accountants in the next room listened while we talked about nothing and leafed through the latest edition of the *Baranov Beacon*. A story by Greta quoted fishery biologists predicting a bad year for halibut. Byron blamed it on *El Nino* and the ozone. I thought the Japanese were to blame.

When the doughnut was gone, I said, "Jim Bohannon is chewing pretty hard on Jack's butt and now he wants to take a bite out of mine. You got any guess as to what's on his mind?"

Byron uncorked his canteen and splashed a little unfluoridated water into his tea. "I guess he didn't like my story last week. He's the guy who's trying to push this riverfront zoning through without a public hearing. You read the story, right?"

I had, but only after reading one of George's sports stories, which tend to numb the senses. Apparently my eyes had glazed over one paragraph in which Byron had accused Bohannon of hatching "a conspiracy of silence" and then described the planning commissioner as "a member of the local Masonic lodge, which indulges in secret ritual and politics designed to bring about the establishment of riverfront zoning and a one-world government."

These charges were nothing new. Byron made them every time he had the chance. The news was that I had not deleted them from the published product. "This could be a problem," I said after rushing through the rest of the story.

Byron was sorry that he caused me any trouble, but glad that he had finally been able to strike a blow for the human race. I gave him the old line about how editors are always "throwing their bruised and battered bodies into the breach just to keep their reporters out of harm's way." He said this was quite noble of me and offered to do me a favor sometime. I said he could do me a favor right now by taking Lindy Sue Baker off my hands.

"I want you to handle the Old Believer trial. I'll probably do some kind of sidebar story, but I want you to be in court and deal with the lawyers."

Byron sipped his unfluoridated tea. Strange cults, dark history and deep suspicions were his very reasons to be. "What do you want me to do?"

"I want you to find out all about the Old Belief and about the people who live at Vygovskaia Pustyn. Father Nick told me they had some kind of fight about watching TV. I want you to find out about that. I want to know all about Ivan

44

Smolensk and Boris Yermak and I want everything fast enough so we can do a big spread on the Sunday before the trial starts. And let's do some kind of story on this Lindy Sue Baker person. She's Ivan's lawyer. Stroke her down real good and maybe she'll be a source for us sometime.''

Byron became so excited he bit into a glazed jelly doughnut. He chewed it a couple of times before realizing what he had done. His mouth stopped in mid-chew, as if the pastry had turned to sawdust. He looked for a place to spit it out. Finding none, he swallowed slowly and said, "What about Jim Bohannon?"

I leaned over so the eavesdropping accountants couldn't hear. "I'll just put Greta on the planning commission for a while. That'll teach 'em. He'll never complain about you again."

The Baranov Municipal Golf Course was wedged between the tidal flats and Myrtle Sheppard's homestead. It was a nine-hole, par thirty-five. On a good day, I doubled par. The fifth hole, which abutted the woods behind Myrtle's cabin, was the toughest, and considered to be the supreme test of a golfer's resolve. Anyone unlucky enough to slice a shot onto Myrtle's property had a tough chip shot during which Myrtle could be expected to blast a round of buckshot over the trespasser's head. Myrtle didn't want to hurt anybody, but she was getting old. Rumors said her eyesight was failing and her trigger finger was suffering from the palsy.

Bohannon, Jack and I exchanged greetings on the first tee, then got right down to business. The planning commissioner scowled into his golf bag. Jack said, "My junior partner here is going to answer that question you had and I'm going to smash this little white ball right down the middle of the fairway."

My senior partner addressed the ball. He is a lean man with lots of silver hair, agile and smarter than most. He'd managed to salt away millions. He moved to Alaska after the Second World War. He worked as a crew boss for the Alaska Railroad and learned a lot about building things under difficult climactic conditions. He saved as much as he could and started a little construction company. The construction business boomed after oil was discovered in the Swanson River basin. He became very rich supplying big oil companies with big equipment and big guys from Texas who worked for the lowest possible wage. Success in this venture subsidized the two joys of his life—newspapering and golf. One of the newspaper's duties was to keep Myrtle Sheppard from closing down the golf course. Jack's drive stopped in the middle of the fairway, about two hundred yards from the tee.

Bohannon was a thick man. He had thick arms, a thick body and a thick head. His club bent into a high arch and crushed his Tru-Flite golf ball into a low cannon shot that veered to the left but landed a good seventy-five yards beyond Jack's ball. Bohannon retrieved his tee and strutted toward the golf cart. Jack was delighted. He preferred beating good players to beating bad ones. I was one of the bad ones. Besides, I worked for him, so it was easy for him to intimidate me.

"Looks like the Masters, Pres," my publisher said to me.

My tee shot looked like one of the pop-ups Reggie Jackson used to hit when one of his home runs went up instead of out. It almost pierced a cloud, took forever to come back down, and landed about fifteen yards away. Seven strokes later, my ball nestled into the cup, where Jack and Bohannon were waiting with waning patience.

Bohannon didn't bring up the subject of Byron Schiller's story until I was fifteen strokes behind him. He and Jack had parred three. I was playing polo instead of golf.

"Where'd you get that Schiller guy?" Bohannon said after smashing another tee shot. "He's about three bricks shy of a load."

I propped my ball up on the tee. The wind gusted and blew it off. Bohannon continued, "Anyway, I think he's got some pretty strange ways about him. I heard how he lives in a cabin over by Nikiski with barbed wire and an ugly wife and a pack of dogs. What's he worried about? There's nothing out there. Now you need to know that I'm a real strong believer in newspapers and the freedom of the press and all of that crap, but who cares if I'm a Mason and what's this shit about a 'conspiracy of silence?' Hell, there ain't no conspiracy about it. We gonna rezone the river for commercial and that's that. Don't you want to be able to buy a Coke when you're fishing for king salmon? The mayor says we could put Coke machines on the riverbank."

I sliced my drive at a perfect right angle from where it was supposed to go. Bohannon and Jack headed down the fairway. I headed for my ball. Eight strokes later, we assembled for the fifth hole, a 465-yard par five with a shotgun-toting grandmother in the rough.

Jack's drive was perfect again, and a good thing too. Myrtle Sheppard blamed him for an editorial I had written praising the golf course and its contribution to the community.

Bohannon addressed the ball. I said, "You don't have to worry about it anymore. I'm putting Greta on the planning commission for a little while. You can talk to Greta from now on. Byron Schiller won't bother you anymore."

I think I saw the hair on the back of his neck stand up. He cleared his throat. His shoulders twitched. He threw all of his frustration into the ball and propelled it deep into Myrtle's spruce grove. I'd never seen a ball stray so deeply into her forbidden woods.

My own drive landed safely in the duck pond situated on the other side of the fairway. Jack walked with me part of the way. He said, "Nice work, Pres. I guess that'll shut him up. But you ever think he might be right about Byron? Sometimes I think that man might be a little high-strung to be your second-in-command."

I agreed that this was so, but reminded him that Byron knew how to spell. Jack respected good spellers in the same way the rest of us respect good nuclear physicists. We joked a bit about the havoc Greta would cause for Jim Bohannon and the other borough planning commissioners. Then I nudged my ball toward the green. Jack's second shot landed in a sand trap while Bohannon's was accompanied by a shotgun blast.

Chapter 6

GRETA WAS DELIGHTED BY HER NEW ASSIGNMENT. GRETA was delighted by all assignments, so long as they didn't require her to work on Sunday. She was a pretty woman of middle age, who'd adopted a brood of children from everywhere. She fed them balanced meals and schooled them in the Way of the Lord. She knew many things that I didn't know and knew them with complete confidence. I envied her for this and that's why I asked her to write the stories no one else dared write.

No one else brought to these stories the same boundless energy, girlish innocence, and rich knowledge of local custom and scandal. Her confidence was a product of her religious beliefs. Like Byron and the Old Believers she too was convinced that the Second Coming was coming soon. For some reason that I do not comprehend, the Kenai Peninsula is a hotbed of apocalyptic fervor. I think it has something to do with the big salmon and the strong tides, with the long nights and the cold winters, with Redoubt Volcano and Kalifornsky Beach. God is never very far away from this place. Sometimes it seems like he never left, so a Second Coming is no big deal.

Greta's religious convictions were her most dangerous weapon. They caused her to believe that if God was to beat the Devil, if Good was to triumph over Evil, she had better be quick about it. Time was a-wasting, and she might as well start with Jim Bohannon and the Borough Planning Commission.

I envied her ability to be so certain about everything. She

was certain that Jesus was close by and certain that the Congregants of God talked to Him in tongues on Sunday mornings. None of these godly qualities stopped her from being the smartest, toughest, most tenacious reporter in my newsroom.

I, meanwhile, was certain about nothing other than my utter fear of fatherhood. I tried to believe in nothing, agnosticism being the favorite creed of journalists, who believe nothing that can't be compressed into a two-page press release. This professional creed is of little comfort to me or any of its followers. It somehow manages to be both empty and heavy at the same time, like a letter to Rachel I wrote but never sent.

But my own lack of faith did not stop me from enlisting the services of the godly. She became excited about the story once Byron persuaded her that efforts to rezone riverfront property for commercial development were the handiwork of the Beast, number 666.

I said the same thing in more muted tones. "Greta, I don't know about this Bohannon guy. Why don't you shake him and see if he rattles?"

Greta shook. Bohannon rattled. Byron spent long hours in the public library and whispered into the telephone at Lindy Sue Baker. Chena slept a lot and barked at rabbits in her dreams. I composed long editorials and took long lunch breaks. Rachel got ready for the halibut opening.

I took Wednesday afternoon off and drove her down to Homer, as she had asked me to do. I invited Michael along for the ride. Michael wanted to catch a halibut charter. I wanted to avoid the subject of children. Rachel glared at the highway while Michael and I talked about fish, murder and the strange ways of the Old Believers. At Clam Gulch we picked up a young college student who had too many hormones and hoped to get a job in one of the Homer fish canneries.

The college student couldn't keep his eyes off Rachel. He prodded her with questions about the wonders of Alaska. She told him all about this and that—about gold in the hills, oil in the ground and big fish in every stream and pond. I said something about Native corporations, but he wasn't interested. Rachel said that last year the price of fish went

49

up so high and the price of oil went down so low that for a while one good size red salmon was worth more than a barrel of crude.

The student seemed to think this was the most wonderful thing he or anyone else had ever heard. Rachel added, "And it's a renewable resource too. It doesn't pollute the environment, like newspapers and other bullshit."

This was the opening Michael was waiting for. "Hey, you got it right, Rachel. Just like darts. Darts don't pollute too much either and I suppose they're pretty much renewable like you said." He turned to the student, "You ever play much darts at that college you're from? I play darts for a nickel a throw."

Michael and the student disappeared into a tavern to play darts while I walked Rachel to the berth where the *Derring Do* was docked.

Red Barnes had given his trawler a new coat of paint that was unable to hide the fact that the *Derring Do*'s days were numbered. No amount of scrubbing could prevent the smokestack from belching out a vile smog that had more to do with the disintegration of the engine than with the cheap fuel Red used. The giant crane which his crew used to reel in the dragnets had been made from the discarded pieces of other giant cranes that had long before been consigned to the scrap heap.

The crew was of a similar composition. The captain's son Barney was the first mate. No one ever listened to Barney, especially me since I had once overheard him refer to me as "that little dude with the bum leg over there."

I do have a bum leg and it pisses me off when people stop pretending that they don't notice it. The people who mention my leg are usually either stupid or hostile. Barney was both. His infatuation with Rachel encouraged him to flex his muscles and refer to me as "that little dude with the bum leg over there" when talking to two old salts who never obeyed his orders. The old salts were from Clam Gulch and had lost their boat to the Internal Revenue Service. They handled the dragnet and the crane unless there was a wild sea, in which case they ran the ship and Barney watched the equipment.

They all deferred to Rachel, who knew how to cook. She arbitrated all disputes, especially those involving the skipper. I waved as the *Derring Do* chugged and belched and farted out of Homer harbor and into the open sea.

Michael and I went fishing too. We booked a halibut charter based on the Homer Spit, a long hocker of land which dribbles out into Kachemak Bay. Michael paid for his passage with money he had won from the college student. I bluffed my way on board with the promise that I would write some kind of story for the *Beacon* that would boost the skipper's tourist trade. For bait, we'd brought along bits of the herring Rachel had brought home from the Ketchikan fishery. Thus does one fish betray the next.

After Rachel left, the day turned cold and gray. We were late getting out because of some engine trouble. Our party included two young lovers, three old ladies and a serious sportsman who carried his fishing gear in a shotgun case. He was mostly red, with red hair, pink skin and red freckles. He wore a red baseball cap which read: "I'd rather be fishing."

The hat spoke a secret truth: fishing for halibut is more like hauling bricks than catching something with a mind of its own. The name comes from the Middle English word "halybutte" or "holy flat fish." The meat was usually eaten on Christian holy days, which was only one of the curses placed upon this singularly unfortunate fish.

Halibut are a species of flounder which evolution has twisted into a grotesque form. They use a vacuum-cleaner mouth to suck scum from the bottom of the sea. They swim on their sides, and consequently the halibut's eyes and mouth have been squished over to the downward side to facilitate feeding. They swim all their lives in bitter cold water eating weeds, turds and dead fish. Their whole lives are spent looking at the bottom of the sea from a distance never greater than ten inches.

Weeds, turds, dead fish. Under these circumstances, a morsel of herring impaled on a mean metal hook must be a treat indeed. Once the hook is sunk, the halibut eats its last meal and then follows the line to the surface. The fish doesn't fight the inevitable. This is understandable considering its miserable existence. The biggest halibut ever caught weighed 397 pounds, a little less than Michael. The tastiest are much smaller and called "chickens."

The guy who'd rather be fishing struck first. "Yea! Yea! Yea!" he shouted. "I got us a little chicken." The sportsman hauled the halibut in. The skipper killed it with an aluminum baseball bat. The sportsman boasted about his accomplishment and the rest of us hunched over our poles.

There soon developed an unofficial competition between Michael and the sportsman. Every time the sportsman caught a fish, he would dance around the boat, kiss an old lady and say, "And that's why they call me the Chicken Man."

Every time Michael caught a fish, he would say, "He'll pay. I'll make him pay. I have to. It's my duty."

After Michael had caught his fourth halibut, I said, "And just how are you going to do that?"

He started to smile, but stopped. "Gimme some of one of them herring bits you brought along."

I handed him the ass end of a dead herring. He impaled it on his hook. He started to smile but stopped. "I'm worried about Father Nick," he said.

It took me a few seconds to follow his thinking. "How come?"

Michael dipped his line into the water, but didn't pay much attention to it. "Well, you know how I'm his handyman and all. So just a couple of days ago I come by to tell him how Andy Sacramentov . . ."

Our conversation was interrupted by the sportsman, who had caught another chicken. He danced around the deck and kissed an old lady. Michael squeezed his pole and finished his sentence:

". . . And so I come by and tell him how old Andy Sacramentov has this old refrigerator that Father Nick can have if he wants it to toss over down on the beach so as the tide won't carry our church away.

"I says we should go and pick it up, but Father Nick doesn't want to do that. He doesn't want to do anything, except run around looking low and sad. That's not like how he is. I should know because I'm his handyman. Usually he says we should go pick up stuff right away, even if it's just an old file cabinet instead of a refrigerator. So then I talk to Tatiana and she says that just the other day he even yelled at the kids. I mean that's not Father Nick. He never yells, especially when it's his kids, which is why I think they're all so crazy, but he says priests' kids are just like that. Anyway, I never heard Father Nick to ever yell, except maybe in church but that doesn't count because that's his job. I figure it's because he's helping the cops with the murder of Boris Yermak."

The charter boat rocked over big swells of gray water. The halibut kept flopping in. I caught two chickens. The sportsman caught five, each of which he celebrated with a dance and a song and a kiss on an old lady's cheek. After Michael had caught his fifth chicken, he said, "I'm gonna burn that asshole."

To do this, Michael dipped his hook into the water and slowly worked his way over to where the sportsman had cast his line. "You've got the magic touch," he said to the sportsman. "What's that you put on your hook?"

The sportsman gave Michael an extended lecture on the properties of rotten pork dipped in salmon sperm. Michael thanked him for the tip, gave his pole a little sideways flip, and then worked his way back to where I was fishing.

"That guy's about to snag the biggest chicken there ever was."

Before I could ask for an explanation, Michael yanked hard on his pole. This caused the sportsman to let out a scream that sounded like terror giving birth to joy. Michael let out a bit of his own line and the sportsman said, "Shit, I think I lost him. I swear but it felt like I had Moby Dick on the line."

"Or maybe it was Moby Michael," I said under my breath.

Michael gave his pole another hard yank. This time there was no doubt as the sportsman released a scream of pure, undiluted terror/ecstasy. "Holy shit! My God! Jesus Christ!"

Michael let him out and then reeled him in. Let him out, reeled him in. Depending on how hard he tugged, the sportsman would squeak, or laugh or groan until the two young lovers and the three old ladies and the captain and his mate had rushed to his side to see why the sportsman's pole had bent into the water like a piece of overcooked spaghetti.

When the crowd had gathered and started some respectful murmuring, and the sportsman had already mounted a 400-pound halibut on the rumpus room wall of his dreams, Moby

Michael filled his lungs with as much air as they could hold and let it all out at once. "Hey killer, you've hooked my line."

The respectful murmuring stopped for what may have been the longest moment the sportsman had ever known before exploding into laughter. There was the twittering laughter of the three old ladies and the private laughter of the two young lovers. The captain and his mate sounded like dueling fog horns and Michael like an earthquake with a sense of humor. I made do with a knowing chuckle and the sportsman turned a shade of red that combined the worst features of anger and embarrassment. His hair wilted and his freckles faded.

The skipper cut the sportman's line, and charged two dollars for the hook he'd lost. The three old ladies decided that no fish could top what they'd just seen and asked for a go-home vote. The only dissenting votes were cast by Michael, who was still in hysterics, and the sportsman, who wanted to restore his dignity by catching another fish.

"You two ain't enough," the captain said. We headed back to Homer.

Rachel returned from her fishing trip the day after I returned from mine. We were supposed to talk about children over lunch at the Rig Café, but at the very last moment Jack said I had to write an editorial about the importance of commercial fishing.

When I came home that night, I did everything I could to avoid the subject of children. I had a briefcase full of work and a lame excuse: "Jack says he needs a newsroom budget right now, as in yesterday." I scribbled during dinner and made a long phone call afterward.

Shortly after midnight, she poked her head into the kitchen. "Look, just come to bed, okay? I'm not going to say a word. Let's just get some sleep."

I ate breakfast in my pickup truck and rushed to the *Beacon* in a hurry to find something important to do. Byron Schiller was almost out the door when I called after him. He snapped back like a yo-yo on a short string, clutching a leather briefcase to his belly. I sat him down and closed the door to my office.

"How's it going, Byron?"

He said it was going okay.

"Are you still working on that Old Believer story?"

He unlatched his briefcase. A ream of paper spilled out. Bail for Ivan Smolensk had been reduced to $500,000. He told me there was an opera by Mussorgsky I should listen to. Byron was always saying improbable things. His conspiracies required them. Sometimes it took some effort to keep him on the right track.

"What are you talking about?"

"*Khovanshchina*. It's supposed to be based on a true story. It's all about this time the Old Believers rebelled against the czar. They thought he was the Antichrist, as usual, so the soldiers trapped them in a monastery and in the last act they all go up in flames. It's quite exciting when they do a big-budget production, but the music's only so-so."

I made the mistake of telling Byron I wanted facts, not fiction. So he gave me some more facts. Not only was *Khovanshchina* based on a true story, but the Old Believers had a tradition of setting themselves on fire in the name of the Lord: 2,700 martyrs on March 4, 1687; 1,500 on November 23, 1688. They believed self-immolation was a shortcut to Heaven.

I told Byron he had done his homework well, but that none of this had anything to do with the murder of Boris Yermak or the trial of Ivan Smolensk. We had more important questions of more recent vintage, the most pressing of which was: "So what's the story with this Lindy Sue Baker?"

Chapter 7

PEEK-A-BOO PETE CONDUCTED MUCH OF HIS OFFICIAL business from a window booth at the Rig Café. He would interview witnesses and jot down notes on the Rig's table napkins, and could sometimes be persuaded to drop the charges, especially if you could pull him over to the Rig Bar, which was next door to the Rig Café.

I ordered orange juice and an English muffin. He had bacon and eggs and sausage and hash browns deep fried in butter and washed down with a pot of bubbling crude.

He shoveled in a load of eggs over easy. A small glob of yolk attached itself to his chin. The rest went straight into his already congested arteries. "So who made you some kind of Sherlock Holmes?"

"I'm not any kind of Sherlock Holmes. I don't know who did it. I'm just pretty sure it wasn't Ivan Smolensk. Father Nick agrees with me."

His eyes narrowed on a tiny link sausage. Some grease squirted out as he chomped it in half. The rest went straight to his prostate gland. While chewing he said, "Well I think he did it. Motive: revenge, on account of Ivan didn't like the way Boris dragged him up and down the street by the scruff of his beard, which must have hurt like hell. Opportunity: Ivan was on the road to Vyg at the time of the murder. We know that's true because of tests we did and because Ivan told us so himself when he called us up to tell us about the body."

"Which doesn't make any sense at all. Why would he call you if he was the one who did it?"

Peek piled a little bit of everything onto his fork. He used hash browns for the foundation and egg juice to glue it all together. "To put us off the track. These foreigners can be pretty clever sometimes."

He was about to shove it all in when I added, "And what about the murder weapon? You haven't found it yet. How can you convict a man if you don't have a witness or a weapon?"

He shoved the food in his mouth, talking and grinding at the same time, so I could see him mash it all together into a deadly goop. "The trial starts Monday, so you just come and watch. We make our case and that Texas woman'll make his and the jury can decide who's right. Of course, if he doesn't defend himself they might think he's hiding something."

"Maybe he is hiding something," Rachel said.

I was mopping the kitchen floor and she was dusting the furniture so that everything would be clean and tidy when her teacher friends came over to talk about going on strike next fall. Rachel was the shop steward at Aleksandr Baranov Elementary. Negotiations with the board of education were at an impasse and had been for the better part of a year. Rachel was a tough negotiator. I can attest to that.

Our conversation had to be shouted from one room to another. A stranger would have thought we were arguing, that our affection was in danger.

"Do you think he did it?" I shouted.

She shouted, "No. Maybe he's hiding something else."

"Like what?"

She stopped dusting for a moment and came into the kitchen. She pointed to a tile that looked clean to me and said I'd missed a spot.

"I told Captain Barnes about the Old Believer murder and he said something strange."

She told me that Red Barnes, capitain of the *Derring Do,* had met another skipper at the Land's End who'd seen a pastel boat called the *Pugachev* steaming back to Homer after last year's Bristol Bay fishery.

I'd rubbed the one tile clean while she told me this. She pointed to another. I said, "That's in the northwest, right?"

57

"That's right. It's the biggest salmon fishery in the world. We get boats from all over, especially the Japanese."

Rachel said that Red said that the other skipper said there was something funny about the *Pugachev:* "It ain't had no crane, but there musta been twenty o' them funny-lookin' people aboard, what with bags of clothes and such. You can't catch fish with all them people, and you for certain have to need a crane."

"Now who said that?"

"This other skipper that Red was talking to. Whatever the Old Believers are doing, it sure isn't fishing. Maybe that's what Ivan is trying to hide, not that men can ever hide anything. I think hiding is mostly women's work, because men are so obvious about everything. Just like you with your chili cheese dogs. You can't hide anything from me. I bet I could hide almost everything from you."

"Like what?"

She went back into the living room and turned on the vacuum cleaner. "Like . . . ow . . . oo . . . uu . . . ee . . . aa . . . eee."

The vacuum cleaner seemed to be sucking up all her consonants. I went into the living room and shouted, "I can't hear you. What did you say?"

She put on one of those know-it-all expressions that women put on when they know it all. "I said, like how come you won't let me have a baby?"

Because I'm ugly. Because I was crippled by polio when I was six months old. Because I have nothing worth passing on to the next generation. I didn't understand why she didn't understand. In the past, she insisted that I wasn't all that ugly or all that crippled and that I had a lot to offer future generations. She was totally deluded by love, and in a way deserved the catastrophe of having a baby from me. I just didn't deserve the blessing of having a baby from her.

Of course, that's not what I said. Instead I said, "I can't hear you with the vacuum cleaner on." When she turned it off, I looked at my watch and said, "Oh shit. I gotta go. I'm late for a meeting with Jack."

And so did my resolve begin to crumble at the very moment when circumstance and my own boneheadedness conspired against me. All this talk about children made me yearn all the more for something pointless and irresponsible, preferably with a woman with spike heels, too much makeup and too many names, a dress that was too small and a voice like hot molasses. But Byron didn't want to talk about Lindy Sue Baker. He wanted to talk about the opera, again.

I looked at Byron. His jaw was starting to twitch, a nerve disorder which often preceded one of his paranoid delusions. "Look," I said, "we're not going to do a story about a goddamn opera. I don't care how many Old Believers set themselves on fire in a stupid opera. It has nothing to do with Boris Yermak or Ivan Smolensk or anything else that's happening right now. What about that profile I asked you to do on that public defender, that . . . what's her name?"

"Lindy Sue Baker."

"Right. Well?"

"Well, I'll make you a deal."

Our deal was as follows. He wrote the profile and I agreed to let him quote passages from the opera as part of a longer story about the cult of Old Belief. We illustrated it with some photographs of the murder scene and of the village of Vygovskaia Pustyn and ran it all as the lead story in the Sunday paper, the day before jury selection was to begin.

Sunday night, the telephone rang. Rachel answered and handed it to me. Her voice was the sloe gin I'd imagined it to be: "Mr. Riordan, this is Lindy Sue Baker. I got a bone to pick with you. Who's this crazy person you got writing stories about me?"

Her spike heels sounded like gunshots as she stomped around the otherwise quiet courtroom. The gallery was filled with Old Believers. Men wearing cossack shirts and heavy knee boots mumbled into their beards. Women in babushkas knitted furiously. Solemn children clasped their hands so they wouldn't fidget. All eyes were on Lindy Sue Baker as she unfurled the Sunday *Beacon* and asked Judge Kramer to move the trial to another town.

A prim business suit could not disguise her essentially Texan nature. She was plump in a voluptuous sort of way and jiggled when she walked. She'd used a black Magic Marker to circle what she said were seventeen errors of fact

59

in Byron Schiller's stories. He'd even managed to misquote Mussorgsky.

"Your honor, I'll confess I do not understand the relevance of opera to this case. It's not my job to second-guess newspaper editors. But at least they could get their Mussorgsky right."

She read the correct passage into the court record, as yet another example of how the *Beacon* was destroying her client's chance for a fair trial:

> So this is how things now stand! The
> Time has come to win a Marty's crown in flames . . .

The *Beacon* had neglected to include the second letter "r" in the word "Martyr's". The public defender asked the rhetorical question, "Who is this 'Marty' person? Does the prosecution intend to call him as a witness?"

She denounced the other sixteen "errors of fact" in equally excruciating detail. Most of them were harmless goofs which she tried to blow up into lies, rumors and innuendo, for which she blamed Byron. Byron blamed me. I blamed our typographer, even though the *Beacon* doesn't have one.

"Your honor, we can't find an impartial jury in Baranov. Not after everyone has read these lies."

Judge Kramer took her motion under advisement and gave himself three days to think about it. By then he had another murder on his hands and I had been sued by Lindy Sue Baker.

Chapter 8

THE MAYHEM BEGAN ON TUESDAY, WHEN BILL HOOPER went fishing. That in itself is nothing special. Bill Hooper always goes fishing. But he didn't always land a king salmon bigger than a small human being, bigger than any king salmon anyone had ever caught before, big enough to be put on display in the lobby of Peninsula Pontiac. Bill Hooper caught that salmon on Tuesday and that's when the mayhem began.

Other things happened on Tuesday which contributed to the catastrophe. Rachel left for the Bristol Bay fishery and Lindy Sue Baker filed a lawsuit against the *Beacon*.

But Bill Hooper's capture of a monster king was by far the most exciting event of that day, and it was to have amazing, if unintended, consequences far beyond the lobby of Peninsula Pontiac.

A little background is in order. The Kenai River is a young river fed by the melting glaciers of the Chugach Mountains. It has many branches, like the Moose River and the Vyg, which wind around onto the flatlands and out to the sea, which splashes against Kalifornsky Beach and the foot of Redoubt Volcano, and claws at the bluff under St. Alexander Nevsky Church.

There are plenty of salmon of all sorts to be found in the rivers and streams of the Kenai Peninsula—silvers, reds and pinks. If you don't mind what you catch, you go for the pinks, which are considered an oily junk fish by salmon connoisseurs. If you want to catch a lot of fish, you fish for reds in the Russian River, where the run is so thick that even the most inept angler can't help but go home with a bucketful.

But if you want to catch just one fish that you can take a picture of and brag about for the rest of your life, you fish for king salmon in the Kenai River. Maybe it's something in the river. Maybe it's something in the air. Maybe it's something else. For some reason, the Kenai River and its basin are the spawning place of the world's biggest salmon, a cunning fighting fish with vicious teeth and clever ways of getting off the hook. On any other river in the world, fifty pounds is considered a king big enough to hang on a wall. But big kings are so plentiful on the Kenai River that a salmon must weigh upward of seventy pounds and be nearly five feet long to be proper for a trophy.

The strong, arrogant king salmon is everything that the slow, fatalistic halibut is not. If the halibut is a load of bricks, the king salmon or chinook salmon or *Oncorhynchus tshawytscha* is a basketful of trouble. Their will to live is the stuff of legend, as they race against death to give birth. They start to die as soon as they reach the fresh water of the Kenai River. They undergo a chemical change that causes the flesh around their mouths to disintegrate, leaving behind a crazed, sardonic jaw full of angry teeth. Once you've hooked a Kenai king, the fight has just begun. They chew on the line and try to drag it into snags on the river bottom. Once landed they snap at their captors even as their brains are being scrambled with a club. They don't give up until they're dead.

The rush of king salmon up the river occurs in two distinct runs. The first starts in May, and signals the opening of the tourist season for Kenai, Soldotna and Baranov. The second batch of kings runs the river in July, accompanied by millions of the smaller red salmon, which charge the shorelines of Alaska from Bristol Bay to Baranov like some Red horde from Siberia. This is how it has been and how it will be until we poison the Kenai River too.

The first run of kings had been relatively uneventful. It started in a different world from that in which we now reside. Boris Yermak was still alive. Ivan Smolensk was not in jail. Children were someone else's problem.

As usual, during the first run the *Beacon* had been full of fish stories about fish issues built around fish statistics.

There was a rematch of the old fight between sports fishermen and commercial fishermen and who should be allowed to catch what. I wrote my usual editorial about how fish are good no matter who hooks them, and let's keep the river clean. Rachel tended to her nets and corrected final exams, and then went chasing after herring and halibut.

With the second run came mayhem. Boris Yermak was murdered and Ivan Smolensk was charged with the crime. The road was thick with Winnebagos and the cash registers sang their merry tune. Lindy Sue Baker was out to get me and Rachel Morgan had left me to go commercial fishing in Bristol Bay.

"Why don't you drive me down to Homer?" she said. "Maybe you can meet the skipper that saw the Old Believer boat."

We headed for Homer early on that fateful Tuesday morning. I'd asked Michael to come along for the ride, for fear Rachel would talk about children if she got me alone on the road. But Michael declined the invitation. I brought Chena along, but she wasn't much help. My old dog, though spayed at an early age, seemed to be on Rachel's side, so I put her in back. I kept on the lookout for hitchhiking cannery workers, but they were all safe in their canneries, scraping scales and sliming innards. I was trapped and we both knew it.

We drove for an hour, but didn't say much. Dark clouds heavy with rain hung over the water and hid Redoubt Volcano from view. For a long time, the only sound was made by Chena, who started to howl and whine and moan when the rain clouds moved inland. I stopped the truck and Rachel let her into the cab section. She tried to shake off the water, but her tired old legs couldn't generate much torque. She fell asleep on the floor. Rachel took off her shoes and rubbed Chena's back with her bare feet.

We still didn't say anything. When I couldn't take it any more, I turned off the radio and said, "Look, you haven't said but two words all day and those were 'Fuck off.' "

That was the chance she'd been waiting for. She waited for a little while longer, so that I would be sure to listen. A big cargo truck passed us just outside of Ninilchik and sprayed muddy water on the windshield. I tried to keep my mind on the road, but it kept wandering back to Rachel's feet, to the way they were covered with wet dog hair.

There was a taffic jam near Anchor Point caused by a cow moose and her nine-hundred-pound offspring. Several motorists had pulled to the side of the road and were shooting away with their cameras. Other drivers slowed down and took that long, close look they usually reserve for traffic accidents. The cow and her calf nibbled on the low branches of trees. Rachel resisted the temptation to say how cute nine-hundred-pound babies can be.

When she finally did say something, it was very simple and difficult to misunderstand: "I'm going off the pill."

I passed a pickup truck with a sailboat in tow. My hands squeezed the steering wheel and I almost ran off the road. When we were safely in our proper lane, I said, "That's okay. I understand. I'll get a vasectomy. I know it's not safe to be on the pill for too long. You could get cancer of the something-or-other."

This produced another thick silence. Rachel pressed her nose against the passenger's window, sighed. A few seconds later, she sighed again, in case I'd missed the first one. "Pres, I'm going to have a baby. Whether you like it or not. If you don't want to be the father, I'll find another man. You can think about what you want to do, but you better have an answer when I get back. If you say no, we're through."

She'd have no problem finding a mate. The crew of the *Derring Do*—every manjack of them—seemed ready to volunteer. They made a big commotion over her when we walked into the Land's End. The crew members were getting in one last bender before leaving on the month-long expedition to Bristol Bay. Barney offered me his chair—"So's you can rest your wooden leg."—and then squeezed between Rachel and me.

"What happened to your leg anyway?" Barney asked.

Rachel looked away. I said, "Nothing. What happened to your face?"

There were six men at the table—four old salts and two young ones. Among the old salts were Red Barnes, the two men from Clam Gulch and a guy who had rubber clothes and a voice that sounded like stripped gears. "Howjado," he said to me.

The two young salts were in love with Rachel. Barney Barnes, the skipper's son, had just gotten a tattoo. He showed it to her. His friend wrapped around her shoulders an arm as thick as an old oak tree.

We ordered some beer and halibut. The young salts looked at Rachel, while the old ones looked at me. "This'll be Big Blow Eddie Miller," Red Barnes said to me while pointing at the guy in rubber clothes. "He's in charge of the *Howling Dog*, the one that Rachel told you about."

Big Blow looked like he'd been fishing for fifty years and smelled like he'd been fishing for fifty more. I shook his hand. It was missing a finger or two. He'd had gotten his nickname from his decision to put out to sea on Holy Thursday of 1964. That was the day before the Good Friday Earthquake, which leveled most of southcentral Alaska and caused a spectacularly destructive tsunami, a tidal wave of sorts. The *Howling Dog* was safely out to sea when the tsunami crashed into port, destroying all but a handful of fishing boats.

Big Blow shoveled in a forkful of halibut. Some butter slid down his chin. "I seen your Old Believers at the last year's fishin' of Bristol Bay. We was coming back to port with a bellyful. The catch was so big we almost snapped a net. There was forty-foot swells and a big blow comin,' so my chickenshit first mate come up and say we should dump some fish so as there won't be no chance that we'd capsize."

The tourists at the table next to ours had stopped talking so they could overhear an authentic Alaskan conversation. They looked away when Big Blow squeezed something out of his nose and wiped it on his rubber pants. He continued: "I say that if we dump a load we start with him, and so he gets all pissed off and disappears down to the engine room. That left me to take the wheel, which I done and that's when I see a kinda blue or purple fishin' boat wit'out no crane. That's about the craziest thing I ever seen, ain't it Red?"

"Pretty much," Red said. "Except for the weird-lookin' gold."

One of the tourists dropped her fork. I looked over at Rachel. She was telling Barney and his friend about the joys of motherhood and her grade-school English class. Before I could ask Red about the gold, Big Blow had started talking again.

"Now any fool from Fooladelphia got to know you can't catch fish wit'out no crane, unless you're like them sissies what hooks 'em one at a time and nails 'em to the wall."

I said, "Rachel said something about people on board."

Big Blow nodded into his beer and spilled some on his chin.

"That's right. So I say 'Howjado' and then I take out my spyglass for a better looksee and what I see is a buncha trouble because not only do they ain't got no crane, but they ain't got no smoke coming outta their smokestack. That's a way of saying they ain't go no power, which is a quick way to get dead with a big blow comin'. They was all on deck wearing funny suits like they got at Vyg and they was waving at me and dancing and lookin' pretty scared, so I come over and give 'em a tow all the way to Naknek Harbor. They was so heavy, I had to dump some fish."

"All of that trouble for some weird-lookin' gold," Red said, mostly to himself.

Before I could ask about the gold, Barney said something about his tattoo, a multicolored mermaid located on the heavy part of his upper arm. He made a muscle which distorted the mermaid into a swollen, ugly thing. Rachel thought it was beautiful. "Now it looks like she's pregnant," she said to me while looking at him.

I turned back to Big Blow Miller, who hadn't stopped talking. ". . . and on the ass end it had a buncha funny letters in a foreign language what I don't understand right under some English letters what I don't understand so I looked it up. First I thought it was the *Boogaloo*, but it really was the *Pugachev*. That's a poor guy what pretended he was the Russian king and led a poor man's army till they all got killed."

Red Barnes said, "I guess it wouldn't have happened if he had some of that weird-lookin' gold, wouldn't you say, Big Blow?"

"That's right. I would say that. So we get into Naknek and that's where the gold comes in. We tie up both ships all secure and I go talk to the skipper, who was one of the Yermak family like the one what got killed in your newspaper recently. They was all jabbering at me in Russian and I was jabbering at them in English. What I was saying is that since I dumped some of my fish and went out of my way all

66

the way to Naknek just to save their Communist butts that maybe they should give me some money, especially since I heard what they say about how all them Old Believers is loaded."

"Loaded with weird-lookin' gold?" said Red.

Big Blow uttered a curse about ten words long and set a heavy coin on the table. That's when Rachel excused herself and headed for the ladies' room. Barney went after her. I went after Barney. We took a leak together. He showed me his tattoo.

When Rachel came out of the ladies' room, she kept on walking out of the bar and toward the harbor. I followed her. Barney followed me. That's when we had the implosion. Not an explosion, but an implosion. Our emotions collapsed in on themselves. Both of us talked, neither of us listened.

She wanted me to say, "I want to have a little girl that looks just like you." Instead I asked her to ask Red Barnes about the gold coin he'd shown me.

I wanted her to say, "No, not that. I'll never leave you." Instead she reminded me to wash the dishes and said she'd ask Red about the gold and call me on the radiophone when she got to Bristol Bay.

I headed back to Baranov. The rain let up, but it was a very long ride and very lonely. My mind ran wild and I went a little crazy. I tried to think about murder and Russian poor guys who pretend to be king, but all I could see on the rainy road before me were phantasm pictures of the wrong people making love. Rachel did it with a commercial fisherman and then gave birth to a mermaid with a throbbing muscle for a belly. I did it with Lindy Sue Baker, who filed a lawsuit claiming I didn't wait until she was done. I took a turn too fast on the north end of Clam Gulch and almost lost control of my big red monster pickup truck.

How could I ever be a father, when I hadn't been much of a son? My own father was so horrified at the prospect of my birth that he left home before I was born. After the polio knocked me down, my mother had worked and slaved to buy me a leg brace so I wouldn't fall down when I tried to stand up. The brace cost thousands of dollars, but I fell down anyway. She sacrificed and suffered to send me to the best schools so I could get the worst grades, and I never even called on her birthday. I was a frazzle, my life was in ruins and Rachel was going to have a baby whether I liked it or not.

Lindy Sue Baker wanted a piece of my ass, and she wasn't being very romantic about it.

A message from Jack was waiting for me that afternoon when I checked into work at the *Beacon*. His lawyer wanted to talk to me about a lawsuit that had been filed that morning in Baranov Superior Court. Ivan Smolensk was the plaintiff, Belinda Baker was his attorney and the *Beacon*, Jack and I were identified as the defendants.

"You got notes and quotes and stuff like that?" asked Ellis Fielding, Jack's attorney. Fielding's parents had discovered Soldotna in 1947 and still considered the riverfront town to be their personal property. Everyone took it for granted that Ellis would be a state senator some day.

"That's right."

"Well this Baker person wants them because she thinks that nutty reporter of yours knows something that will get her client off the hook. You got a problem with that?"

I addressed my comments to Jack. "We can't do that. It goes against every rule in the book."

Jack stood up and looked out the large picture window that dominated the eastern wall of his office. The window faced the Baranov Municipal Golf Course, where he wanted to be. He turned back to us, leaned against the windowsill and said, "Ellis, this is a small newspaper."

Jack always reminded us that the *Beacon* was a small newspaper whenever anyone asked him to spend any money. He said that when Augustine Volcano erupted and he was too cheap to send a photographer to take a picture of it. He said it every time I asked for more money for the newsroom and he said it when we needed a new wax machine.

Now he said it again, just in case we hadn't heard him the first time. "You know that, Prester. You know we're just a small newspaper. Why hell, this conversation alone is going to suck up half our budget for legal. Now I want you to talk to this Lindy Sue girl and get her to drop the suit. Work out some kind of deal that'll make everybody happy."

I didn't want to talk to Lindy Sue Baker. I knew that if I

talked to Lindy Sue Baker, something bad would happen and no one would be happy. It might be something bad that felt good, but that only made it worse.

It was a distinctly Texan pain. It's not that I was infatuated with Texan women. I'm infatuated with all women. But in that summer of my great pain, Texan women had become infatuated with me. Until that summer of my great pain, I'd mostly led a virtuous life, mostly for lack of sufficient temptation.

But in that summer of my great pain, something incredible and totally unexpected happened. After thirty-eight years of being short, fat and crippled, I'd become attractive to women. That summer I learned that the late thirties are when short, fat, ugly guys come into their own. These are the years when women who still entertain illusions of happiness enter a time of desperation having to do with ovaries, wrinkles and the ticking of their biological clocks. When it's almost too late, women finally realize that all men have flaws and they suddenly begin to appreciate the relatively harmless afflictions of homeliness and clumsiness and bashful confusion, with which I am well supplied.

This extraordinary development had a Texas flavor because the oilfields make Baranov a Texas place. A waitress smiled a little wider than my cheesburger called for. A bank teller admired my new haircut. A gum-snapping lady with big hair and a station wagon full of drywall winked at my big red monster pickup truck.

You can imagine my surprise. This took a little getting used to after a lifetime of longing for, dreaming about and being rejected by women in all their lovely forms and fashions. Back when I was a craven teenager, the girls treated me like a freak—Quasimodo without the bells. Now would come the Hunchback's Revenge, and I might as well start with Lindy Sue Baker, who filed her lawsuit at the very moment when the stars conspired to punish me with my own sordid fantasy.

No. Absolutely not. I wasn't going to do it, even if it was all Rachel's fault because she wanted me to be a father when I hadn't been a very good son.

*   *   *

The eventual catastrophe was delayed but not prevented by Bill Hooper, who went fishing that day. I didn't call Lindy Sue Baker to talk about the lawsuit because everyone was in a frenzy over Bill Hooper's fish.

The news was all over town. Ronda took a picture of Bill and the monster king he'd pulled from the Kenai River. The fish was as tall as Bill, and weighed more than Ronda. Byron Schiller interviewed the angler, who said he'd keep the meat and lease the skin and bones to Peninsula Pontiac, which would have them enameled and put on display.

We held a news meeting to discuss our handling of the story. Ronda would follow Bill Hooper, and Joe would follow Ronda. Byron was assigned to interview other famous fishermen and compose a chart listing the ten biggest kings that were ever caught and the fishermen who had caught them. Greta would get comments from local celebrities and George would devote his entire sports section to the king salmon, also known as the chinook salmon, also known as *Oncorhynchus tshawytscha*. I would write an editorial and then go fishing for king salmon and a king salmon color story.

George didn't like that idea. He wanted to go fishing too, but I left him in charge of the composing room. After the meeting broke up, I explained my thinking to him. "I seem to remember a few weeks ago when you wanted me to get more involved in the news. Well that's what I'm doing. Getting more involved."

Chapter 9

I CAUGHT UP WITH MICHAEL AND THE BIG BELUGA AT THE Rainbow Bar in Kenai. They smelled of fish and beer. So did the Rainbow Bar. It was packed to the gills with cannery workers. Michael said, "Hey, how you doing, Shorter-Than-I?"

"I'm doing okay, Michael. Let's go fishing."

The Big Beluga turned away from the pretty young cannery worker he'd been romancing. "It's too late now, Pres. The skeeters are out and the run slowed down for the night."

Michael had a better idea. "Let's go drinking first, and then we'll go fishing when we're done. By then it'll be too early instead of too late and we'll get the biggest goddamn king fish there ever was."

We took the big loop through the bars of Baranov and then the bars of Soldotna and then the bars of Kenai until we found ourselves back at the Rainbow. Michael pulled out his darts and began fleecing the cannery workers while the Big Beluga danced with a red-headed girl with no shoes on. She was of Texan extraction, he a collection of disorganized bones. She was made of tightly-packed curves and jiggled when she bopped. The Big Beluga was a tall, skinny man with a scruffy black beard. His seemed to be dancing in two directions at once.

He danced over to me. "You shoulda seen it, man. The river looked like the L.A. freeway. Everybody heads over to Bill Hooper's fishing pole, and there's old Bill saying, 'What's the big deal?' like he's Mister Cool."

Then he danced over to the dart board and wrapped his arm around the cannery worker Michael had chosen to be his latest victim. "Nice shot, Slimer. Where you from?"

Slimers are people who are paid by the hour to scrape away fish guts. This one was from Milwaukee, where he attended Marquette University. He and a classmate had come up north to grow their first beards, play darts and smell like fish for a while. He'd spent the last sixteen hours "squeezing Harry," which is cannery talk for removing the internal organs of a halibut.

The student thought removing fish guts was a great way to spend the summer. The Big Beluga thought he was some kind of idiot, but didn't say so at the time. Instead he waited until the cannery worker had tossed another dart and said, "Nice shot, Slimer. Buy us a beer and I'll let you tell me how you got so good."

Although I was a bit groggy, Michael and the Big Beluga seemed to be in full control of themselves when the bars closed down. We all climbed into my big red monster pickup truck and drove down to the Soldotna boat ramp. We slept in the truck for a couple of hours, until the fish began to stir.

Michael nudged me awake. "Hey, Shorter-Than-I. It's time to move."

The Big Beluga had already started the engine of his flat-bottom riverboat. Michael led me into the boat and handed me a life jacket. The Big Beluga hit the gas and we started to ease upstream. It was still dark, but in summer the Alaska dark never lasts too long.

I asked Michael, "So how's Father Nick?"

I heard his weight shift and felt the boat rock. "I'm worried about him. The cops want him to speak Russian at the Old Believer trial and it's got him feeling bad somehow. I asked him what's wrong and he won't say nothing, but I bet it's got to do with that Old Believer. He still hasn't picked up that old refrigerator that Andy Sacramentov wants to donate to the church."

"Father Nick thinks the Old Believer is innocent. What do you think?"

"Yeah, maybe. I don't know. Let's go kill some fish."

The Big Beluga cut the motor and we threw our heavily-weighted lines in the water. We drifted with the river current in the opposite direction of the kings.

There's lots of ways to kill king salmon, but only a couple of them are legal. One of them is called trolling, and that's what we started to do. Trolling is drifting with the current as it heads out to sea, in the opposite direction of the salmon. The bait is supposed to attract the kings and the heavy weight is supposed to bang them on the head so they get pissed off and bite out in anger. The angler's job is to hang onto the pole, look at the world floating by, and tell improbable stories until something improbable happens. Trolling works best when the fish are in a big hurry to get to their spawning grounds, but it didn't work that morning. The world upriver started to glow as the Big Beluga passed around a thermosful of coffee. We each poured ourselves a cup and watched the lights of Soldotna. The Big Beluga took a leak over the side of the boat. He called this "an offering to the fish god."

Dawn turned the sky gold, the river valley green and the mountains blue. By this time we had reached the mouth of the Kenai River without so much as a nibble. The Big Beluga idled the motor and said, "Okay, now it's time to try some official Big Beluga salmon jism and then we'll head back upriver and make another pass."

Michael and I pulled our lines from the water. The Big Beluga grabbed our hooks and baited them with a slimy combination of bright red salmon eggs and gooey white salmon sperm, a concoction said to be as attractive to king salmon as it is repulsive to human beings. Thus provisioned, we headed upriver and prepared to take another ride on the current.

The dawn was full now and the river was coming to life. Dozens of boats just like ours drifted toward the sea and dozens more were just getting ready to push off from the Soldotna boat launch. The Big Beluga pushed his boat into overdrive and the chilly morning air blew through our bones. Our bait and hooks bopped the bottom of the river, but they didn't bop against the head of a homeward-bound king and piss him off so we could kill him. "Goddamn, will you look at this mess," the Big Beluga said as he eased into the seaward-bound current and cut back on the gas.

Michael grunted agreement, and we settled into an expectant hush. The Kenai River was indeed like the L.A. freeway. Traffic was snarled by the tangling of some fishing lines and the air smelled of outboard motor fumes. Hundreds of fish killers hunched over their poles in a prayerful posture, looking for the same kind of king Bill Hooper had caught. We watched a Styrofoam cup follow us downriver. At the mouth of the river we turned around and it slipped out to sea.

Michael said, "Jeemanee. We catch us a king and it'll have five hooks in it. I bet Bill Hooper's laughing in his beard right now."

The Big Beluga adjusted his hip-waders and yanked his line out of the water. "This is bullshit. Too many boats. There's just too many boats. I bet there'll be a crack-up and somebody gets hurt. I say we head for my fishing hole."

A fishing hole is a quiet spot in the river where the kings pause to rest from their heroic charge upstream. It seemed a little early to give up on the current, but the Big Beluga knew his business and so Michael and I agreed. We headed back upriver, causing some commotion as the waves we made slapped against the sides of the trolling riverboats. Just outside of Soldotna, the Big Beluga cut the engine and pulled next to another boat decorated with a smiling salmon and the inscription, "Henry's Kenai King Charters."

"Hey, Henry," the Big Beluga yelled, "you seen anything?"

Henry shook his head. His boat was full of eager Japanese men, each with a pole tugging on the water. "I seen a net up by Ed's Fishing Hole, but I bet it was some guy who'd hooked himself a log." A net up indicates that someone in the boat has hooked a fish. It's a warning for others to stay clear.

They talked about Bill Hooper's fish and the trouble it was causing. One of the Japanese had caught a fifty-pounder yesterday, but threw it back because it wasn't as big as Bill Hooper's fish. Henry whispered to the Big Beluga, "Fifty pounds and he throws it back, and then says, 'How come you not take us to place with big fish?' Big fish. Now they want their money back if they don't catch Codzilla."

The Big Beluga hit the gas and headed for his fishing hole. He leaned on the wheel and smoked a cigarette.

74

Michael asked, "Hey, Pres, ever hear how the Big Beluga found his fishing hole?"

He'd told me about fifty times, but that didn't stop him from telling me again. The Big Beluga had had a boat full of insurance agents when he discovered his very own fishing hole. It was a slow day for drift fishing and the insurance agents had started to grumble, so they headed upriver and planned to scout the other side of Big Eddy.

The other side of Big Eddy had several of the deep pockets of still water where the salmon stop to rest from their labors. They came to an unclaimed fishing hole and threw out their lines. Their grumbling got louder when another boat hooked a king and put its net up. It was a small boat, so word got around fast and the word was that the Big Beluga didn't know where the big fish were, or if he did he was saving them for himself.

But the talk stopped cold when one of the insurance agents screamed and his pole bent into the water. The Big Beluga put his net up and dropped his jaw when the fish surfaced. It wasn't a fish at all, but a beluga whale that had strayed upriver from its saltwater stomping grounds in Cook Inlet.

The whale took a big gulp of air and headed back under. The insurance agent's reel spun like a top on fire. "Cut the line! Cut the line!" the insurance agent said.

"Are you crazy?" the Big Beluga said. "Reel it in! Reel it in!"

"Cut the line or I'm gonna let go!"

"The hell you are," the Big Beluga said. He'd paid a lot of money for that fishing pole.

The reel kept spinning and the line kept disappearing into the water. The Big Beluga grabbed the pole and held on until the line ran out. Then the whale yanked him into the river. The whale got away and the untended boatful of insurance agents drifted into a snag of tree roots over by Big Eddy. That's how the Big Beluga got his name and found his very own fishing hole. Or so legend has it. The Big Beluga isn't about to deny it, since it's good for business. Michael says it's true, but then the Big Beluga also says that the stories they tell about Michael are true. I wonder if they have an agreement.

* * *

But on this particular day, the Big Beluga's fishing hole did not belong to him alone. It looked like an upriver parking lot. We saw a couple of nets up, but didn't get too excited. The Big Beluga hung his head and cursed Bill Hooper's fish. Michael yanked his bait off the hook and threw it in the river. He wiped some salmon jism off on the cuff of his lumberjack shirt.

"So, what'll it be, guys?" the Big Beluga asked.

Michael said, "Let's go over to Pres' house and watch a little TV."

To which I said, "I got a better idea. Let's go down the Vyg River. We can catch some fish there and maybe find out how come Father Nick is feeling so bad."

"What's the matter with Father Nick?" the Big Beluga asked. The Big Beluga wasn't much for church, but he liked the archpriest. Most residents of Baranov liked Father Nick, except for the merchants and the pioneers who considered it their duty to look down on Natives.

I told him about the murder. Michael told him about the refrigerator. The Big Beluga seemed to think the refrigerator was the more important clue. He'd donated a cannibalized Buick to the cause and remembered how grateful Father Nick had been.

"I bet it has to do with the old Grand Lady," the Big Beluga said.

He let it go at that, as if everybody knew about the old Grand Lady. Everybody but me. "What old lady?" I asked.

The Big Beluga found a slow current and put the engine in a low gear so it wouldn't interfere with his story. He liked to tell stories, and wanted everything to be just right when he started out on one.

"I met a guy on the river one time who fell in love with an Old Believer girl. He went to Baranov High and she was on the Vyg High School girls' varsity volleyball team and he talked about how their uniforms were all Old Believer dresses with numbers on 'em. She wore her blond hair in a ponytail and chewed bubble gum. That's what he said, anyway. He asked her to marry him and she said she'd like to, only the old Grand Lady had to give the okay. The Grand Lady. That's what he said she said."

"What Grand Lady? Who is that?"

The Big Beluga took a long pause, and gunned the engine

for dramatic effect. "That's where the story starts to break down. He says he never could marry the Old Believer girl because this Grand Lady person never said okay because this Grand Lady person was still back in Russia, or the Soviet Union is I guess what they call it now. I figure there is no Grand Lady, and the Old Believer girl just said there was so she wouldn't have to marry Louis, who isn't the best-lookin' guy around."

Michael unzipped his fly and made his own offering to the fish god. When he was done he reeled in his equipment and said, "I don't understand how the Grand Lady is supposed to be in charge if she still lives in Russia. I mean, how can she boss everybody around in Vyg when she's way over on the other side?"

I couldn't answer the question and neither could the Big Beluga. But I said that maybe if we followed the Vyg River to the village at its mouth we could snoop around Vyg and maybe figure it out. Michael thought that this was okay and the Big Beluga agreed for reasons of his own. The mouth of the Vyg had a good fishing hole.

Chapter 10

THE FISHING HOLE AT THE MOUTH OF THE VYG RIVER WAS about fifteen miles south on Kalifornsky Beach from the mouth of the Kenai. It was a good fishing hole because of its location in relation to the Kenai River and its many branches. The Vyg was the southernmost of these branches. Therefore each of the hundreds of millions of red, pink, silver and king salmon which coursed through the river system each summer swam up or by the Vyg. Bill Hooper's Kong of Kings didn't go up the Vyg, but it may have rested for its date with destiny in one of the deep pockets of calmer water to be found in and near its mouth.

Michael and I had helped the Big Beluga scout the Vyg earlier, in the spring of that year, before murder and Lindy Sue Baker came along to complicate my life. The Big Beluga scouted the Kenai and its branches in the spring of every year, to see how the frozen chunks of winter and the melting chunks of breakup had changed the river system, piling rocks here and scattering them there. All this geologic commotion had a lot to do with the location of good fishing holes. Last year's glory hole might be filled with silt, while this year's might be newly made and awaiting discovery by some guide.

I tried to remember our spring scouting expedition as we moved upriver through the traffic jam. Lots of trees and a chill in the air. Chunks of melting ice clung to the roots of the trees along the bank, trees that were dying as river trees die.

River trees die in their own river way. The current and the

rushing chunks of melting ice chew and pound at the bank, just as the tide and its flotsam chew and pound at the bluff under Father Nick's church. The roots of the trees which grow along the bank are exposed by this erosion but the trees grow anyway, getting their nutrition from other roots on the landward side. As time goes by, there's less and less bank to support still bigger trees, which is when gravity takes over. The trees lean toward the water. Then they're called sweepers, because they might sweep you off the boat if you don't watch out. But it's not over yet. The tips of the trees take a sky-bound turn and keep growing until the last root is severed and the tree collapses into the embrace of the river, which carries it out to sea, or into somebody's fishing net.

The Big Beluga scooted past the sweepers and around the occasional rapids as we rushed to the place where the Kenai River branches into the Vyg. We passed dozens of boats filled with hundred of anglers, but only saw a couple of nets held proudly up, signaling the good luck of some man and bad luck of some fish. The traffic thinned out on the other side of the Soldotna bridge. The boat maneuvered a path to Three River Bend, where the Kenai branched both north and south. The north branch was called the Moose River, the south was called the Vyg.

Although lots of fish come up the Vyg, most sportfishermen avoid it because the channel is too quirky for casual navigation. The channel is mostly deep and narrow, with lots of deadly rapids, until it spills onto the great flatlands which roll down from the Kenai Mountains and out into Cook Inlet. For a while the river is so wide and so shallow that you can scrape the bottom off a flat-bottomed boat if you don't know what you're doing.

The Big Beluga knows what he's doing. At one point he stopped the motor and ordered us out. We carried his boat through a few hundred feet of foot-deep water, until he was sure it was safe. After that the Vyg gathered itself up into a proper river again and started its rush to the sea. We navigated around sweepers and white water.

"These are mostly new rapids, that weren't here last year," the Big Beluga said. "New or old, it don't really matter. Split this boat right in half. That's how come you

79

need El Beluga Grande at the wheel if you want to fish the Vyg. I can run these rapids with my eyes closed."

"Bullshit," Michael said. "I bet you ten you can't."

"Show me the color of your money boy, and I'll go back to where we was and do it right now."

Michael asked me to lend him the money. I refused to do so. The Big Beluga enjoyed a big belly laugh that occupied him until he found an easy current about eight miles upriver from the mouth of the Vyg where the Old Believer village and lots of good fishing holes were located.

We figured to troll our way there. The Big Beluga loaded up our hooks with salmon eggs and salmon jism and we dropped our lines in the water. The sun climbed higher and burned away the morning mist, warming our bones. I interviewed my companions for the story I had promised to write. They talked on the record about Bill Hooper's fish and the trouble it was causing. Then I dozed a bit and dreamed of pregnant mermaids and Texan women until my line snapped tight and my pole bent toward the water.

"Ho!" I screamed. At first I thought it was a Texan mermaid, but I quickly came to my senses. The Big Beluga put his net up, although there were no other boats around that needed to be warned away from our lines or advised of our good fortune.

The king yanked me to my feet. The Big Beluga revved up the motor and turned the boat around. We played with the fish a bit, and started to follow it upriver. The tug on my pole felt like the tug of a willful fish, undiscouraged by the fact that it was fighting for its life against the combined strength of the boat, the river and me. One time, the line became slack as it charged back at us, hoping to tangle my line in the blades of the outboard motor. Another time, it caused me to slip on a glob of discarded salmon jism. I fell down but held on tightly to the Big Beluga's $250 fishing pole.

"It's a lunker! It's a lunker!" the Big Beluga said. He always said this even when he wasn't working. There's no percentage for a guide to oversee the capture of a small king salmon.

Michael added, "Way to go, Shorter-Than-I."

I pulled the king to the surface and the Big Beluga snatched it with his net. Michael clubbed it to death with a cop's nightstick the Big Beluga carried for that purpose. The king weighed about fifty pounds. It was nothing for Bill Hooper to write home about, but it was the biggest fish I'd ever caught, except for a halibut, which doesn't really count. The Big Beluga took a picture of me and my fish with his Instamatic.

Kings are so big and so special that once you've caught one you've caught your daily limit. That's the law in Alaska. I dismantled my fishing pole and settled down in a nice, sunny corner of the boat to watch the sweepers slide by. It was a good moment, one of the best. The sun was warm. The sky was blue. The water was green and I was the killer of a magnificent fish. Michael and the Big Beluga addressed their own poles with more serious intent, now that they were sure there were lunker kings in the Vyg.

I dozed again and dreamed some more. Lindy Sue called Boris Yermak to the stand. I tried to tell her that Boris was dead, but she couldn't hear me.

Boris looked like he'd been beaten to death with a knout. "And is it true," Lindy Sue asked, "that you crave Texan women for no other reason than you shouldn't have one? And isn't it true that you contemplate adultery while your true love is away at sea?"

Boris collapsed and his family was ashamed. I jumped up out of nowhere and said, "No, leave him alone. I'm the guilty one. But it's not my fault. Texan women have lovely breasts. They talk like sugar and aren't afraid to smile at me."

I was about to say something about mermaids getting pregnant when my dream was interrupted by a great shaking and a big booming and the dissonant screams of Michael and the Big Beluga: "Mutherfuckergoddamnsonofabitchwatchwhatyou'redoingstop."

When I came to my senses, the boat was rocking as if from a great wave. Michael was reeling in his line. His pole was slack and he seemed more disgusted than excited. "That asshole cut my line," he said, to which the Big Beluga added: "I pay good money for them lures, and salmon jism ain't cheap, you know."

I looked upriver and saw a figure in black in a boat moving away from us at a rapid pace. He had wild black hair and a

81

wild black beard and seemed to be dressed from head to toe in black leather. He made a big noise, took a sharp turn and disappeared behind a bend in the river.

"Did you get a number?" I asked.

Michael and the Big Beluga looked at each other, then shook their heads together. Michael said, "But I seen his boat good enough. He's got a Riverking Cruiser with a fifty-five-horsepower Riverking outboard."

To which the Big Beluga added, "Motor like that is against the law, by the way. The limit is thirty-five horsepower on the river system now. If there wasn't a limit the Kenai would be like a blender back by Soldotna with all of the boats that're out today. What I want to know is where is that trooper-dork Peek-A-Boo Pete. He's always around when he thinks I got an illegal fish in the back of my truck, but then here comes a real criminal and I bet he's out back of the K-Beach burger place picking his nose and eating it."

Our boat was still rocking in the wake of the Riverking Cruiser when Michael pointed downriver and said, "Hey, look over at that!"

The Big Beluga and I looked. We saw a huge cloud of black smoke billowing from the mouth of the river, just about where the village of Vyg would be.

The water near the mouth of the Vyg was covered with a fine gray soot. The Old Believers had formed a bucket brigade linking the river to a large fire which was consuming two small buildings and some low lumps scattered along the beach. The fire and the villagers made a great, roaring, incomprehensible noise punctuated by the wailing of a small gathering of women, who held one another and looked at the blaze with frightened eyes.

"Fedor! Fedor! Fedor!" moaned a plump woman with a missing tooth. Her peasant dress was wet with tears, and soiled by the ashes in the air.

The Big Beluga eased his boat past the woman, toward a flat part of the bank several hundred yards downriver from the confusion, near the place where the river became the sea. The boat bobbed up when Michael jumped ashore to tie a line to the roots of a sweeper.

We ran to the fire in a state of great excitement, as if it was some carnival attraction. The Big Beluga made the distance in a few long strides, followed by Michael with his blubbering waddle, and then me with the hop-skip-lunge I've employed all my life thanks to polio. This hurried limp has the absurd effect of making me look most silly when I am at my most serious. I stumbled more than once, but kept on scrambling.

I took a few pictures with the Big Beluga's Instamatic, and then joined my friends in the bucket brigade. The Big Beluga waded into the river, where his long arms were well suited to the task of dipping buckets into the water and swinging them ashore. I handed the buckets to Michael, who passed them on to an old man with a great gray beard. The man seemed to regard us as a necessary evil because our arrival had freed three of the Old Believers to join another fire crew who were splashing sea water on one side of an Old Believer church with a golden-colored, onion-shaped dome on top. The church was near the fire but as yet had not been touched by the flames.

The heavy work was clearly a strain on Michael. His fat wobbled and his face became slick with sweat. I thought he was going to die, but his heart kept pumping squirts of blood to his fat but very strong hands. As for me, my heart was strong but my hands were tender, and soon started to blister.

The Big Beluga had no problem at all. He seemed to regard the work as some sort of game, the object of which was to pass buckets to me faster than I could pass them to Michael. His long arms were a great whirling water wheel and more than once I was stunned or knocked down by a bucket I wasn't ready to receive. Likewise was the Old Believer perfectly suited to this line of work and it seemed to me that an unspoken bond developed between him and the Big Beluga, as if they were drawn together by shame for the two weaklings who struggled between them.

We passed buckets for more than an hour without having any apparent effect on the fire. At one point, the village elders decided to give up on the burning sheds and pointed our bucket brigade at the church, which had started to smolder in one spot and seemed to be in jeopardy. After this, the fire did its work quickly, consuming the shacks and then itself until all that remained was smoldering ash out of which poked a few charred bits that wouldn't burn. I looked at my hands. They were rubbed raw and smeared with blood.

Peek-A-Boo Pete and the Baranov Volunteer Fire Department arrived shortly after that and tried to take credit for saving the church. The volunteers were thrilled at the chance to display their skills. They unrolled their hose in no time, plugged it into a pumper truck and covered first the church and then the ash heap with a fine rainbow of water. The ash heap quickly became a sticky black bog from which no spark could ever hope to escape. The woman with soot-stained tears was still crying for Fedor, whoever he was.

Peek-A-Boo Pete led his troopers in an official stomp around the village. They asked everyone who Fedor was. If any of the Old Believers understood him, they didn't let on. Peek's constant question was met with silence, a shrug and a hostile stare. After a while, he came over to me and said, "What the hell are you doing here?"

When I told him we'd been fishing, he gave the river a wistful look and said, "I ain't been fishing yet since the second run started. This trial takes up all my time."

I said, "Sorry to hear that, Peek. You'll be sorry too when you figure out you've arrested the wrong man."

Peek removed his glasses and wiped away a smudge. He shook the glasses at me. "Oh, we got the right man, all right. And we'll nab the guy that did this too. You know anything about what's going on here? I mean, who's this Fedor person and where is he?"

Before I could say that I didn't know, the Old Believer with the great gray beard poked Michael with his elbow and pointed at the devastation that the fire had left behind. "Fedor Yermak," he said.

Peek took a notebook out of his back pocket and wrote something down. "So this Fedor Yermak started the fire, huh? Is he any relation to Boris Yermak, the guy that Ivan Smolensk killed?"

The Old Believer didn't understand the question, so he pointed at the ashes again and again said, "Fedor Yermak."

"I'm gonna take a real good guess and say that just maybe those sheds belong to Ivan Smolensk or his brother or his father or some other Smolensk and that Fedor Yermak burned them down to pay some back for his brother or father or son getting killed. Follow me, Riordan, and I'll show you some real police work in action."

I followed Peek. Michael followed me. The Big Beluga

didn't follow anybody. He went back to his boat and took a nap while we investigated the incident.

Peek asked every Old Believer in Vyg where Fedor Yermak was. And just about every villager said something in a language we didn't understand and pointed at the ash heap. The only villager who didn't point at the ash heap was the woman who had been wailing and weeping and crying out his name. When Peek asked her where Fedor Yermak was, she only cried louder and beat the ground with her fists.

"It seems like we got plenty of witnesses," Peek said. "Now we just need to find this Fedor fellow."

Father Nick was delivered to the scene in a patrol car driven by a rookie trooper who saw some need to announce his arrival with a screaming siren and a full display of revolving lights. The archpriest looked tired and sad. The Old Believers looked away when he stepped out of the squad car.

Peek explained the situation. "We got an arson fire here. From what I can gather it was set by Fedor Yermak. I expect that Fedor Yermak is related to Boris Yermak and the fire is some kind of revenge for the way Ivan Smolensk killed Boris, which just about ruins your theory that Ivan is innocent. What we need here is to find Fedor so I can arrest him."

Peek ordered his troopers to round up all the villagers so that Father Nick could question them. The old man with the soot-stained beard stepped forward and looked the archpriest in the eye. Father Nick asked him something in Russian and the old man mumbled something and pointed at the black bog that the Baranov Fire Department had made from the smoldering ashes.

At this, Father Nick dropped to his knees and began to pray out loud in Russian. The Old Believers whispered among themselves. Peek waited patiently until the archpriest was done praying. "Okay, Father. Enough's enough. Where's Fedor Yermak?"

The archpriest looked even sadder than before. He dropped his eyes and pointed to the place the fire had destroyed. "He's in there, Peek."

*　　*　　*

The Yermak women wiped away sooty tears with sooty handkerchiefs as they watched a young state trooper wade into the black ash bog. He pulled away some charred bits of stuff that wouldn't burn. Tied to a blackened pole with a blackened chain and a blackened lock were the blackened bones of a human being.

Father Nick said another prayer and made the sign of the cross—first with two fingers, then with three. One of Peek's men started to unfurl the yellow evidence tape which the state troopers used every time a member of the Yermak family was murdered.

When Father Nick had finished his second prayer he walked up to Peek and said, "Do you think Ivan Smolensk killed this man too?"

Chapter 11

PEEK-A-BOO PETE'S OFFICE WAS PLASTERED WITH CERTIF-
icates, commendations, flattering news reports, and the enameled remains of a king salmon that had run afoul of the
law. A picture of his family had an honored place next to his
electric pencil sharpener. He asked me and my two fishing
buddies to sit down on a brown leather couch.

"If you have any information, it's your duty as citizens to
tell me. I'm trying to solve a murder, not sell subscriptions
to that liberal rag of yours."

"I don't have a liberal rag," Michael said.

"Me neither," added the Big Beluga.

Peek didn't care much for my deposition. It was mostly
about the heroics of the village bucket brigade and an opera
by Mussorgsky where the Old Believers kill themselves
while singing one more song.

"I read about that in your newspaper," Peek said. "It
didn't make any sense then and it doesn't make any sense
now. I hope you're not saying that this dead Believer's a
martyr, or maybe it was Marty." He laughed at our typo-
graphical error for what must have been the fiftieth time.
Ashe put my affidavit on the bottom of his pile. "I appreciate
your comments, Riordan, but I think I know what's going
on."

"Oh, yeah? And what's that?"

"Vendetta."

"But these people aren't Italian. They're Russians, remember?"

Peek adjusted his gun belt so that it squeezed his belly in.

87

"It's all the same to me. I don't care what you call it. I'm saying this is nothing but a good old-fashioned family feud. Like the Hatfields and McCoys, only with Communists."

"They're not Communists. That's why they're here."

"Whatever."

"I hope you're not going to tell me that the man we saw on the river was an Old Believer? Please don't try to tell me that."

His gun belt had slipped down again and let his belly swell out. "That's what I'm saying and if you say I said it I will deny it and never talk to you again. Now you'll have to excuse me so I can interview these other so-called witnesses."

It was not present when my friends made their official statements, but was able to obtain photocopies from a trooper who owed me one. We printed part of Michael's deposition in oversize type and ran it next to a picture I had taken of the bucket brigade with the Big Beluga's Instamatic. The statement read, in part:

"He looked like a bear with big teeth and mean, like a biker from Nikiski. When he cut my line I yelled at him and he looked right at me and I froze up. His hair was black and maybe his eyes were a little slanted. He had a short leather jacket with lots of buttons and knobs."

The part we didn't publish went like this: "I'd know him for sure if I ever saw him again, but first I'd probably have to pee in my pants the guy was so scary."

I wrote an editorial about death and justice and truth and salvation. We put it all together, and threw it on the page. The headline machine started acting up, turning capital O's into capital U's: FIRE CLAIMS LIFE UF ULD BELIEVER. It took Joe a while to fix the machine and we missed deadline by an hour and a half. The pressmen didn't mind. They smoked cigarettes, talked about fish and made some easy overtime while we struggled in the composing room.

I went home exhausted, but couldn't sleep. The ceiling of our bedroom became a fast-forward movie—fish, fire, death, man. The Big Beluga's Instamatic. Fish, fire, death, man. Blisters on the bucket brigade. I rolled over on my side, but the movie just moved faster—fish, fire, death, man. The woman who wept for Fedor. Fish, fire, death, man. A boatful of peasants and a coin made of gold. I couldn't slow the movie down. Our bedroom started to spin and I could hear my heart beating hard and fast, then harder and faster, as if it might explode.

Chena I went for a walk, and my mind started to slow down. We saw the moon make a gauze halo of some steam from Redoubt Volcano. We went to the 7-Eleven and bought some chili cheese dogs, and then to the *Beacon* to watch the paper come off the press.

The truck drivers smoked cigarettes and talked about fish and made some easy overtime while the pressmen struggled with huge stacks of newspapers. Chena took a leak on a pile of scrap paper while I went inside to get a copy. The press was a concert of motion and noise as it gobbled up great white rolls of paper, smeared them with ink and then cut and folded them down to size.

I grabbed a copy from a pile from a test run that had been discarded for having too little ink. My Instamatic picture of the bucket brigade didn't look like much, but the story was okay. I turned to an inside page as I walked out into the night, where I was greeted by slow clapping and the crisp, nasal voice of the upper crust: "Author. Author."

The voice was prep school all the way, as if the speaker's nostrils were pinched together with a clothespin. It came from a man standing in the bright yellow glow of a streetlight Jack had installed to warn the careless truck drivers away from his azalea bushes.

I called Chena and headed for our big red monster pickup truck, but the man gave another slow clap and again said "Author. Author." Chena thought he was talking to her and went over to sniff his shoes.

He was a tall man, rather thin, with blond hair and pale skin made more blond and more pale by the unreal yellow beam of the streetlight. He extended his hand to me. I shook it. It was cold and hard and thin, like a skeleton wearing a surgical glove.

"Do you like to read your own stories, Mr. Riordan?" There was a lockjaw quality to his nasal whine, as if his teeth were cemented together.

"Who are you?"

Chena finished sniffing his shoes, and went off to sniff

something else. "I represent your government. My name is Jon Jones."

I didn't ask but knew in my gut that this Jon spelled his name without an *h*. "My government?" I said.

"That's right. Customs and Immigration. Do you know the penalty for smuggling?"

"Smuggling what?"

"Smuggling anything. People, perhaps. Or ancient artifacts." He dipped into a pocket and pulled out something that sparkled almost as much as his teeth. He handed me a coin. It was heavy for its size. I held it up to the light. It had the profile of a man I didn't recognize and funny letters I didn't understand.

"Have you ever seen a coin like that, Mr. Riordan?"

"What is it?"

"It's Romanov gold. A thousand of these were minted more than three hundred years ago, when the boyars elected Michael Romanov to be their new czar. There's not many left now. They're worth quite a lot."

I gave it back to him. "You're a little far afield, aren't you Mr. . . . ah . . . Jon Jones?"

He tried to laugh, but couldn't squeeze much merriment between his clenched teeth. "Not at all. There are many Russian artifacts around here, and some of the Natives run a vigorous black market with their cousins from Siberia. It comes from across the Bering Sea. The superpowers are neighbors up in this part of the world, you know. There's an American island in the Bering Sea that's only three miles away from the Soviet Union. You can walk right over when the water freezes up."

I told him I'd heard something about that, but that I hadn't seen any Romanov gold. Chena'd run out of things to sniff and had started to sniff at me, her way of saying "Let's go." Jon Jones walked us to our big red monster pickup truck. When he stepped into more normal light, I saw that he had a trim mustache that was almost the same color as his translucent skin.

"I suggest you be careful, Mr. Riordan. Your government is keeping an eye on you."

Chapter 12

THE TRIAL OF IVAN SMOLENSK BEGAN. PEEK-A-BOO PETE, prosecutor Larry Wilkins and Judge Kramer could hardly admit to the boys at the Baranov Barbershop that they had arrested, charged and indicted the wrong man. The boys at the barbershop weren't about to press the issue, since they had already voted to convict.

The real jury was hardly less certain of the truth despite the *Beacon*'s frantic efforts to persuade them otherwise. They wanted to convict Ivan as quickly as possible so they could go back to fishing for a king salmon even bigger than the one Bill Hooper had caught. The fact that the king salmon fishing season would close in ten days lent a certain urgency to the legal proceedings.

Judge Kramer dismissed Lindy Sue Baker's motion that the trial be moved to another town. "I understand your motion," he said, "but we don't believe everything we read in the paper, especially when it's the *Beacon*," the judge proclaimed. The *Peninsula Clarion*, our chief competitor, quoted him at length.

A Riverking Cruiser with a 55-horsepower Riverking motor was found abandoned in a slough behind Harrison's Place in Cooper Landing, a fishing town about eighty miles upriver from Baranov. Harrison's Place is run by a guy named Miller and a confusing assortment of relatives. One of the younger Millers took a flatboat into the slough with a young girl from Moose Pass. Their flatboat bumped into the Cruiser, which had been scuttled in shallow water. None of the Millers remembered anything about a man in black who looked like a biker from Nikiski. The demolished boat was traced to Jerrold Walker of Soldotna, who'd reported it stolen two weeks before.

Jury selection began. Prosecutor Wilkins was looking for twelve people who didn't like Natives or Russians or any foreigners whose claim to Alaska predated their own. Wilkins was an angry man who hated fish. He'd never caught one. His great desire was to become a state senator and he believed that his prospects would improve if he could convict Ivan Smolensk of a crime he didn't commit.

Ivan mumbled into his beard. He didn't seem very interested in the proceedings. On his left sat Father Nick, who had been commissioned by the court to translate the proceedings for the defendant. Behind him, praying for him, sat many people from Vygovskaia Pustyn, including the family of Boris Yermak, the man he was said to have killed.

They looked like Pugachev's army—sullen peasants brooding over a thousand years of persecution. There were a few children, but most of the Old Believers were old. Dried-out men stroked long gray beards with leathery hands. There were three old women wearing babushkas, with fat happy cheeks and melancholy eyes. All of the Old Believers had melancholy eyes, but the three old women had other qualities. Their bodies had been made wide and soft by the birth of many children, their breasts heavy and low by constant motherhood. Knitting was their only revenge and they went at it with inspired fury as they listened to Father Nick's translations and passed them on to the back benches.

To Ivan's right was Lindy Sue Baker. She had lush curves, short legs and the disposition of a pit bull. She tended to point her left breast at the person she was talking to and asked the same three questions of each prospective juror:

"Do you read the *Beacon*?"

"Do you believe the *Beacon*?"

"Do you think Russian immigrants should be allowed to live on the Kenai Peninsula?"

I cornered her in the lobby when the court adjourned for lunch. "Miss Baker, my name is Pres Riordan. I'd like to talk to you."

She pointed her left breast at me. "I know all about you,

Mr. Prester John Riordan. I read all that crap you write. Anything I have to say to you, I'll say in court and if you want to listen it'll cost you more than that piece of shit newspaper is worth, unless of course you give me all your notes right now."

A police artist made a composite drawing of the man in the black leather coat. They gave him a big black beard and wide Slavic cheeks of the sort found in abundance in Vyg, and in some of the Native families where the Russian blood still ran thick. The drawings were posted in grocery stores and gas stations from Baranov to Soldotna. A biker from Nikiski was arrested, but they let him go.

That afternoon, Rachel called me on the *Derring Do*'s radiophone. "Hi, Baby. How you doing? Over."

"I'm doing fine, Rache. How's the catch?"

There was a long pause full of static. A radiophone is different from a regular phone in that you can't talk and listen at the same time. Finally, Rachel said, "You forgot to say 'Over.' Over."

"Sorry . . . ah . . . Over."

"I asked Red to tell me about the coin, but he didn't know much. He's a little mad at me because his son Barney has gone a little crazy and won't leave me alone. Red says it's my fault. Are you there? Over."

"Yes. Over."

"But there's something else. We saw the boat that Red's friend was talking about. It's a real beauty painted mauve. Over."

I played dumb, which I was. "What's mauve? Over."

"It's kind of a purplish-rose color popular with the Russian royalty. I read about it in a book called *Nicholas and Alexander* about the last days of the Romanov dynasty. It's a very sad story. They had a bunch of children but they all got murdered. The other thing about this boat is that it doesn't have a crane, just like Red's friend said. You can't catch fish without a crane, unless you're Bill Hooper. Is is true what I read about Bill Hooper's fish, that it's in a case over at Peninsula Pontiac? Over."

"It's true. Over."

"That about circles the square on the world's biggest

king. Beer, cars and little boy games. Don't you men ever grow up? I've got to hang up soon so I'll tell you about the boat. It was headed northeast. Siberia-bound, which doesn't make any sense. Do you miss me? Over."

"Of course, I do. Over."

"Well that's too bad because I was thinking maybe I'll stick around after the opening's over and maybe work on one of the processing boats. A Polish skipper offered me twenty-five dollars an hour to supervise some slimers from Washington State. We could sure use the money, unless you want me to come right home right now. Over."

"I guess. I don't know . . . ah . . . Over."

"Right. Maybe you need some more time to think. Have you been thinking about having a baby at all? I mean, if you have, what do you think? Over."

Crinkling static stopped conversation, but the static was all in my head. "Rachel? What was that? I can't hear you. Over."

Larry Wilkins called a number of expert witnesses to the stand. The first was Peak-A-Boo Pete. Peek testified that Boris Yermak had been beaten to death and that Ivan Smolensk was the only person in the vicinity. He testified that when Ivan saw Boris' body, he uttered a single Russian word: knout.

Larry trotted over to the jury. Some of the jurors were paying attention. Others were dreaming of fish. "Your honor, for the benefit of the jury I would like to point out that a knout is a heavy whip."

He spun back to Peek. "What country is the knout from, Officer Roberts?"

The trooper squared his shoulders and straightened his tie. He still looked like a slob. "The knout's from Russia. It's a Russian whip." Larry slapped his hand against the railing of the juror's box, but failed to stir the more determined fish-dreamers.

"Thank you, Officer Roberts. I have no more questions, your honor."

Lindy Sue Baker's cross-examination was a sort of verbal jujitsu. "Officer Roberts, you said the knout is a Russian whip. I bet you know a lot about Russia."

"I know enough," he replied. "A knout is a Russian whip, like I said."

Lindy Sue went back and leaned under the defense table. The men in the jury who weren't dreaming about fish got a good look at her breasts as she leaned under the table and pulled out a brown shopping bag. The contents jingled when she dumped them on the table. It was a whip. She picked it up.

"Like this?" she asked Peek.

The Alaska State Trooper shifted in his seat. He mumbled under his breath. The judge made him mumble louder. "Right."

"Right, a knout like this?

Peek nodded. "Right. A knout like that, but that better not be the one or you've been hiding evidence."

Lindy Sue rattled the whip under his nose. The leather straps were tied into knots. "Don't worry. This isn't the knout you're looking for. It isn't even a knout. It's a cat-o'-nine tails and it was used by the English. Now how much Russian history did you say you knew?"

Peek didn't say anything. Lindy Sue went on. "I brought this whip to illustrate a point. The point is you don't know what a knout looks like because you haven't found the murder weapon. Are you sure it was a knout that killed Boris Yermak? Maybe it was a cat-o'-nine tails?"

"Maybe it was. But Mr. Smolensk over there said it was a knout and I figure he should know."

Lindy Sue had a little more trouble with the next witness. Harrison Carter Morgan was a professor of Russian history and language at the University of Alaska–Fairbanks. Larry called him to the stand and asked him to talk about the role of the knout in Russian history.

The professor was a plump fellow who sweated a lot. "It was introduced by the Rurik dynasty, a family of mixed Slavic and Viking blood who ruled Russia before the Romanovs. Ivan the Terrible was a Rurik. He used the knout to punish criminals and dissidents. It's a heavy whip made of parchment soaked in milk and dried until it becomes hard and sharp."

Larry leaned against the witness box. "Parchment soaked

95

in milk? That doesn't sound too bad. It can't hurt too much."

Harrison Carter Morgan made four smiles—one with his lips, the others with his chin. "On the contrary. The knout is a most painful and deadly device. A few blows can skin a man in minutes if administered properly. The Communists prohibited its use."

The jury's mood became more foul as the afternoon wore on. They fidgeted and frowned and took turns watching the clock. The proceedings were slowed by Father Nick's translation of the testimony into Russian, so the defendant could understand what was happening to him. Ivan Smolensk didn't seem to care. He looked at the jury with heavy eyes, which might have bothered them had they dared to look back.

Father Nick spoke to Ivan in a stage whisper so the Old Believers attending the trial would also know what was going on. Each of his whispers moved around the room from lip to ear, starting with three babushkas knitting in the front row. From lip to ear, lip to ear, the information moved around the room until it reached an old man with a red face who seemed a little deaf. When the word got to him he would bellow it in coarse Russian so everybody could hear, including the judge, who tolerated the situation, and the jurors, who did not. Every now and then Judge Kramer would tap his gavel, but the old man never heard him.

A doctor testified as to the cause of death. A theologian described the religious significance of the cross shape in which the body had been laid. A television repairman from Homer told the court that Ivan's brand new TV had been smashed to smithereens by a man named Boris. Six Old Believers were called to the witness box and cited for contempt of court after they refused to testify.

Lindy Sue Baker mounted a spirited but ineffective defense. She made several strong objections, some of which were sustained. She subjected some of the state's witnesses to vigorous cross-examination and challenged the credentials of others. Nobody had found the fabled knout; nobody but Lindy Sue seemed to care.

As the trial entered its final days, the public defender showed signs of desperation. She called a long list of expert witnesses in an effort to wear down the jury. They didn't have much to say, but took a long time saying it. This only made the jurors more anxious. Her closing argument made a stirring appeal to justice, reasonable doubt and her client's right to remain silent. The jury thought about it for almost an hour before returning a verdict of Guilty-Let's-Go-Fishing.

Sentencing was set for the following Monday. That's the same day the power went out and the same day Rachel sent me a postcard from Dillingham. Her postcard said there was no more talk about weird-looking gold and no other sign of the Old Believer boat. Red seemed to think it was heading for the Bering Sea. Barney was in a constant state of passion and the red salmon were fighting through nets and river currents for the chance to lay some eggs. Rachel wrote, "Try to imagine millions and millions of fish struggling to give birth to a new generation."

And then they die, I added to myself.

Judge Kramer gave Ivan a lecture he didn't understand and a sentence he couldn't serve: ninety-nine years with a chance of parole after twenty. I cornered Lindy Sue Baker after the sentencing. She'd tied her hair back up and was chewing bubble gum. This time she agreed to talk to me.

"I'll call you tonight," she said. "But we're not dropping the lawsuit. We plan to appeal and we'll need that reporter's notes to overturn the verdict."

That was the night that the power went out. A storm blew out of Siberia and across the Bering Sea, bringing high winds and horizontal rain. The real trouble started in Anchorage, which got its wires crossed and managed to suck all the electricity out of everyplace else before bringing the whole system down. Baranov, Soldotna and the rest of the Peninsula were plagued with pulsating power failures as utility workers struggled with the elements. In some places, the wind was so strong the linemen refused to climb up the power poles for fear of being blown away.

The first blackout came about 9 P.M. Somebody in the newsroom had ordered a pizza and we were putting the paper to bed. I was writing an editorial about the injustice of it all and thinking about what I would say to Lindy Sue. I folded Rachel's postcard in half and tucked it in the pocket next to my heart in the hope it might have the same effect on Texan women that garlic has on vampires.

All of a sudden, my green computer screen flickered some gibberish and then went black. So did the rest of the building. The central computer uttered some sort of metallic whine and then became quiet. The reporters uttered a collective groan and began to curse the dark.

Ronda lit a candle she always kept nearby and Greta angrily stuffed some papers in her briefcase and announced: "I'm leaving now. I've got young children at home who are afraid of the dark."

The rest of us gathered around the candle and the pizza to exchange power failure anecdotes. Blackouts are a common occurrence on the Last Frontier. Too few Alaskans are spread over too much Alaska, taxing a power system designed for dense concentrations of people. Ronda had been relieved of her virginity during a blackout. She said this for Byron's benefit, but Joe was the guy who was listening so hard he almost fell onto the pizza. Byron Schiller believed that power failures were the mischief of unseen hands. I said this one was the judgment of the Old Believer's God come down on the people of Baranov.

The wind howled and the rain splatted against the windows to remind us just how weak we are. Then the lights came back on and the computer coughed awake, like a smoker in the morning. I called a meeting to assess the damage. How many stories were destroyed? How many could still be saved? Where was Greta and what she been working on anyway?

"I've got the lead," Byron said. "The Old Believer trial. I wrote the story already, but I think the computer ate it when the power went down. I'll write it again, but I'll need some overtime."

We went to our desks and started to patch up the next day's news. But then the wind blew somewhere else and the lights went out again. Joe made an animal sound and slammed something against something else. Ronda relit her candle and Byron started to tell her a story about a ghost called the Illuminati, the Illuminated One. Nothing was getting done, and the pressmen—who made twice as much money as any of my reporters—were already into overtime. I came out of my office and made a little speech.

"Okay, okay. First of all, who's here?" They sounded out their names: Byron, Ronda, Joe and George.

"Look, I'm not going to pay you to sit around and wait for the electricity to come back on."

George started complaining while I handed out the assignments. "You get me a story about the power failure and you get me a story about the storm. Byron, I want you to type your Old Believer story on paper and we'll figure out later how to get it into the computer."

Byron and I assembled our typewriters around Ronda's candle while the others scattered to their duties. We pecked away in the dark while the storm raged over the flatlands. Primal chaos brought out in Byron the philosopher that was never too far from the surface: "I think the dark puts us in touch with our animal nature. I feel like a terrified savage crouching in his cave. The Neanderthal man lived his whole life in a world like this. No wonder he believed in God."

We pecked away in the dark some more, until I said, "Hey, Byron. Have you ever heard anything about Romanov gold?"

Byron Schiller had heard something about almost everything. He thought for a minute and replied: "Geneva, 1926. The Communists accused the royal family of stashing away billions in a Swiss bank account. They wanted the gold back, but the Swiss said they'd have to produce Czar Nicholas or one of his heirs, which the Reds couldn't do because they'd murdered them all."

I wanted to ask another question, but before I could do so the telephone rang. Byron fumbled for the receiver and whispered into it. That's when I noticed we'd been whispering ever since the lights went out, as if the darkness was alive and angry and might hear us if we talked too loudly. "It's for you," Byron said.

Her voice sounded like all the trouble I'd never had. "Mr. Riordan, this is Lindy Sue Baker. I'll meet you at the Rig in fifteen minutes."

Chapter 13

THE MANAGEMENT OF THE RIG TRIED TO MAKE UP FOR THE shortage of light with an abundance of beer. Music came from a portable radio. Dozens of candles gave the place a medieval feel—like party time at the Olde Mead Hall. The crowd was giddy and excited. Shadows slid past twinkling flames. The biggest shadow of them all moved like a ship in the night and belonged to my friend Michael Gudunov. When I walked in he switched from coffee to beer and sat on the stool next to mine.

"Hey, what's the word, Shorter-Than-I?"

The power failure was hitting him hard. His voice had the frayed tones of a television addict in need of a commercial. I asked him if he seen a Texan lady and he said yeah, he'd seen a dozen or so.

"Hey, Mike. Are you okay?"

"What're you talking about, Shorter-Than-I?"

"I'm talking about the television, Mike. I can see you got the jitters because you can't watch TV. That's not good."

Michael had never been angry with me before. He became angry then. The dark got a little darker. "Well, you're a fucking asshole. I like the TV so you better back off."

Michael was different in the dark. When you couldn't see his big lumbering body, he sounded like a little boy who'd lost his puppy. "I figure you'd understand, you being a cripple and all. But you don't understand. Father Nick don't understand. Nobody understands that the great thing about TV is that it don't look back at you. The tube never calls me fat and ugly and it never makes fun of me because I'm a

Native or Russian or both. TV just gives me the pictures and the sound and I can turn it off or change the channel when it pisses me off and later I can turn it back on if I feel like it. What you don't understand is there's been a million nights when the TV was my only friend. What about you? How many times. . . ."

The lights went on again. The candle flames faded and the sliding shadows solidified into human beings. The jukebox cranked up a rock and roll song and a pinball machine that had been in the middle of a jackpot when the power went out picked up where it left off, all garish lights and bells. Michael got up to finish the game. I remembered we had two hundred pounds of frozen halibut melting in our basement. Michael scored another jackpot. I looked around for Lindy Sue Baker. Then the lights went out again.

Michael sat down at our table and picked up where he'd left off. "So don't talk a buncha shit, okay? I'll let it slide if you buy me some beer."

I bought him a whole rancid pitcher. Michael had lost his glass, so he took a deep swig straight from the pitcher and then passed it over to me.

"How's Rachel?" he asked.

I touched the pocket with her postcard in it. "She's fine, I guess. Considering."

Michael listened patiently while I told him about pregnant salmon and the trouble with women.

"That's where you need the TV," he said triumphantly. He had learned from two hours of soap operas every day that women are crazy and can't be understood by anyone as sensible as men. "It's just like 'All My Children.' Natalie loves it when they treat her like shit. But if you're nice she'll walk all over you."

I resisted the temptation to remind Michael that he found all his women at the Flatlands Boom-Boom Cabaret. He added, "And another thing about the TV is you always got the music to let you know what's going on. There's bad guy music for the bad guys and hero music for the heroes. I mean out in the world you can never know who's who because real people never have their own music."

I was going to tell him about Romanov gold, but before I could there descended over the table a cloud of perfume that smelled like all the flowers that had ever bloomed.

My mind made some trouble music, the theme from "Dragnet": "Da-Du-Dun-Dun."

The flame of our candle was agitated by the disturbance in the air. "Is that you, Mr. Riordan?" the disturbance said.

She sat down and pulled the candle over to her side of the table. She'd undone a button of her blouse I'd never seen undone before, flashing me a nice view of her left breast as she pointed it at Michael. "What's your name?"

We exchanged pleasantries and information. I told her about the *Pugachev,* and how it didn't have a crane and carried people instead of fish. She told me about the defense fund which the Yermak family had set up for the man convicted of killing Boris. I told her about Rachel's latest fishing expedition.

She understood. Her husband was an oilman who left her alone for weeks at a time while he pumped crude from Prudhoe Bay. She said her job as a public defender helped to atone for his petroleum sins. Some of them, anyway. Other sins had to be atoned for in other ways.

"But Ivan's only sin is he won't talk to me or you or Father Nick or anybody else. I want to help him, Riordan. He's innocent."

Michael told her about the black leather man we'd seen on the Vyg. She told Michael about the Great Grand Lady.

"The what?" I said.

"A person I know—I can't say who—told me a story about this Great Grand Lady. That's what they call her. She lives in Russia and is very wealthy. She's very old and uses Romanov gold to help the Old Believers."

"Help them do what?"

"Maybe to bribe the Communists and help the Old Believers escape on board the *Pugachev.* Do you know very much about the village of Vygovskaia Pustyn?"

The candle melted into rivers of wax and the soft light danced in her eyes. She had gone to the village a couple of times and checked the borough record books. A strange thing had happened in Vygovskaia Pustyn: the population had doubled in the last ten years, but most of the people were very old.

"So?"

"So how did they do that? Old people can't have babies. Any fool knows that. I think this Great Grand Lady they talk about has set up some kind of underground railroad to smuggle the Old Believers out of the Soviet Union. I bet they use the *Pugachev* for transportation. The question is, how do they get through the border?''

"Kotzebue," I suggested.

"Or Diomede," Michael said.

Michael hadn't said anything for a while. I moved the candle over so we could see his face.

"What did you say?" I said.

"Little Diomede, Michael replied. "It's an American island way up over in the Bering Sea. It's just three miles away from Big Diomede, which is owned by the Russians. They have some soldiers there, but it's almost like an open border. I know because I saw a story on the TV news that says they're gonna make it into a park now that we're friends with Russia again. A crazy guy from California tried to walk right over to Russia when the water froze one time. Maybe the Old Believers just walk the other way. What I'm thinking is that if the Great Grand Lady that you're talking about is sneaking Old Believers over, maybe she sneaks 'em through the Diomedes, just like those crazy people from California.''

"I heard about that," Rachel had said. I said I'd heard about it too, although I hadn't, although my job was to hear about everything. The *Beacon* is a small newspaper covering a small world. If it washes on our shores, it must be news. If it doesn't, it isn't.

Michael got up to talk to a lanky shadow that could have been the Big Beluga. Lindy leaned back so the dark covered her face. The uneasy light of the candle illuminated her breasts. Her left one was pointing at me. She leaned back over the candle with something on her mind.

"Okay, Pres. I've got a deal we can talk about if you want to cut a deal.''

I forget when we started using first names, but it was a bad idea. "Okay, Lindy Sue. Like what?"

"I think Michael's right and I think it has to do with the man you saw on the river and I think it has to do with Ivan's refusal to defend himself. Here's the deal: You go to Kotzebue or Little Diomede or wherever you have to go to do a story about why Ivan won't talk. Find out what's going on and I'll drop the lawsuit.''

I complained about the money; Jack would have wanted

me to. Lindy Sue said the Ivan Smolensk defense fund would pay for my transportation. "Look, the Yermak family gave me ten thousand dollars to help Ivan. I can use it to sue you and make your life miserable, or I can use it to send you on a big news story that'll make you famous and get my client out of jail. I don't want to put a lot a pressure on you, but Ivan Smolensk is an innocent man."

I think it was a hallucination. Or maybe it was a confused memory from a fantasy I'd always had. Or maybe it really happened. I thought I saw Lindy Sue Baker play with another button of her blouse and say, "I need your help, Pres. Don't make me take you to court. I've really liked some of the stories you wrote, and sometimes you seem like a pretty good guy. It's too bad you're taken."

I thought about too many things in too little time: about Texan dreams on a lonely night and the way Lindy Sue's bosom peeked out from behind undone buttons; about all the girls I'd never had and dying at the end of an unlived life. My heart did a troubled fandango. I tried to touch it with my hand to see how it was beating. Instead I felt the postcard Rachel had sent me. I excused myself and went to the bar for an unspoken purpose. I stopped for a while to talk to Michael. The lights came on before I could say or do something I didn't want to say or do.

If Jack was surprised, he didn't let on. "Now about these Diomede Islands. Isn't that the place where fruitcakes from California walk to Russia to be Communists? How do they do that, anyway? Let's play for twenty."

I waited until Jack hit his tee shot and then replied. "I guess the sea freezes in January and then they just walk over the ice. But it's summer now and the sea's melted, so I don't think that'll happen."

Jack thought something was up, but he didn't know what it was. He sliced his chip shot onto the mudflats which abutted the second green. "She says she's gonna pay all that money just so you can go over there. Isn't that against journalism ethics or something?"

It was, but I made it sound like it wasn't. My own iron shot slammed into a tree and careened toward the green. "Give me ten strokes and I'll put twenty bucks on this round. I feel lucky today."

Jack stopped worrying about my ethics and concentrated on his short irons. My ten-stroke handicap faded, but it didn't fade fast enough. Jack's drive on five landed in Myrtle Sheppard's backyard. He took the penalty stroke. Word was, she was gunning for him. The penalty stroke won me the game. I'd never beaten Jack before and he didn't like it much. I made him pay up right away and promised to frame the twenty-dollar bill.

"Okay, fine. Let's play another round."

"Sorry Jack, but I gotta pack, unless you want to get sued."

Chapter 14

THE NEXT DAY WAS DEVOTED TO AIRPLANES AND AIRPORTS. I hate airplanes. They seem so unlikely. I love airports. They have purpose and passion. They are places where strangers share primitive emotions, where the fear of takeoff mingles with the relief of landing, where sad good-byes are made in the vicinity of joyous reunions.

The Baranov Municipal Airport is a tidy, busy place. Oil workers commute to their new jobs at Prudhoe Bay. Tourists come in from Anchorage bearing fishing poles and shotguns, and are greeted in the lobby by wildlife stuffed and mounted in big glass cases—a brown bear, a caribou and the world's fifth or sixth largest king salmon, their fierce scowls frozen forever in the moment of their death.

I rode to Anchorage in a twin-prop Cessna. It was a bright, clear day and the Cessna was as light as a kite. A crosswind buffeted it, making it dip and slide. The sun sprinkled the blue mountains and the gray seawater with a million twinkles of mirrored light. The green flatlands rippled in the wind.

The Anchorage airport also has the obligatory animals stuffed and mounted in glass, and a collection of Native artifacts donated by Potter MacKenzie, in memory of Edna. But these Alaskan touches are overwhelmed by the general atmosphere and design, which is the same as that found in any of a hundred American cities. There's a row of booths offering rent-a-cars and a cafeteria featuring all sorts of food wrapped in plastic that tastes the same, whether it's labeled salad, sandwich or onions and peas. People shuffle about and wait for something to happen. Inoffensive music waltzes through cavernous rooms made of inoffensive plastic. The bar is full of tired travelers, who soak their anxiety in alcohol.

I do not like to fly. Planes seem too heavy and too slow for flight, but heavy enough and fast enough to explode into fireballs. The sun dipped behind Mount Susitna, the Sleeping Lady, as we pulled into a long, slow turn and headed for Kotzebue on the northwest coast. The universe collapsed in on itself and dropped into a cold, black hole. Death was a bump in the night followed by a white hot explosion and the scattering of our charred remains. I do not like to fly.

I tried to hide my anxiety from the old Native woman who sat next to me. I ordered some beer and brandy so that if we did crash, I'd be too drunk to feel any pain.

The old woman hid her own anxiety behind a calico babushka and the latest edition of *Reader's Digest*. She pulled out a pack of cigarettes as soon as the "No Smoking" light flickered to black. She'd soon churned out enough smoke to cloak the bog in a Sherlock Holmes adventure, and read a "Drama in Real Life" while I rummaged through my memory for something to distract me from the fear in my belly—from wondering about how a pilot could land such a big plane on such little wheels, and what would happen if he was unable to do so.

The beer and the brandy and the baritone hum of the engines lulled me into a fitful sleep. First I dreamed that I forgave Rachel for telling me that I wasn't enough, that she needed a baby, too. Then I dreamed that I forgave my father for leaving my mother before I was born, for setting me adrift in a hostile world. Then I dreamed that I was Dosifei the Old Believer in the grand opera *Khovanshchina* by Modest Petrovich Mussorgsky.

The prince was played by my sports editor, who tried to foment a rebellion against Czarevna Sophia, played by Lindy Sue Baker. The prince promised me and Rachel and all the other Old Believers freedom of worship if we would join the insurrection. Rachel and I enjoyed soprano love and suffered baritone treachery. There was a great deal of killing put to music. Prince Khovansky was arrested by the royal guards and I led the Old Believers in the prepara-

107

tion of our funeral pyre as the Czarevna's troops surrounded us.

> Those bugles herald eternity!
> The time has come to win
> A Marty's crown through fire and flame.

"Who is this Marty person?" says Czarevna Sophia, played by Lindy Sue Baker. Rachel lit the fire and we all jumped in. The audience applauded as the grim baritone of the late-night plane to Kotzebue joined our crescendo of perdition and song.

I was drenched with sweat when I woke up. The old woman in the calico babushka watched me out of the corner of her eye, her toe bobbing like a cork in a storm. The rest of her face was buried in a book entitled *The Yearning Leaves*.

The engines screamed and the cabin shook as the late-night plane to Kotzebue dropped like a stone before leveling off into a bumpy landing. As we left the plane the stewardess handed us fancy sheets of bonded paper which read, "This is to certify that the bearer has traveled north of the Arctic Circle, to the friendly city of Kotzebue, Alaska."

The summer sun was rising, and began to roll around the horizon like the little white ball of a roulette wheel. The place was chilly and gray, quiet except for a sleepy boy in a Chevy van who drove us to the Vu-Nik-Luk Hotel. The windows of my room were covered with aluminum foil and heavy plastic to keep the light out and the heat in. The bedsheets were crisp and as cold as ice. When my body heat melted them, I fell asleep.

Chapter 15

THE VU-NIK-LUK HOTEL WAS OWNED BY THE NUVIK REgional Native Corporation and operated by Al "King Kotz" Hundley and his wife, Olga. Nuvik and the thirteen other Native corporations had been established as part of a settlement with the Inupiat Eskimos and the Athabascan Indians to allow the construction of the trans-Alaska oil pipeline.

"Nuvik she run by boneheads," King Kotz said to me. He was a member of the Nuvik board of directors and had been a territorial senator before Alaska was admitted as the forty-ninth state of the Union. The summer sun and winter wind had given his face the color and texture of an old pair of shoes—wide at the smile and wrinkled at the eyes.

His wife Olga needed a tooth or two and claimed to be related to the Russian explorers who came over from Siberia in 1815 with Otto von Kotzebue. She cooked us a breakfast of salmon and biscuits while her husband and I talked about the fate of the world, or at least this frozen and neglected corner of it.

King Kotz continued, "So as our big part of the pipeline deal, Nuvik gets this Three Sisters zinc mine way up in the hills where the river comes from. I say, who cares? But everybody else says we gotta work the mine so our children can have a little something too. But I say the mine'll just bring more people to Kotzebue, and what we need is not so many people. I always notice that Alaska does a lot better when there aren't so many people. More room for the moose and the fish and such is how I look at it, but I'm just one vote on the corporation board. So we're going to work the

109

mine. So now we got to build a road to get to the mine, only nobody ever built a road up here. This is the Arctic, you know. Nobody knows about roads up here. So we build the road and now they say the price of zinc is going down so we can't afford to work the mine. We're supposed to sit around for ten years until the price goes back up. But ten winters is going to chew up that road like a piece of fried fish. Speaking of which, that smells pretty good, Olga. You ready? We're ready if you're ready.''

Olga poked her head out of the kitchen. It was a gray head with a round face. "Your yelling won't help, you know. If you want to eat, then let me do my work." Then she said to me, "He yells at me just like I'm on one of his boats back in the whaling days."

King Kotz puffed out his chest and set his chin at a regal angle. "She's talking about when I used to run this town. Back then my father was a mostly white man who used to fly a plane." His hand took off from the table and banked into a slow turn to pick up the coffee pot. "We would hunt for whales like a team with my father in his plane to find them and me and my brothers in a boat to throw the harpoon and haul them in. We got so good at killing whales they cut down the season to almost nothing, which is how it is now. They called my father King Kotz because that plane made him the King of Kotzebue and then when he died they called me King Kotz, too, and elected me to be a senator when Alaska was just a territory."

Olga carried in a steaming tray piled high with fish and biscuits and gravy and some kind of meat I'd never had before. Off to the side of the tray was a small plate on which were placed three small cubes of black rubbery stuff that jiggled every time one of us bumped the table.

Olga said, "We're worried, of course, about the young ones. They watch TV and they never read and some of them drink alcohol and smoke dope and don't want to go to school."

She picked up the plate and waved it under my nose. It smelled like old tires. "Here, have some muktuk."

I picked up a piece. It had the consistency of overcooked jello and was oily to the touch. "Muktuk?"

King Kotz grabbed a piece and sucked it into his mouth. "Yeah, that's right. Whale blubber. Our crew caught this one over by Barrow in the last season. We didn't catch anything this year, though, and it's all because of the Japanese. They hunt whales with guns and stuff while we use real ivory harpoons and give the whale a fighting chance."

The whale blubber tasted like salty axle grease and chewed like rubber bands. I chewed until I couldn't chew any more and then forced it down.

King Kotz and Olga started to laugh but were interrupted in mid-guffaw by the entrance of another guest.

Jon Jones looked less pale in the daylight. His legs seemed longer and his shoulders wider than I remembered. My impression that he was scrawny was replaced by an impression that he was wiry. His mouth smiled but his eyes didn't.

He pretended he didn't know me. King Kotz introduced us. I almost coughed up my muktuk and had to chew it a second time when he looked me right in the eyes and said through clenched teeth, "I don't suppose you've seen a blue fishing boat in the vicinity? It's a bright pastel and it might look purple if the light hits it a certain way."

I shook my head and paid close attention to a piece of biscuit as I pushed it through a clot of cooling gravy. When I looked up again, Jones was still looking through me. "I haven't seen anything but the inside of my room. I just got in last night."

There was a big question hanging in the air. King Kotz asked it of Jones. "How come you're here? You here about the whaling treaty? Then I got some words I need to talk at you."

Olga disappeared into the kitchen with an armful of dirty dishes. The stranger shook his head. Olga came back and plopped a cube of muktuk on his plate. "No, I'm with Customs and Immigration. We're investigating a complaint filed by the Soviet government. They think someone is smuggling Russian artifacts in the country." He looked at me again. "You haven't come across any artifacts have you, Mr. Riordan?"

"No. Like I said, I just got in last night. But if I see any artifacts or a bright blue boat or anything that looks like it's any of your business, you'll be the first to know." I nodded at his plate. "Don't forget to eat your muktuk. It's good for you."

* * *

111

King Kotz gave me a guided tour of Kotzebue. We started on the outskirts of town, where the main road dropped into Kotzebue Sound. The city limits were marked with an enormous sign painted red, white and blue that read: "Welcome to Kotzebue, a 1981 All-American City."

King Kotz explained, "We won that 'cause we built the airport hangar for all the bush pilots like my papa used to be. They sent us a certificate and everything."

We drove back the other way until we ran out of land again, this time at a body of water called Hotham Inlet, across which could be seen low brown tundra which eased up toward a barren plateau. King Kotz gazed over the water, hunter's eyes peeking through a narrow slit. "That over there is an official U.S. American national monument with lots of old graves and some whalebone knives. The Native part of my family lived over there for a pretty long time, but now the whales are mostly dead because of the Japanese."

We stood on a point of land. I saw gray and brown and gray and blue and gray and gray where King Kotz saw remarkable detail. "Now that over there is where the Kobuk River comes from and the Native company owns a jade mine. And over there is where we keep the reindeer herd for sausage we get sent to Anchorage. You can't see it from here, but way over there is Siberia, where the Russians came over and discovered us. Lucky us. Kotzebue was the captain of their boat, just like the name of our town. I think it's funny how us Eskimos name everything and even themselves after the snow and caribou and salmon and the stars while white people always name everything after themselves. Olga says it's because white people are always afraid to die. Not that it does them any good. I mean Kotzebue's dead anyway, right?"

We finished our tour with a visit to the city museum, the Ootukahkuktuvik, which means "Place Having Old Things." It had old women who did an old dance and and old men who used an old blanket to toss a young boy into the air.

King Kotz said, "That blond man sure has a strange way about him."

I nodded agreement. "You think he's on the level?"

King Kotz gave me a look that made me wonder if I was on the level. "I think he's with the government, you bet. He made a lot of calls to Washington and he's got a way of asking you to do something where you don't want to do it but you do it right away anyway so as he won't come back and ask you a second time."

I took a walk along the beach, which slid into Kotzebue Sound. The place was so flat and low that I could stand on a rock and see the whole world. I could see the tide bang against the shore and the sun roll along the horizon. I could see the low tin shacks of downtown Kotzebue and the brown tundra flats rising into brown hills. I could see the vast forever of the Arctic Sea on my left and the vast forever of the Alaska mainland on my right. I could see everything but Jon Jones of Customs and Immigration, who snuck up behind me and said, "Good afternoon, Mr. Riordan."

I almost fell off the rock I was standing on. Jones grabbed my elbow to steady me. "What happened to your leg, Mr. Riordan? If you don't mind my asking."

I did mind, so I lied about it. "It got frostbite in the winter of '82 so they had to cut it off." Actually, I'd had polio in the summer of '52. I was six months old at the time.

He was so tall and stood so close to me I had to hold my neck at an awkward angle to look him in the eye. He said, "I see. I see. And what brings you to Kotzebue?"

I picked up a rock and threw it at the sea. "I'm a newsman. I'm doing a story on the whaling treaty."

"No, you're not." He turned and walked away. I followed him, taking two steps to his every one. It was hard work. I said, "I'm not?"

"No, you're not. You're looking for the *Pugachev,* just like me. And maybe some Romanov gold."

I scooted up ahead and stepped in his path so that I could confront him face-to-face and stop all this walking. I was short of breath. The afternoon tide splashed salt water on my shoes. "What's with you anyway? Why are you checking up on me?"

"Just doing my job, Mr. Riordan. I think you should know that the penalty for smuggling antiquities can be quite severe. You'll get several years in prison and a fine that's a lot stiffer than you can afford." He paused to let the tide splash on my shoes again. "And the penalty for smuggling people is even more severe, especially when they're enemies of the state. You wouldn't betray your country, would you Mr. Riordan?''

I found King Kotz and Olga over by a tiny wood smokehouse. Red salmon were hung out to dry on a network of fishing lines which circled the smokehouse.

King Kotz poked a slab of fish with a stick. "We got no sun today. You can't dry fish very good if you got no sun, and the rain that's coming in from over there don't help too much either."

The smokehouse belched forth a rich fog of salmon smoke that made my mouth water. King Kotz asked, "So how come you want to go to Little Diomede? My cousin is the new mayor there and even I don't go there much. Nobody goes to Little Diomede unless they live there or they're a crazy person from California and it's February. You're not from California, are you?"

My host had become darker, more sullen. Maybe it was the bad weather and maybe it was the government man. I almost slipped on a smudge of salmon slime. "I'm with the newspaper in Baranov and I'm doing a story on the whaling treaty."

King Kotz looked at me with seal hunter's eyes that saw things I didn't even know existed. "That may be so. And maybe you're another liar. You and that other white man from the government. I seen you talking to him."

Before I could say something in my own defense, he turned away and yelled at the smokehouse. "Hey Olga, come on out here. The rain's coming up real quick now."

We wrestled with the fish meat as a black storm rolled in from the sea. When we were done, we were covered with slime from our knees to our chins. A big wind blew against the door of the smokehouse.

King Kotz said, "I want to thank you, Mr. Riordan. There's not many white men I know who will smear themselves all up with fish just to help a Native man, like you done for us. How come you have to lie like you did?"

Olga said, "Now, King . . ."

"He's right, Mrs. Hundley," I cut in. "Look, King, I need to talk to you. There're some things you might want to know."

*   *   *
114

I told King Kotz all about it. He said I could probably stay with his cousin, the mayor. I booked a flight to Little Diomede with the only pilot who flew that way, and then listened to the bad weather slam against the windows of the Vu-Nik-Luk Hotel. The wind came from every direction at once. A dusting of summer snow was starting to stick to the ground. "The flight'll be canceled, right? We can't fly in this."

Olga patted me on the shoulder and said, "Now, don't you worry, Pres. Doug Gatlin flies like a killer whale swims. He'll run through just about anything."

When I got the airport, Jon Jones was playing chess with a cousin of King Kotz Hundley. Everyone in Kotzebue was a cousin of everyone else to one degree or another. This cousin had a knight advantage and a clear road to the government man's back row. I asked him to direct me to Doug Gatlin.

He moved his rook before replying, "I don't know where he is."

Half of the townspeople had crowded into the cavernous tin shell which served as both the Kotzebue airport terminal and a parking garage for some of the smaller airplanes. The townspeople milled around and talked to each other in flat tin echoes. Some were waiting for relatives to arrive on the plane from Anchorage. Others were waiting to leave on the very same plane. Three wooden benches that looked like they'd been lifted from the bleachers at Wrigley Field were reserved for a gathering of chubby old men who were waiting to wait. Among them was King Kotz, who winked at me and then continued telling his friends a story which required broad, sweeping gestures.

Behind the men were two vending machines and a ticket counter made of painted plywood. A thick, bronze plaque behind the counter announced that I was in the John Cross Memorial Airplane Hangar, built by the state in 1981 in honor of his many years as a northwest arctic Alaskan bush pilot. A thin woman with a wide face and Asian eyes appeared from behind the ticket counter. "Can I help you, sir?"

I asked her if she knew where Doug Gatlin was. She pointed to a broad-shouldered white man fussing with a pushcart full of boxes. I walked that way.

"Are you Doug Gatlin?"

"Yo."

"I'm Pres Riordan. I talked to you this afternoon."

"Yo."

Gatlin checked the boxes against a list on his clipboard. He didn't seem like a typical Alaskan bush pilot. He not only looked like he could read, he looked like he did so on occasion. He wore a neatly pressed lumberjack shirt, an Air Force flight jacket, worn but spotless blue jeans and fancy basketball shoes. His jaw was heavy and thick as a brick. He was of medium height and weight, but wide on top. He said "yo" a lot.

"I'm supposed to hitch a ride with you to Little Diomede."

He nudged a box with his toe and checked it off his list. "Yo."

"Do I have time to go back to the hotel? I'd like to say good-bye to the lady who runs the place."

"No. We're ready to go. There's another storm cooking up in the Chuckchi Sea. If we don't get out now, we might not get out at all. You got some money?"

I handed him a check for fifteen hundred dollars that had been signed in advance by Lindy Sue Baker. I hoped the Yermaks would get their money's worth, but I couldn't see how. Gatlin interrupted my reverie. "How about lending a hand here?"

We dragged the pushcart to a large vehicle which looked about as flightworthy as a mobile home with wings. One of the wings was green, the other brown. Through the windshield I could see a pair of fuzzy dice dangling from a hook in the cockpit. Gatlin called her "The Leapin' Lizard."

"Nice plane," I said weakly.

He ignored the compliment. "I rigged her up myself. It's mostly an old C-130 Herc that the Army didn't want any more. That's where she got the green. They used her to deliver munitions to the Russians in the Second World War. She knows the polar route by heart."

That was at least forty-five years ago, I said to myself. I tried to remember if I'd ever been in a forty-five-year-old car.

"She likes the cold," the pilot added.

Gatlin pulled on a shank of rope and the plane's belly

116

bounced open with a heavy clang. We loaded the boxes into the cargo hold and heaved the belly door closed.

I prayed to a God I'd forgotten long ago as Gatlin cranked his machine up into a fierce, grinding roar that made the hangar rattle like a garbage can rolling down a cobblestone alley. The residents of Kotzebue looked our way and waved. King Kotz directed the other old men to open the great tin doors.

"Goddamnit," Gatlin said. "Look at that."

I looked. The right propeller was as still as a frozen body sinking into the Bering Sea. "Hang on a second," he said. "I'll be right back."

I watched in horror as the pilot jumped down to the ground, stepped up on an old packing crate and used a large screwdriver to pry open a small panel next to the reluctant propeller. He fussed and banged for five minutes before returning to the cockpit.

"It's hard to get spare parts for these old military planes," he said, as if this would ease my mind. "The companies that make them are used to dealing with the Pentagon, so they charge a fortune and take forever. Let's try it again."

The left propeller roared to life, followed thirty seconds later by its hastily repaired companion. King Kotz and the other old men wrapped their faces in their hands as the hangar filled up with the swirling storm of dust and snow and ice fog that ushered us onto the runway. A crosswind buffeted the *Leapin' Lizard* at it lined up for takeoff.

I screamed but couldn't hear myself above the sound of the engine: "Isn't this a treat? Snow in August."

Gatlin mouthed a soundless "Yo" and released the brake. The *Leapin' Lizard* crawled, and then raced, and then bumped, bumped, bumped until a final violent bump launched us into a slow climb over the water of Kotzebue Sound. A small snow flurry was illuminated by the soft light of the cockpit and the harsher beams of the plane's headlights. We made a big turn and leveled off.

Gatlin eased the engine to a drone, then laughed and turned to me. "It takes about twenty minutes to die once you hit the water. If you've got a life jacket, that is. They say it's a great way to go. First you get numb so you can't feel a thing. Then you get light-headed and the last thing is you start to dream. Sometimes I wonder what I'd dream

117

about if it happened to me. High school football, I suppose. I used to be the quarterback. How about you?''

I told him about the trouble with women. About the Texan dreams and an unborn child. Gatlin made a sad face, as if he knew how I felt, and said, ''Yo.''

We rattled and bumped into the thickening storm. Motion was an illusion, a hoax perpetuated by the millions of puffs of late summer snow which raced at the windshield but never seemed to hit it. It was as if we were the only living things left in a hostile dimension which tossed us around to see how we liked it. The sun had set wherever it was and the gray night became a black night which hated light and wanted to squeeze us out because we were the last two flickering sparks in all creation. Somewhere down there, the night congealed and the sea was silenced too.

I looked at Gatlin, who seemed lost in thoughts that had nothing to do with the flying of an airplane. ''Okay if I look around?''

He tapped one of the meters with the blunt end of his screwdriver. The dial on the fuel gauge went from empty to full. ''Yo.''

I steadied myself by clinging to the straps which hung in a row from the curved fuselage. I was on my own for a step or two where the straps had broken and been left unmended.

The cargo hold was illuminated by a red trouble light and packed to overflowing with the stuff of modern life. Boxes and duffle bags shifted against one another every time the plane bumped against the wind. Some of the boxes were sealed with masking tape and looked like care packages from the people of Kotzebue to their cousins on Little Diomede, where the westernmost outpost of the American Empire was only three miles away from the easternmost outpost of the Soviet Empire.

The United States purchased Alaska from Russia in 1867. This was shortly after President Lincoln freed the slaves and Czar Alexander II freed the serfs. Back then, nobody cared too much about these two godforsaken islands in the middle of the godforsaken Bering Sea. The buyer and the seller just drew a boundary line between the two islands and forgot about them. A hundred and twenty years later, they still didn't care, although journalists would get excited when a crazy person from California flew to Little Diomede in the

118

dead of winter and walked across the ice bridge into enemy territory.

The *Leapin' Lizard* hit a cloud or an air pocket or something else that made us drop a couple of hundred feet. By the time we regained our equilibrium, my legs had turned to jelly. The boxes and duffle bags which Gatlin was delivering to Little Diomede strained against the heavy chain net that held them in place.

I took a quick inventory of the shipment: two Honda three-wheelers, a Sony color TV and a handful of heavy crates packed with the various parts of something called the Texatron Remote Power Supply System. There was a crate full of material from the Bering Straits School District and a Red Cross locker filled with medical supplies, Oreos, generic rice and Coca Cola. Box by box, piece by piece, the twentieth century was coming to Little Diomede just in time for the twenty-first.

The other centuries had passed the place by. No one knows for sure how long the Natives had lived there. They'd already been there for a very long time when the Russian explorer Vitus Bering "discovered" the place on St. Diomede's Day, 1728. The Native legends are unclear. Some say the islanders were dropped from the sky by an eagle. Others say the islanders were stranded fifteen thousand years ago when the Ice Age melted and the land bridge connecting East to West became submerged again. Still others say the people of the Diomede islands came there in their kayaks to get away from it all.

Now *it* was coming to get them. Free television at the cost of free thinking; junk food at the cost of nutritious food; rock and roll videos at the cost of a durable culture which had stood the test of fifteen thousand of the harshest winters this planet can contrive. The refuse of modernity was washing onto these forgotten shores.

Maybe it was the air pocket. Maybe it was fear of death or of the future in general. I felt a little sick and headed back to the cockpit. Gatlin looked at me and said, "Yo."

We bounced around for another hour or so before he turned the *Leapin' Lizard* into a long, slow descent. I expected a controlled crash, but instead we enjoyed a rough but uneventful landing. We tied down the plane with grappling hooks so the wind wouldn't blow it away.

119

Chapter 16

A THIN LAYER OF SNOW COVERED THE LANDING STRIP OF Little Diomede. The landing strip was narrow and made of gravel and seemed like a big driveway shoveled by the beams of the dozen-or-so flashlights that rushed out to greet us. The rest of the island was a mystery cloaked in swirling snow and darkness, except for a handful of sparkles clustered together in the distance; house lights, I guessed. My ears were turned to glass by the chill of a wind that howled from six directions at once.

The flashlights had a small army of chubby men at the source of their beams. The men opened the belly of the *Leapin' Lizard* and spilled its cargo onto the runway. Their bodies tilted this way and that so as not to be carried away by the shifting arctic winds. I wedged myself close to the skin-covered doorway of an old toolshed. To the south and east, and gray sea heaved up a gray dawn. The new day melted into a heavy rain, which was wetter than the snow but seemed no less cold.

Six of the islanders stomped away with the various parts of the Texatron Remote Power Supply System. Four others quickly unpacked the Honda three-wheelers. They assembled the vehicles and fed them from five-gallon gas cans before speeding off in a spray of mud. The wind bounced the boxes around until the rain flattened them against the ground.

Three more men were left to attend to the rest of the cargo. I almost froze to death, or maybe I almost drowned, while they debated who should carry what. After much waving of their thick, stubby arms, the men picked up the rest of the boxes and filed toward the house lights, which were already fading into the stronger light of dawn. I followed them and Gatlin followed me, towering over us all.

After a short walk, we arrived at the mayor's house, which also functioned as the "L. Diomede Village Hall" according to a sign hung above the door. The house was like one of those modern works of art in which the odd bits of various garage sales are fused together in a humorous way: a telephone with a plastic blue banana in its cradle or books popping out of a toaster. The main room was the husk of a Continental Trailways bus which had been relieved of its wheels, seats and engine. A half-dozen beds—mine included, as it turned out—had been made from the overhead baggage area. Ground level was cluttered with the stuff of colliding cultures—ivory carvings and a picture of John Kennedy, sealskin wall hangings and an imitation oak coffee table littered with *Women's Day* magazines. Two hunting rifles were piled in the same corner as a handful of rusting harpoons. The emergency exit had been cut away and now opened into a kitchen area made of corrugated tin where a giggly, jiggly woman cooked ancient recipes on modern appliances. Beyond the kitchen was a long round tube that looked like it used to be the business end of a milk delivery truck. Here is where the mayor and his wife slept and where their uncountable children sat transfixed by a television set. The bathroom was a brisk walk in the open air.

"Pres, I'd like you to meet the mayor of Little Diomede," said Gatlin, pinching his cheeks to get the blood moving again.

His name was Phil Kropotkin. English was his second language and he was very glad to meet me. He was even shorter than I, but wide, strong and full of a bouncing vitality. He laid down the boxful of medical supplies he'd carried from the *Leapin' Lizard* and used a harpoon to scrape the mud from his boots.

"Yeah, sure. Great. What's your name again?"

"Pres Riordan."

The man laughed at a joke I didn't understand, is if "Pres Riordan" meant "Bonehead" in the Eskimo language. "Yeah, sure. Well, we welcome you here to Little Diomede, you bet. Big city people we don't get much here, but this place is lately getting to be a real tourist attraction, if you know what I mean. What happened to your leg?''

"Mauled by a brown bear," I replied.

The mayor seemed unconvinced. He slapped his hands together over a coal stove implanted where the dashboard used to be and peeled off his rain gear. The thin beak of a baseball cap protruded from under the hood of his dark red sweatshirt. He pulled back the hood. The mayor was a Dodgers fan.

Some children came into the room and smiled at Gatlin, who pretended not to notice them. Finally, the smallest one tiptoed up and started poking at his pockets. Gatlin gently nudged the child away. When the urchin came back for more, the pilot swept him up in his arms and nuzzled him in the face with the stubble of his beard.

"Cut it out, Uncle Gat," the child squealed in some combination of pain and delight.

Gatlin raised the child up on his shoulders and started twirling around on his heels saying, "You think you're pretty tough, huh? Well you can have it if you can find it."

This was the cue the other children were waiting for. They rushed up and pulled the pilot to the floor, burying him in a warm mound of hugging laughter. After a minute or two of roughhouse, a younger child of indeterminate gender screamed "I've got it!" and rushed away from the confusion with a videotape cassette. The victor plugged the tape into the television set. It was the 1956 science fiction classic, *Invasion of the Body Snatchers*. But before the opening credits were done, their mother stopped her almost constant giggling and ordered them to turn off the television set.

They had work to do and Gatlin and I needed some sleep. We crawled into the overhead sleeping area of the refitted Continental Trailways bus while the Kropotkins went out into the day. A luminous clock on the wall said 4:48 A.M., but time didn't matter in this place, where it snowed in the summer and dawn arrived just a few hours after sunset.

Gatlin was gone when I woke up. He left me a note saying he'd pick me up on his next cargo run six days hence, adding "And don't you go wandering over to the other side. The Russians have a place for people who do that. It's called Siberia.''

122

The morning sun and a southerly breeze had made a shirtsleeve day by boiling away the snow, the fog and the clouds. I jumped up on a big rock and saw that from Little Diomede, Big Diomede looks like the only other place in the world. The sea was flat and still, the sky a constant forever. The horizon was a perfect line curled in a perfect circle until it bumped into the Soviet island. Big Diomede looked like something the sea had made. It was gray like the sea and mostly smooth, as if the Bering Sea had heaved up a big swell which then became frozen in time and space. A low mist held onto the place, although the sky was crisp and without clouds. The two and a half miles separating the islands didn't seem like much at all up there in the lonely north, where the sea and the sky go on forever.

I walked down to the beach so I could look at the Soviet island from a closer spot and a different angle. Little Diomede was as barren as Big Diomede looked. The beach was made of sand and stone and millions of tiny rocks made flat and smooth by the action of the tides that had deposited them here. A few hardy weeds had fought their way into the sunlight, but otherwise only stone and sand held sway. Stone, sand and human beings, the tougher stuff of nature.

I had the distinct impression that someone was following me. My neck tingled and my breath became slow and short. I remembered Jon Jones: the way he was in Baranov and again in Kotzebue, his habit of turning up in improbable places at a very bad time. I turned around quickly, but saw nothing. My heart pumped faster than it needed to.

The beach was busy. Festive three-wheelers sped back and forth. Children splashed in the tidal pools and their mothers exchanged vital information while walking along the shore. The mayor and some of his constituents had gathered around the Texatron Remote Power Supply System to argue about how to install and maintain it. The sun was strong and seemed like it would stay strong forever. The late summer snow of the night before must have been a dream.

I selected a flat pebble and flung it sidearm at the Soviet island. It skipped three times and then went under. I got ready to fling another one when someone else's pebble shot past me and danced on the water for more hops and a longer time. When it sank, a young boy yelled in my ear, "That's a tenner, you bet. Did you see?"

The boy looked like one of the uncountable Kropotkins. He was small and thin and wore a Los Angeles Dodgers baseball cap. "A tenner?" I said.

He picked up another stone. "You bet. Ten skips, you know. I did a fifteener once, but Davey wouldn't say so even though he saw me do it. I got a knuckleball that just won't quit. When it's warm out we play baseball on the beach with an official major league rubber baseball."

The boy was indeed the mayor's son. His name was Fernando Valenzuela Kropotkin. He had four older brothers named after the Dodgers' infield of the glory years. Steve Garvey Kropotkin was the first mate on the family fishing boat. His little brothers were the crew: Davey Lopes Kropotkin, Bill Russell Kropotkin and Ron Cey Kropotkin, who had a way with seals and could pound a Rickie Saroff curveball into the Bering Sea.

"Papa had a fit when they all got old and the Dodgers started to trade their infield away. For a while he didn't know if maybe he should get rid of my brothers or find a new baseball team. Mama said he shouldn't do nothing so he ran for mayor instead. My papa's a big man, you know. He beat Alfred Saroff in the big election to be mayor and now he's gonna run to be president of the village corporation too. He should win too, you bet, so long as my Uncle Fred don't die. Rickie Saroff just turned eighteen so he can vote now, but there's a lot of Kropotkins these days. Papa figures he should win just so long as Uncle Fred don't die. Are you with the big black leather man?"

I was about to launch a rock when he asked me this. I stopped in mid-throw and almost wrenched my arm out of its socket. "What did you say?"

Fernando picked up one stone, discarded it. He found another more to his liking and threw it into the sea. It took one giant hop and then many little skips. Each left behind a widening ring. "I asked if you're friends with the big black leather man. He came up here the other day in a Lear jet over at the airport. We don't get too many people coming here on account of this is such a dull place, but now we got two people here at once. You and the black leather man. My brother Ron says he's a big creep and Ron should know because he's a big creep himself."

"I don't know anything about him. What's he doing

124

here?" I tried to throw a rock, but my shoulder ached too much. The stone landed with a dull plop and didn't skip at all.

"Well, I can't tell too much because he's kind of a grumpy guy and probably doesn't know anything about baseball. He just sits in a tent on the north end of the island over there and doesn't talk to anybody. My brother Ron tried to talk to him to see if he wanted to play baseball, but he didn't seem like the type. Where you from anyway?"

I started with the present and worked my way back: Baranov, Anchorage, Milwaukee, Kenosha, Chicago, Milwaukee, Chicago, Willow Springs.

"That's a lot of places. Chicago won the American League pennant in '59. The Dodgers beat 'em three to one in the World Series. I bet you can't name their starting lineup."

"Aparicio, Fox, Kluzewski . . ." I ran out of names after that.

Fernando rattled off the rest of the lineup, and then listed the Dodgers' too. "I know a lot about baseball because of Papa and besides there's not too much else to do around here except watch sports on TV."

"Will you take me to where the black leather man is?"

He thought about it for a second. "I don't know. Maybe tomorrow. The sun's out now. Let's go play some baseball."

Logic would dictate that my being crippled is a serious handicap when it comes to participant sports. But logic would be wrong. In most sports, the heavy metal brace which kept my right leg from flopping about like a cooked noodle offered me some unique advantages. For one thing, its very heaviness made it a force to be reckoned with. There's no better way to break up a double play in baseball or to discourage an opposing basketball player from going to the hoop than to flail about at knee-level with twenty pounds of steel.

The brace also gives me a psychological edge. Some kindhearted opponents feel sorry for me and give me plenty of slack. I feel sorry for myself and give them none in return.

But the most important benefit of being crippled is that I operate under a special set of expectations that are easy to meet. A crippled man doesn't need to do much to gain the admiration of friend and foe alike. The most humble accomplishment becomes an awe-inspiring thing. Likewise, the most catastrophic blunder is readily excused with the simple observation, "Well, what do you expect? He's a cripple, after all."

Of course, these things mean nothing when the other athletes are children, who don't seem to understand my rules. The children of Little Diomede gave me no slack whatsoever and took great joy in my long afternoon of sports humiliation.

They played a variation on baseball much like a game known as "Swift Pitch" in Chicago. A strike zone had been painted on the flat face of a big rock. A ball pitched inside the box was a strike, while one pitched outside was a ball. Most of that afternoon's endless argument had to do with whether or not a ball had been pitched in or out of the box.

The infield was a slope of round, flat stones packed down hard by a hundred thousand ground balls hit in two hundred thousand innings. The bases were an old tennis shoe, a garbage can lid and a copy of the *Anchorage Daily News* weighed down with a stone. The rock on which the strike zone had been painted also functioned as home base, which made a close play at the plate a thing of great danger and excitement. The beach was the outfield and anything that landed in the Bering Sea was a home run, unless the tide was too high, in which case it was only a double.

That day's game, like every day's game, featured the Kropotkins versus the Saroffs. I was made an honorary Kropotkin. The Saroffs took great pleasure in striking me out until the fourth inning, when the Kropotkins insisted I be made an honorary Saroff, so that they too would have the opportunity to strike me out. I had as much trouble with the Kropotkin knuckleball as I'd had with the Saroff curve. Everyone took turns, including Maria Kropotkin, Fernando's very pregnant older sister.

By the seventh inning, the score was something like 52 to 38 in favor of the Saroffs, although the Kropotkins had been coming on strong ever since I switched to the other team. After Maria struck me out again, I took a seat on the bench next to Rickie Saroff, the captain of my team.

Rickie pounded his glove and then sprayed a little spit in the pocket before pounding it some more. Fernando had said that Rickie was a great lover of women. Although this sort of thing didn't go too far on Little Diomede, it had apparently gone as far as Maria Kropotkin. Rickie's eyes had the moody innocence of the natural rake, and whenever he pitched to one of the Kropotkin girls, he displayed the sort of boyish charm which compels normally stable women to press roguish men to their bosoms. Fernando also had said Rickie was number one on his father's shit list.

I took a wild guess. "I hear you've been over to the other side."

"Who told you that?" he said.

"So it's not true?"

"I didn't say it ain't true. I just asked you who said so."

A Saroff girl smashed a line drive down the left field line, but a Kropotkin boy made a diving catch to end the inning. Rickie started walking toward the mound. I chased after him.

"How do you do it?"

He showed me the ball. "I put these two fingers across the seams and snap my wrist real hard."

"Not that. I mean how do you get over to the other side?"

Rickie gave me one of those boyish smiles he usually reserved for Kropotkin girls. "I know what you mean. You gonna play baseball or what?"

The game ended about two hours later. The Saroffs won, but there was some dispute as to the actual score, which was bigger than the national debt. As we limped away from the playing field, Steve Garvey Kropotkin, the oldest brother and captain of his team, said, "Screw it. We ain't gonna play anymore if that's the way it's gonna be." Nobody seemed to believe him, so he quickly changed his tack. "Oh yeah, well tomorrow we're gonna rub your face in it real good. You can even have Mr. Riordan on your side for the whole game and we'll still kick your ass."

Some baseball players had a loud and lengthy debate about who had struck me out and how many times they had done so, while some others watched *Invasion of the Body Snatchers*. The mayor's wife instructed two unlucky daughters in the preparation of a thick, pungent soup. The mayor and I talked about politics and baseball and what it is like to live only two and a half miles from the Soviet Union.

"Not good, not good." He adjusted his baseball cap, as if

giving the signal for the hit-and-run. "When I was a little boy, nobody cared too much about us and we could go over there any time we wanted and visit all the relatives we had over there. It's a bigger place, so it had more people. But then they had this Cold War and then they figured out that maybe there's some oil around here so the first thing is the Russians won't let anybody go across anymore and they take all our relatives and make them move to Siberia instead. This is not good. Neighbors should be neighbors, especially when there's nobody else around here to be neighbors with."

The mayor's wife sent a shy daughter over to ask me if I needed anything. She seemed relieved when I said no. The baseball players cheered as a hysterical woman was transformed into a contented pod person. I asked their father, "So nobody goes over any more?"

He opened his mouth but didn't say anything. He noticed a small commotion over by the television set and left the table to investigate. He didn't come back until his wife had assembled their children for dinner. The mayor sat down and said grace.

We all bowed our heads, except for Fernando and a sister about his age, who seemed to be trying to kick each other under the table while their father said the blessing: "And we would like to thank You for having such a good run of fish this year, you bet, although we probably could do with a few more salmon and a few less pollock, if You don't mind. And we still want You to have your people in Washington and Moscow open up the border between us and Big Diomede so as we can ask the soldiers to come over here for potlatch and not have to worry we'll get shot at. Amen."

He looked at me. "All of us men on the island that are over eighteen years old are in the Eskimo Scouts National Guard, but they won't ever let us have any bullets because they're afraid we might take a shot at a Russian soldier and maybe start World War Three."

After we'd passed the food around, I asked my question again. "Does anybody ever go over to the other island anymore?"

Everybody looked at Steve Garvey Kropotkin, who turned a bright red and started to examine his food very closely. "Would you please pass me the bread, Mr. Riordan?" the mayor said.

He continued, "Me being the mayor and all, us Kropotkins go by all the laws, even the bad ones and they've got plenty of those. I catch anybody going over there with Rickie Saroff and his bunch and they'll find themselves stoking the coal furnace all night, ain't that right Steve?"

"Yeah! Yeah! Do it, Papa!" Fernando said. As the youngest it was his job to keep the stove hot all night. He later explained to me that he usually performed this task in a half-sleeping state and rarely remembered getting up in the middle of the night. Still, he hoped Maria would have her baby quick so someone younger would inherit the job.

It was a night full of fire, family, and contended pod people. We finished watching *Invasion of the Body Snatchers* and then went off to bed. The mayor and his wife settled into the back end of the old milk truck. The girls slept in the overhead compartments on the left, while the boys and I slept in the overhead compartments on the right. I had decided there were between eight and ten children in the family, not counting the unborn one which Maria carried in her belly.

A strong wind rocked the old Continental Trailways bus back and forth and forced its way through a tiny hole near my feet. I had to assume the fetal position to keep warm. Some time in the middle of the night, Fernando stumbled down from his bunk and over to the old oil drum that the mayor had made into a coal furnace. He threw four shovels full of coal into the fire and then went back to bed. He scratched his face, but was careful not to rub the sleep from his eyes.

I took a bone-chilling walk to the outhouse to relieve myself and then dreamed of sometimes happy, sometimes angry, always lively Natives who watched too much television and were thereby transformed into bland but contented pod people. There came a new disturbance and Mama emerged from the master bedroom and started puttering around the kitchen. I was lulled back to sleep by the delightful melody of banging pots, matronly grunts and seal blubber sizzling on a propane stove.

Chapter 17

WHEN I AWOKE AGAIN, FERNANDO VALENZUELA KROPOT-kin was dressed for play and had suspended himself by his elbows from the side of my bunk. "Come on, let's go. It's time to play more baseball."

When I came to my senses, I replied, "First I want you to take me to the black leather man."

We crouched behind an oddly-shaped rock that was much too small to hide us from anyone, particularly the black leather man. He had taken the highest ground on Little Diomede, a large slab of flat stone which jutted up and over the beach. He had a good view of the Soviet island across the way.

His tent was a jungle green color and of a type I'd never seen before. In front of it was the blackened scar of an old campfire and a heavy spyglass mounted on a tripod. A thin gray wire was stretched between two hooks which he had jammed into flaws in the rock.

Fernando picked up a small stone, whispered "Watch this" and threw it at the tent. It caused a light ripple in the fabric and summoned forth the loudest, angriest dog I've ever seen. It was a large brown thing with the wide chest of a German shepherd, the ears of a Doberman pinscher and the soul of a pit bull. It charged right at us, all slobber and noise and teeth. I searched the ground for a stone and found one that wouldn't hurt a sparrow. I pushed Fernando away and prepared to smack the beast with my legbrace, or at least shove the metal between its jaws.

Fernando screamed.

The dog leaped.

The scream sounded like laughter and the dog came within two feet of my neck before reaching the end of its tether. It snapped back and collapsed into a pissed-off, frustrated heap and became tangled in its leash. The dog got up and charged again, even meaner and more pissed-off than before, but again it reached the end of its tether with the same result.

Now the dog got up and became very still, regarding me with a hot fury, as if memorizing my face and my scent for a future comeuppance. Fernando was delighted by my terror and the dog's rage. But in a slow second, he choked on his glee and the dog's growl subsided into a wimper. I followed Fernando's eyes.

Like Michael said, he was black all over, as if black-hearted angels had fashioned him from the black of night itself. Black beard, black leather, black eyes relieved only by the white skin around his eyes and the heavy silver lumps which studded his leather pants. He looked just like a motorcycle enthusiast from Nikiski.

"Go away," he said. It was a flat voice without accent or inflection.

Fernando tugged at my elbow. Our eyes locked and my limbs froze, but before I knew it we were down on the beach running like the wind against the wind.

The mayor was both angry with his son and proud of the way he managed to find trouble on an island which usually offered so little opportunity for adventure. "That guy come here in his own Lear jet, you bet, about a few days before you came, too."

It was Saturday afternoon in most of America, but not yet mid-morning in its most western village. The mayor and I hunched around the television set to talk about murder and watch the NBC game of the week—the Yankees hosting the Red Sox. Mayor Phil Kropotkin told me his middle names were "Scooter and Rizutto because my papa was a Yankee fan."

The Red Sox jumped out to a big lead. During the commercials I told the mayor about the Old Believers and how they were killed. We talked about rumors of Great Grand Ladies and Romanov gold.

131

The mayor looked around to see that no one was looking and put his feet up on the coffee table. "Maybe he's come here to see the boat come through, you bet. It's just about that day, you know."

To myself I said "What day?" To the mayor I said, "The *Pugachev?*"

Before he could reply, the Yankees came up to bat. They put a small dent in the Red Sox' lead, but a double play snuffed out the rally.

"Well, we don't call it the *Pugachev*. Uncle Fred even has a wise man's story where we call it 'The White Man's Trawler Without No Crane' these last thirty years or so. We used to call that story 'The Little Boy Without No Soul,' but we don't go hunting so much anymore because everybody else killed the whales. When the *Pugachev* boat started coming to visit us, Uncle Fred switched the words around a little bit."

"Thirty years?" I leaned on the coffee table, which creaked under the weight of my shoulders and the mayor's feet. I thought I saw some worry in his eyes. I eased off the table and again said, "Thirty years?"

But by then the Red Sox had come up to bat. They went down in order. The mayor's wife came in and scolded the mayor for scuffing up her coffee table. When the coast was clear the mayor put his feet back up and said, "That's right, thirty years. Almost since I was a boy. They come every year about this time, just when the salmon are finished running through Bristol Bay. And without no crane every single time, which ain't too smart for a fishing boat. It sure is pretty though. It'll be purple or blue depending on where the sun's coming from."

Uncle Fred lived in a prefabricated garage on the eastern side of Little Diomede, the side that faced away from the Soviet island. From a distance, it looked like an old hut covered with skins and painted a dirty yellow. But when the mayor knocked on the door, it sounded like cheap tin. Admission was granted by the use of a Genie Automatic Garage Door Picker-Upper.

The mayor went in first and talked for a bit with the old man. A few moments later, they invited me in. The wide

132

door rattled shut with the push of a button which Uncle Fred kept close at hand.

The mayor said, "Uncle Fred, this is Pres Riordan. He's a newsman come here to do a story on the boat."

The old man leaned up from a pile of sealskin bedding jammed into a corner of the room. He extended his hand and I shook it. "Are the Giants in first yet?"

"Yes, Uncle Fred," the mayor replied. "They're still in first." In fact, the San Francisco Giants were mired in third.

"Does McCovey have his thirty home runs yet?"

"Yes, Uncle Fred," the mayor said. In fact, Willie McCovey hadn't batted for the Giants or anybody else in many years.

"Is the election tomorrow yet?"

"No, Uncle Fred. The election ain't gonna be tomorrow yet until October. That's two more months still. You just stick around until October and then we'll have the election and you can watch the Giants in the World Series."

The old man slumped back into his bedding. He seemed to sleep for a second, but then his eyes cleared up. He looked at me and said, "I hope you die in a big TV car crash when you're seventy-five years old."

It sounded like a curse, but didn't feel like one. I looked at the mayor, who understood but couldn't explain. Uncle Fred leaned up at me and said with a wet whisper, "It's a bitch to be old, you bet, my friend. Life hurts a lot, but this is worse. There's gotta be something more than this because this is a bunch of shit."

He dozed off again. His cubicle was full of odd little things: a whale jawbone and some old books; a box full of clothes and a shotgun; a half-eaten sandwich made of white bread and Velveeta, which is considered a delicacy on Little Diomede. One whole wall was covered with photographs, including a team picture of the mayor's children standing in front of the flat rock where they had struck me out the day before.

The old man came back to his senses and said, "Scooter?"

The mayor leaned close so he could whisper too. "I'm right here Uncle Fred."

"Can I go now? Is the election over? Did we win?"

"Not yet, Uncle Fred. First you gotta tell your stories to

my friend. Tell him the ones about the boy and the white man's boat.''

Uncle Fred's wasted eyes looked past the ceiling and past the clouds and past the stars and all the other things a man can see. His breath smelled as if a part of his guts had already died. Here's the story he told to me:

Once upon a time, long before Man made the mistake of becoming People, there lived in the Great Green Land a Young Boy who wore no clothes. This was not an unusual thing in the Great Green Land because the Wind there felt like the daughter of a well-tended Fire. The Young Boy was the Blessed of God in the Great Green Land and the Wind was so warm that the Joyful Plugging Up of Women would be performed in the Open Air, which is quite exciting and allows others to compliment Man on the size of his Plug. But life was not perfect in the Great Green Land. The Wind blew so warm that there was no Snow and there was no Ice and sometimes every now and then, there was no Water.

Now Young Boy was the son of Eagle and Halibut, which is a prescription for trouble right there. His parents gave him the power to fly and swim, which only made his trouble more troublesome when there came the day that Young Boy became Man and was required to do a Brave Thing so he could begin the Joyful Plugging of Women and the ostentatious display of his Plug.

Halibut said, "Get me some water. I feel that I'm out of my element." And indeed, Halibut was out of her element for she plopped on the ground and flopped about in the Open Air where the Blessed of God could see how ugly she was. The comments of Caribou were particularly unkind.

So Young Boy flew around the World seven thousand times looking for some water in which Halibut could hide and swim. On the seven thousand-and-first time, he tripped on Cloud and fell into the Great Only Pool, where all the Beloved of God bathe, drink and otherwise refresh themselves. Then a great crime was committed. Young Boy killed Seal so that he could put the Great Only Pool in Seal's bladder and carry it back to Halibut.

The Beloved of God made a great complaint. Moose and Sheep and Caribou and the many Salmon Sisters said, "Do not do this great crime, Seal-killer. If you take away the Great Only Pool, we can't bathe and drink and otherwise refresh ourselves and we'll smell like a bunch of animals."

But Young Boy did not listen to their complaints and carried away the Great Only Pool and gave it to Halibut. And to this day the Beloved of God smell like a bunch of animals and to this day Halibut swims at the bottom of the Great Only Pool and to this day . . .

Here is where the story splits off toward two separate conclusions. In the old version, called "The Boy Without No Soul," the Beloved of God banish Young Boy to the Southlands, where his skin turns white and he becomes very lonely because none of the animals will talk to him. In the new version, called "The White Man's Trawler Without No Crane," Young Boy becomes a blue fishing boat that never catches any fish and never touches any land and every August passes through the narrow channel separating Big Diomede from Little Diomede.

Uncle Fred coughed up something green and wet. The mayor wiped it off his chin. Uncle Fred said, "Now you bet it don't matter which story you like to believe because either way the moral is this, 'Don't be an asshole.' Now remember that, my children, and you'll be pretty smart."

There's only one telephone on Little Diomede. I asked the mayor if I could use it. He looked as if I'd asked for the hand of his favorite daughter and mumbled something I couldn't understand.

"I'm sorry, Mr. Mayor, but I didn't hear that."

"I said, you'll have to ask my wife." He hollered at the kitchen, "You come in here, woman." His gruff tone was betrayed by sheepish eyes.

The mayor's wife listened to my request with grave concern, one of the few times during my visit to Little Diomede when she was neither laughing nor ready to do so on a moment's notice.

"We don't let men use the phone around here. Last time

135

we did, Albert Saroff traded a boatload of bottomfish for an electric power windmill that still don't work. Cost him the election, you bet. Now we got a rule where just women use the phone for talking about babies and marriages and only important stuff.''

The mayor said something about the village pride and I explained to his wife how important it was. She said they'd have to put it to a vote, but promised to speak on my behalf.

The only telephone on Little Diomede was always busy. It had a room of its own in the village school and was guarded twenty-four hours a day by trusted women of the ruling family. A blackboard was used to keep track of everyone's turn, the general pattern of which alternated between Kropotkin and Saroff and back again. All calls were limited to fifteen minutes and broadcast over large stereo speakers so that every woman who crowded into the room could enjoy the conversations made on this public utility.

The maneuvering required to make my telephone call was an example of power politics on Little Diomede. The Saroff women said I should not be allowed to use the phone at all. They were outvoted by the Kropotkin women, who supported my request on the condition that a woman from the mayor's immediate family give me her turn.

The mayor's wife told her pregnant daughter Maria to let me call Kotzebue during the fifteen minutes allotted to her. This produced a disappointed clucking from the audience, who expected Maria's call to be one of the evening's most exciting.

I made poor use of the opportunity. I connected with King Kotz at the Vu-Nik-Luk Hotel, but he was unable to find Jon Jones. We talked for a while and he promised to find the government man and have him sit by the phone to await my next call. An egg timer sounded the end of my fifteen minutes and a surly Saroff woman demanded that I hand over the phone.

The Kropotkin women threatened to abandon my cause if the mayor's pregnant daughter was again prevented from making her eagerly-awaited call. The mayor's wife presided over a confusing round of negotiations whereby her sister made a trade with her aunt for the rights to a phone call three hours later originally assigned to one of the Saroff women.

After a while, the women became more at ease with my presence and started to chat among themselves. They were divided into three groups. The mayor's wife presided over a gaggle of Kropotkins, who shook their heads and clucked dismay whenever some Saroff scandal was broadcast over the stereo speakers. A second group of Saroff women gave a similar treatment to the broadcast of Kropotkin blunders and embarrassments. A third group of younger women seemed to be composed of women with divided loyalties who enjoyed everyone's problems but their own.

Maria Kropotkin's telephone call was of a different sort. The pregnant girl was due soon and needed a husband fast. She called an old boyfriend in Nome who'd once said he'd like to marry her. She held her tummy and shuffled her feet while trying to suggest that his proposal would be accepted if only he'd make it again.

The audience gave this conversation a different sort of reception. The Kropotkin women became quiet because she was one of them. The Saroff women became quiet because the scoundrel who had shamed her was a member of their clan. The younger women of divided loyalties became quiet too, perhaps because they had flirted with the catastrophe which now swelled in Maria's belly.

The old boyfriend didn't get the hint or didn't want to. When Maria hung up, her sobs produced a great female commotion. Women of all sizes and families and ages looked at me for a long, still moment and then broke out into a magnificent babble. Kropotkin women and Saroff women and Kropotkin/Saroff women all gave witness to one irreducible germ of truth: Men are jerks. Whether they are Kropotkin men or Saroff men or Kropotkin/Saroff men or crippled strangers from Baranov, men are jerks.

Who was I to disagree? I waited for another hour or so. The commotion subsided and the room regained its usual rhythm until I was summoned to the phone. A silence swelled and became heavy. I longed for the comfort of a male voice.

"Vu-Nik-Luk Hotel." It was Olga.

"Olga this is . . ."

Before I could finish, she was gone and Jones was on the line. "What's the problem, Mr. Riordan?"

I gave him a quick accounting of the black leather man, and accused him of the murders of Boris and Fedor Yermak. I was only guessing, of course. But what else could I do? Somebody had killed the brothers, and Michael had seen this man racing away from Vyg. All this was broadcast over the loud speakers to an increasingly horrified gathering. The women glared at me. Jones said, "Uh-huh," to urge me over the rough spots and asked a question every now and then. Finally, I said, "And now he's here, like he's following me."

"Or you're following him. I suggest you be very careful, Mr. Riordan. As I told you, the Soviet government is very anxious that neither their artifacts nor their citizens be smuggled into the country."

"You mean he's in the KGB?"

He laughed a laugh made even more hollow by the echoing effect of the telephone room. The women of Little Diomede were quiet and still. "The KGB?" He laughed some more. "Nothing so dramatic. As I told you, this is a matter for Customs and Immigration. I believe the gentleman you described is a Mr. Vladimir Chen of the Soviet border police."

The egg timer announced the end of my fifteen minutes, but this time no Saroff woman demanded that I hand over the phone. "What are you going to do, I mean about the murders and all?"

His words sounded crisp and certain, as if they'd been stamped out by a tool and die machine. "I'm not going to do anything, Mr. Riordan. I assure you that Mr. Chen has not murdered anyone. He's here on the invitation of your government, and besides, murders are not my jurisdiction. I believe that's being handled by your own state troopers. We're only interested in ancient Russian artifacts and illegal aliens. Now tell me, have you seen the *Pugachev* yet?"

Although the women continued to comment on the fortunes and misfortunes of others, they did so with little joy. I was trying to persuade the mayor's wife to let me make another call to the FBI or the CIA or someone with guns and authority when a commotion burst into the room.

The commotion's name was Fernando Valenzuela Kropotkin. His breath was labored and his face was flush with excitement. The women stopped chatting among themselves and listened to his announcement:

"I seen it! I seen it! The blue fishing boat without no crane. It's coming right now. I seen it myself. I was the first one too, no matter what Davey says."

Chapter 18

THE BEACH WAS ALREADY CROWDED WHEN THE *Pugachev* could only be seen as a twinkle on the southern horizon to the left of Big Diomede. Saroff and Kropotkin women herded their fathers and husbands and children onto the beach which faced the Soviet island. Very old people sat on lawn chairs and very young ones sat on their laps. The others milled around and talked with excitement while pointing to the place where the ship was coming from.

I could barely see the vessel, despite the assistance of the powerful eyeglasses I've worn since age eight. But the old seal hunters and their children and their children's children could not only see the boat, but could also distinguish subtle details from what to me looked like nothing more than a blip on the thin line separating the sea from the sky.

"I think it looks like she got a new coat of paint," said a Saroff to a Kropotkin.

"Can't be," the Kropotkin replied. "She got new paint last year I'm pretty sure, you bet."

Uncle Fred was carried to the beach in a sealskin hammock by three of the mayor's infielders. They set him down in a place of honor reserved for the island's oldest resident. Everyone gathered around to hear what he had to say.

"Look's like she's got a new coat of paint, you bet. Now everybody sit easy and I'll tell you the story of the Boy Without No Soul, which is also called 'The White Man's Trawler Without No Crane.' "

The people of Little Diomede made circles within circles within circles around the dying man. The first circle was made of babies and toddlers who weren't quite sure what the excitement was all about but were excited nonetheless. Around them was a circle of young children who were just starting to understand Uncle Fred and therefore gave him their complete attention. Around them came the magnificent confusion of adolescence in which boys and girls and men and women and sane and insane and new and old becomes jammed so tightly into awkward bodies that they almost can't take it anymore. The members of this group tried to act either younger or older than they really were. Many pretended an indifference to the story they did not really feel. Next came the young-marrieds and the well-marrieds and the too-marrieds. Then came the old people and then came me. I could now see the *Pugachev* as a tiny blue smudge to the south.

". . . and the moral of the story is, 'You always better be sure what you're looking for because you just might find it.' "

I heard sniggering from the adolescent circle. A young boy elbowed his way into the first circle. It was a pubescent Saroff who had struck me out with a curve ball on the inside corner of the plate. "But Uncle Fred, I thought the moral of the story was 'Never listen to a Halibut, even when it's a relative.' That's what you said last year anyway, I think."

Uncle Fred cracked a smile that for a second made him look like he would live forever. "That was last year's moral, son. A good story must have many morals, especially when you got a television in the house."

The immortal smile disappeared and a gray film clouded the old man's eyes. The villagers broke up into small groups to discuss their favorite morals to the story. The mayor gave a speech in which he took personal credit for an abundant harvest of pollock and blamed the Japanese for a poor seal hunt. When he was done, Alfred Saroff stood up to address the population. He blamed the mayor for the poor seal harvest and credited God for the abundance of pollock.

"And another thing, I think," he said. "I notice how Scooter Kropotkin didn't say nothing about how come we still can't get no bullets for the Eskimo Scouts. He sure blamed me for that a lot when I lost the election last time."

Half the population applauded. The other half watched the hull of the *Pugachev* glide along the International Dateline, that imaginary tightrope separating Tuesday from Wednesday, America from Asia, the United States from the Soviet Union and Little Diomede from Big Diomede.

Big Diomede kept a careful silence while the people of Little Diomede ran along the beach, flapping their arms and hollering soprano greetings as the *Pugachev* eased into the narrow channel. The Old Believers paid no attention. They dropped anchor and huddled on the stern.

Alfred Saroff spoke: "Now keeping with my idea that we should be able to go to the other side, my son Ritchie is gonna go out in his kayak and say hello to the White Man's Trawler Without No Crane."

"Now wait a second," the mayor said. An animated discussion ensued. There are laws, you bet, the mayor said. What laws? the elder Saroff replied.

"We ain't supposed to go over to the other side."

"He ain't going over to the other side. He's just going over to the middle, which is where the boat is."

The argument caused a lot of grumbling and cheering and laughing among the Saroffs and Kropotkins. But the arguments and the agitation stopped when Rickie Saroff ran to the beach with a kayak strapped across his shoulders. He was covered from his toes to his neck in a lumpy, bright orange outfit which I later learned was a North Sea Survival Suit. He threw the kayak into the surf and jumped aboard. The villagers hushed as the magical energy of his double-bladed oar propelled him forward.

When he was halfway to the *Pugachev*, Rickie performed an Eskimo roll, an astonishing maneuver in which the kayaker spins headfirst into the water, floats upside down for a bit and then spins back to the surface to complete the 360-degree maneuver. There was a scattering of applause from his relatives. "Showoff," some Kropotkin said.

Then silence again, except for the tide and Uncle Fred, who had fallen asleep and was snoring. It took Ritchie about fifteen minutes to reach the *Pugachev*, but it felt more like fifteen days or fifteen years. I tried to remember what Jon Jones had said on the phone, but I couldn't think very well. I was fascinated by Rickie and his kayak acrobatics. Sometimes when his shoulders leaned into the double-bladed paddle, my shoulders leaned too, as if that would help him move along.

142

When Ritchie got close to the *Pugachev*, he raised his paddle. He must have shouted too, because the Old Believers turned away from Big Diomede and rushed to the side of the boat their visitor was approaching. When they were all assembled, he performed an Eskimo roll for their benefit. The Old Believers started waving their arms at the youth. Maybe it was applause. Maybe it was hospitality. Maybe it was something else.

We'll never know, because all of a sudden the sky spat out a small Lear jet. The jet took one pass over the *Pugachev* then turned around and dived toward the fishing boat. As it made a second pass, it blasted out a red bolt of something hot which buried itself in the blue belly of the White Man's Trawler Without No Crane. A fireball exploded and the *Pugachev* blew into a hundred million sizzling bits. Rickie tried another Eskimo roll, but this time he didn't come back up.

There followed another quiet, a sinister one. It was one of those lost and found moments like the death rattle of a prehistoric bug forever trapped in amber. The explosion had set fire to the sea.

The mayor broke the spell with a barrage of commands that sent dozens of young men scurrying to their kayaks. They looked like a toy armada. The Lear jet banked into a low turn and headed for the American mainland as the young men of Little Diomede searched for human beings in the thin layer of smoldering ash that covered the water where the *Pugachev* and Rickie Saroff used to be.

Alfred Saroff tried to blame me for what had happened to his son—for no reason other than I was a white stranger, just like the black leather man who had done the deed.

"I say we take a vote," Saroff said.

"On what?" the mayor replied.

"On whether we go like I think, which is we give this man who helped kill my son a kayak and kick his ass off the island."

"But he'll die," the mayor said.

"Just like my Rickie," Alfred Saroff replied.

"Can I make a telephone call?" I asked.

Saroff pressed the point. "White men kill each other fifty

143

times a night on the TV set. Now they killed my son and maybe your son's next. Let's take a vote.''

"Can I make a telephone call?" I said.

They asked Uncle Fred for guidance. The other villagers gathered around his stretcher as he told stories and suggested useful morals. None of them seemed to apply neatly to white strangers and Lear jets armed with missiles. In the end there was no easy answer, so Mayor Kropotkin asserted his authority.

"I'm in charge of the law, and there's no law saying we can do anything except call the state troopers and report what happened."

They called the troopers, who promised to investigate. I called the hotel in Kotzebue and various federal government offices in Anchorage, Seattle and Washington. Nobody in the U.S. Department of Customs and Immigration had heard of Jon Jones. In desperation I asked directory assistance for the telephone number of the CIA.

703-555-1100. A woman answered. I asked for Jones.

"And who may I ask is calling?"

"Pres Riordan."

"One second please."

The phone made a funny noise. When the noise was done, she said, "Is that Riordan, Prester J., Social Security number 344-40-8114 calling from the village of Little Diomede?"

I thought about hanging up, but figured it was already too late. "That's ah . . . Yes, that's right."

"And what is your business, Mr. Riordan?"

I told her my business. Never once did she seem worried or surprised that a Soviet agent was slaughtering Old Believers. When I was done, she said "uh-huh" and I said "Well?"

"Well what, Mr. Riordan?"

"Well, can I speak to Mr. Jones?"

"No."

I waited for her to say something else, but she never did. "Is that 'No, you can't speak to him' or 'No, he isn't here' or 'No, we don't have a Mr. Jon Jones working here'?"

"No."

"No, what?"

"No. Will that be all, sir?"

Chapter 19

IT MIGHT NOT HAVE HAPPENED IF I HADN'T HAD TO PEE IN the middle of the night.

Peeing on Little Diomede is no small thing, especially at night. The mayor's wife did not allow the use of chamber pots because she thought them to be immodest and unsanitary, especially considering the errant aim of her fourth son, Davey Lopes Kropotkin. For this reason, a pee in the middle of the night on Little Diomede required a major expedition over the rough terrain separating the mayor's house from the mayor's outhouse, a reconverted telephone booth that had been covered with canvas for privacy's sake and put upon some high ground above the western beach.

The situation was compounded by my affliction. If I couldn't hold it, I had to either strap my leg brace back on or make do without it, which required a one-legged hop that is both tiring to perform and ridiculous to observe.

The situation was further compounded by the can of beer which the mayor pressed on me just before we went to bed. We sipped and talked about the day's events, the end of an era for the people of Little Diomede.

"I was just a boy, you bet, when it was the first time the boat came to visit us. I remember it right away. My father and Uncle Fred were on the beach and I was helping with the chores. We were mending a net that got all torn up in the fishing at Bristol Bay. My father and Uncle Fred were talking about the M&M boys, which was Mickey Mantle and Roger Maris. My father was a New York Yankee fan, which is how come he named me after Scooter Rizzuto. He used to play shortstop.

"Anyway all of a sudden, they both start talking and look at the sea. 'Go get your mother,' my father says, 'and then go get the mayor,' which back then was Abner Saroff, Alfred's older brother. So I do what he told me to do and by the time we all came back to the beach, we could see what they had seen, which was the very same boat that got blown up yesterday.

"By then everybody was on the beach and everybody seen what happens every year. They waited for a little while and then when it's dark we heard a speedboat that sounded like a 55-horsepower Evinrude come from the Russian island and go right next to the . . . what's that you call it? The *Pugachev?* Every year since then when the sun comes up the next day, the boat is always gone away, but it will always come back about the same time next year, when the salmon was done running through Bristol Bay. They always did whatever they did in the dark, so we never saw what was going on. What do you think it is?"

I told him I thought they were smuggling Old Believers to freedom and were being helped by an old woman with a fortune in Romanov gold. Scooter Rizzuto Kropotkin said it didn't matter if what I said was true or not, it would make a great story anyway.

"If you don't mind, I think I'll think up a moral or two and tell the story to everybody every year after Uncle Fred croaks. We're gonna miss Uncle Fred."

I tried to fall asleep before the beer filled my bladder, but my mind was stuck on instant replay. Drop by drop my kidneys distilled the brew. I saw the mauve ship explode a hundred times. Sometimes I could hear a dull thud, but mostly it was a silent flash in Technicolor. Time after time a split second turned the beautiful White Man's Trawler Without No Crane into a million sizzling bits of wood and flesh and bone. Time after time I saw Rickie Saroff roll into the water and paddle upside down for a couple of yards, except for the last time, when he never rolled back up and his upside-down kayak started drifting with the tide. I remembered these things again and again, time after time, until I had to take a leak.

I put on my leg brace and went outside. It was about 3:30 A.M. The night was breaking into another dawn. Across the channel, Big Diomede lurked above the wet smudge where the *Pugachev* used to be. The tide had scrubbed the beach and then retreated, leaving behind a few scattered tidal pools. Something howled somewhere, a dog perhaps, or maybe a seal.

The wind came through a dozen tiny leaks in the old plastic telephone booth as I peed through a hole which had been cut into the floor to provide access to God's own plumbing. When I opened the accordian door, there stood Rickie Saroff, seducer of Kropotkin women and master of the Eskimo roll. His orange survival suit was torn in places and not so lumpy anymore. He said, "You gotta come with me right now, Mr. Riordan."

I heard the wind whistle through the holes in the old plastic telephone booth. Each hole had a different pitch and together they made a weird, atonal harmony. "I thought you were dead," I said.

The young man was proud that he wasn't, but still a bit nervous and excited. "I think I almost was and would have been if I didn't have the suit. We always wear survival suits ever since a few years ago when our fishing boat sank and we lost the whole crew from dying of the cold."

His breath was short and labored. Each word became a puff of smoke and disappeared. "The ship blows up and then I do my roll and I got real lucky because when I came up I got tangled in some fishing net. I guess if he'd have seen me floating there he'd have thought I was a buoy or a plastic bag or something else because the suit makes you look like a balloon more than anything else. Only at first I wasn't so lucky because I was floating facedown."

He'd said all this without taking a breath, as if his lungs were reliving the experience. He sucked in another big load of air. "So I started paddling with my arms and got myself faceup and straightened out. Then I got lucky again because the tide was going into Big Diomede and I can't believe it but the tide lets me down just about right where my great-grandfather lives. The fishing net and me got all tangled up with some rocks. I was working to get free when my great-grandfather came to fetch me and warms me up with brandy and soup. Now he says I'm supposed to come fetch you."

He grabbed me by the elbow and started tugging me toward the beach. "Where are we going?" I said, not really believing what I had just heard.

Rickie Saroff looked down at the beach. He kicked a pebble into a tidal pool and then looked back at me. "We gotta go see Ivanovich Chuckwuk. He's a great man who's very old and he says he's gotta talk to you right away."

We had by then reached a lean-to propped up against the side of a big stone. Again I asked, "Where are we going, Rickie?"

Rickie ducked behind the lean-to. He banged around a bit. There was a heavy scraping sound as the lean-to produced first one kayak then another. Rickie next produced two double-bladed paddles. He handed one to me and said, "You asked me before if I ever go over to the other side. Well, I been there lots of times and now you're going with me."

My knees started to wobble as if my ligaments were made of rubber bands. "How do you drive these things?"

He towed me into the surf with a heavy rope he had tied to the front of my kayak and the back of his. With slow, strong strokes he propelled us at an angle into the wind, so the wind and the waves would not knock us over with a broadside. Large waves heaved up and tossed us around, but our kayaks were as light as corks and just as unsinkable. I couldn't hear much because there wasn't much to hear besides the low, gray heaving of the deadly Bering Sea.

Dawn gave a low, brooding shape to the Soviet island. It was hard for me to tell how far we'd gone, or how much farther we had to go. Rickie leaned into his work, a human paddle wheel. I mimicked him, but found his easy strokes were not so easy to perform. Salt water splashed into the hollow of my kayak and sloshed around my feet. My good foot became cold, my bad foot became numb. Rickie paddled on.

We slipped through the wet smudge where the *Pugachev* used to be. There wasn't much left: just some murky water, a few wood chips and a bit of white cloth that could have been canvas or could have been the shirt of a dead peasant. I kicked my numb foot with my cold one, and wondered what would happen to me: maybe I would freeze to death, or disappear into the bowels of the world's most notorious police state like that Swedish diplomat who disappeared after World War II, only no one would remember me; maybe I would be the guest of honor at a wild vodka celebration, like that crazy person from California who walked over the ice one February; maybe I would win the Pulitzer prize and sell the movie rights and become rich, famous and overindulged; or maybe I would be beaten with a knout until my bones showed through, or torched, or blown to smithereens with a highly explosive missile of Communist manufacture.

None of these things happened. I kicked my numb foot with my cold one, but didn't feel anything. We paddled into a small cove and onto a beach made of the same sort of flat pebbles as Little Diomede. I looked across the water and felt like I'd just stepped through Alice's Looking Glass. The American island was smaller, but looked just as gray and gloomy as Big Diomede had looked from over there.

We made land and started walking. The first few steps on my frozen foot didn't feel like anything, as if the limb had turned to wood. When the blood started to move, it felt like a stream of angry ants taking thousands of little ant bites as they squeezed into my foot. I hopped around and stomped the ground until the ants calmed down and my foot came back to life.

"You okay there?" Rickie Saroff said.

I grumbled my reply. "Well, let's go. What are you waiting for?" I hate it when people worry about me.

We walked through a maze of odd-shaped rocks and beach debris until we came to a clearing in front of a wall of rock that angled up into the low mountain which covered most of Big Diomede. Against the rock wall had been pitched a domed tent made of canvas, plastic and animal skins. It seemed like a hovel and looked like a hairy blister.

Rickie peeled back one of the animal skins and we crawled into the tent, which was empty except for another animal skin that covered a second hole in the part of the tent that faced the rock. Rickie crawled through this hole. I followed him into a dream. Slowly, over millions of years, but as surely as the tides which scratched at the land under Father Nick's church, the wind and water and ice had carved into the side of the mountain a magnificent cave of many lofty caverns.

The first cavern had been left in its natural state. Stalac-

149

tites hung from dark folds in the ceiling and dripped down onto stalagmites, one of which looked like a limestone ice cream cone gone bad. The center of the cavern was dominated by a thick but irregular pillar made where the two phenomena had touched one other. Some of the mineral water had settled into a crystal pool. Rickie cupped some in one hand, pinched his nose with the other, and took a noisy slurp.

"Try some. It's good for you."

The water smelled like rotten eggs, but tasted sweet enough if I held my breath. My throat was dry. I tried some more. "What is this place?" I asked.

Rickie didn't answer, but instead walked toward a dark part of the cave. Some more sealskins covered another hole. He went in and I went after, into a tunnel as wide as my shoulders, and just high enough to crawl through. It was pitch black, slick and cold. I slipped a few times and became coated with some slimy stuff. We soon came into a blast of warm air and the bright light of the most marvelous apartment I have ever seen.

The second cavern was as wide and vaulted as the first one, but had been paneled with plastic that looked like varnished walnut. A stalactite protruded from a neat hole that had been cut in a false ceiling. A stalagmite had been chiseled flat to make a clever table on which were arrayed chess pieces in the middle of a game. The place was softened with tapestries, plush rugs and stuffed chairs. Polished wood tables and a china cabinet were cluttered with knickknacks and gewgaws. Heat was provided by a wood stove modified for coal. A full assortment of the latest American appliances were energized by the now-familiar hum of the Texatron Remote Power Supply System.

The lord of all this splendor was an old man with a toothless smile. He was taller than most of the men on Little Diomede, but old beyond time, bent and wrinkled like some wizard who grows more potent with age. His handshake had the dry, leathery strength of a man who intends to get very much older. He wore a red velvet smoking jacket and smelled of whiskey, tobacco and stale feet. I looked down. He was barefoot.

"Pres, this is my great-grandfather, Ivanovich Chuckwuk."

150

"I speak your language very well, but come into my home. White American, you must be. That is not someone who I have seen since before since Arkhangelsk, I think, even though I'm older than . . . How do you say it, Rickie? . . . Older than sin itself. I was an old man already when the Japs attacked your Aleutian Islands and I got a medal fighting for the czar in the other big ugly white man's war before that. I fought the Germans of Kaiser Willie and that's pretty goddamn old. Let me get you something to wear that doesn't have all the crud all over."

He gave my hand one more shake and then let go. Rickie and I were smeared with a green fungus like that which collects on the glass of a goldfish tank. We removed our outer garments and were given housecoats that smelled like whiskey, tobacco and feet.

The two men babbled for several minutes in a language I didn't understand. It wasn't Russian. The consonants were too soft, the vowels jammed too tightly together, except for the words that didn't have any vowels at all. They seemed to be talking business. I learned later that Ivanovich Chuckwuk and the Saroff family operated a flourishing black market which smuggled American products to Soviet army officers stationed in Siberia.

The old man poured some Jack Daniels and sat us around a coffee table with narrowing legs ending in lion's feet. He sniffed his liquor and took a sip. Rickie and I did the same, like placid English gentlemen gathered at the club to talk about the empire and the lazy habits of the working class.

The old man said, "Rickie says to me you come here from over there on the Kenai Peninsula and the Baranov town that the Russians built. He says you came over and saw how all the Old Believers got croaked by spies."

I nodded. "That's right."

They talked again in their strange language, with lots of *n*s and *g*s. The old man said, "Now I think Rickie says he's pretty sure that you're not doing any business with the spies who got the jet plane and how you might even be a friend of the Old Believers that got croaked."

As I told him about the Yermak brothers and how they'd been killed, he rubbed the back of his lean brown hands—to keep them warm, I guess. His grip was too strong for arthritis and he was not the sort to indulge in nervous

151

gesture. He was, in fact, the calmest man I have ever met. Rickie watched his great-grandfather carefully, laughing when the old man laughed, scowling when the old man scowled. Ivanovich Chuckwuk sighed. So did Rickie. I sighed too and the circle was complete.

"I fought for Nicholas against the Kaiser Willie in the First World War until Lenin came back home. Then I fought with the White Russian army and the Great Grand Lady against the Red Russians too, even though our Little Father Czar got croaked by then. We all went to Arkhangelsk after the war when some American soldiers came to Siberia to help us fight the Red Russians. But the Red Russians were too smart for the Americans, who just wanted to go home. Now I'm a Red Russian too, you bet, and I have been ever since Arkhangelsk. That's when I met my beautiful Tosh."

He told the story over Jack Daniels and smelly feet.

Tosh was a Siberian Eskimo, and so related to Yupik Eskimos and Inupiat Eskimos and Canadian Eskimos and Greenland Eskimos and the whole fraternity of northern people who have round faces, eat raw meat and love the outdoors. In the famine years after the Revolution she fled to Arkhangelsk and into the loving arms of Ivanovich Chuckwuk.

Chuckwuk described her great bouncing bosoms by bouncing on his chair. "The end of the line it was, I think. The Americans were there to save us from the Reds, but they wanted to go home. We held on to Arkhangelsk for a while because the Red Russians had lots of other problems.

"I made us an ice cave near Khabarovsk and killed us a bear to eat. Tosh was a maid to the Great Grand Lady and I was in the White Russian Army, although the Red Russians seemed like they were not too ready to fight but plenty ready to let us starve to death. Me and Tosh did some Joyful Plugging and she made me a baby who doesn't always visit me at Christmastime."

The Americans abandoned Arkhangelsk in the summer of 1920, and so did the White Russian officers loyal to the Czar. The soldiers were left to fend for themselves. Some were slaughtered. Others vanished, as Ivanovich Chuckwuk and his infant son had done. Others fought a bitter battle from the hills and the mountains of Siberia. Still others were converted to the Communist cause.

"But the Great Grand Lady says she'd never go away and she never did. My lady Tosh stayed with her all the time so that when the Red Russians got to take over Arkhangelsk they got arrested."

"Were they killed?" I left plenty of space between the words so that Ivanovich could stop me.

He didn't stop me. He laughed instead. So did Rickie. "Oh, no. Not that. The Red Russians never croak them two. They need the Great Grand Lady because she's got all the Romanov gold stuck away someplace."

"Did they go to jail?"

The laughter got louder. "Oh, no, not that. Never that neither."

There was a ringing in my ears. Not the kind of ringing you hear, but the kind you feel. Maybe it was the whiskey, or the kayak trip, or the crawling around on my hands and knees. "What happened to them?"

Ivanovich Chuckwuk stopped laughing and looked straight into my heart. His great-grandson did the same. Ivanovich said, "Tosh died, you bet, and the Great Grand Lady waited for seventy years. Now she's done waiting, and she's ready to go to America, only the spies blew the boat all up into pieces so she couldn't get away. Now she says she wants to see you, only you got to be a gentleman and very polite. She's a Great Grand Lady, you bet, and a Romanov too just like the Little Father Czar that got croaked a long time ago."

The ringing in my ears became louder and more shrill. Rickie Saroff watched me through the bottom of his whiskey glass as his great-grandfather bounced up from his chair and shuffled to a sealskin tacked onto a low part of the farthest wall. Ivanovich pulled the skin back from a black hole and crawled in. Moments later, he crawled out followed by five heavily-armed Soviet soldiers and a frail old woman wearing a babushka and a coarse peasant dress.

A soldier helped her to her feet and then he and his mates snapped to attention. The old woman had proud eyes and a baggy, wrinkled face. She held her chin up straight with great effort because her back had shriveled into the shape of a question mark. Her hands were shriveled too, and held a bulky canvas bag close to the hollow under her weary breasts.

Ivanovich Chuckwuk motioned me closer and said, "Now, Mr. Prester John Riordan of America, this here is the Grand Duchess Natasha Nicholovna Romanov of Russia. She's a Pretender to the Throne and a princess too. But you can call her the Great Grand Lady if you want."

The grand duchess clutched her bag with her left hand and extended her right to me. She wore heavy rings of jeweled gold that hadn't been removed in many years, so bent and swollen were her knuckles. I took her hand in mine. It was light and withered, like a dry leaf that might crumble if I shook it too hard. When I let go, her cool blue eyes mocked mine and I realized I was supposed to kiss her hand, not shake it. I mumbled an incoherent greeting.

She said something in Russian and the soldiers stood at ease. She said something else and Ivanovich translated: "The Great Grand Lady says, 'What's wrong with your leg?' She says to me to say to you that she used to work in a hospital during the First World War and she saw many cripples all the time. She wants to know what war crippled you."

I usually lie when people ask me this. Polio has no magic or mystery, and the truth is something I resent. "Grenada," I said. "Ronald Reagan gave me a medal."

The Russian soldiers marched into a back chamber with a new bottle of Jack Daniel's and a videotape movie the boy had brought over from Little Diomede: "*Streets of Fire,* a rock and roll fable." They cheered at the sex and laughed at the violence and tapped their rifles to the beat of the drum.

Ivanovich Chuckwuk, the grand duchess and I sat around the coffee table. The old woman rested the bag on her lap and talked to me in dense Russian which Ivanovich translated into garbled English.

I said, "Why am I here? What do you want me to do?"

Their Russian sounded like the uneasy mating of angry bears. Even the shortest remarks took forever to translate. I began to suspect that Ivanovich's Russian was as tortured as his English. "The Great Grand Lady says she is a faraway cousin of Nicholas, the last of the Little Father Czars. They had too many Romanovs back then. Now they don't have enough. This Romanov lady was a young girl and played dolls and guns with Anastasia and Alexis until she became into an Old Believer. The Old Believers believe she is the real Anastasia Romanov, but the Great Grand Lady says this is not so. But she says it's all okay if the Old Believers think she's Anastasia because it doesn't matter and people believe what they want to anyway."

Ivanovich paused for a second. I looked at the grand duchess. She nodded severely and seemed to clutch her bag a little tighter. Ivanovich continued: "The Great Grand Lady says to me to say to you that she wants you to take her to the Old Believer town in America called Vygovskaia Pustyn so she can die with her friends."

His rendition of the town's name was as twisted as mine, which confirmed my suspicion that Russian did not come easy to our host. I said, "I don't understand these soldiers here. First the guy in the jet tries to kill her and then these soldiers try to help her. I don't understand. It doesn't make sense."

It took them almost twenty minutes to explain it to me. Ivanovich and the grand duchess growled back and forth for several minutes before the old man threw up his hands in defeat. He went into the back chamber and came back with Rickie Saroff in tow. The three chewed over my question in a combination of growling Russian and clucking Eskimo. Ivanovich became agitated and the grand duchess became very still. Rickie shrugged his shoulders and went into the back chamber. A moment later he returned with a tall soldier sporting a mustache so neat that it seemed to be painted on rather than grown.

I expected another round of clucks and growls. But instead, the soldier took off his hat, squared his shoulders and said to me in the perfect, sterile English foreigners learn in school:

"I regret that I cannot introduce myself, Mr. Riordan, but our mission is not sanctioned by all factions of the Supreme Soviet. But ask me your question and I will answer it as candidly as I can."

The soldier had high, Slavic cheeks, but his hair was jet black and his eyes looked like they might have been left behind by soldiers of Tamerlane or some other Mongol warlord. I asked him my question and he replied at length.

"They tell me it's hard for you Americans to understand that we have our disagreements too, because we don't have them on television. Our tradition is to conduct our most

155

important political arguments behind closed doors. I am here because the old generals who know war have had enough of killing. It is the younger generals who've never had a real war and the bureaucrats who . . .''

It was at this point that the grand duchess emitted a dainty cough. Such was her air of natural authority that the soldier stopped in mid-sentence to listen to her instructions, which were forthcoming in whispered Russian. Her mouth was tight and sometimes she looked at something that wasn't in the cave.

When she was done, the soldier said, "Citizen Romanov thinks you should know that you are in a dangerous situation. The attack on the Old Believers which you witnessed yesterday was performed by an agent of the KGB. His name is Vladimir Chen. He is part of the war faction and his mission is to make sure that Citizen Romanov does not reach her friends in Baranov because she is in possession of certain . . .''

The soldier and the old woman growled at each other in Russian before he came up with the proper word. "In possession of certain 'information' which they do not wish to be known. You should also know that he is being assisted by agents of the American war party. As you have seen they have already killed several innocent people in an effort to intercept Citizen Romanov and I am certain they will kill again if they decide it is in their interest to do so. You must be very careful, Mr. Riordan.''

The grand duchess coughed again and uttered what sounded like a curse. The soldier started to translate, but Ivanovich Chuckwuk beat him to it. "The old Great Grand Lady says that all these spies with three letters like the KGB and the CIA have to have secrets and war because without secrets and war they never have any more reasons to be and would have to get real jobs.''

The soldier smiled at Ivanovich. "That's a somewhat amplified translation, but basically accurate and sufficient.'' With that, he made a courtly bow to the grand duchess. She tilted her head ever so slightly and dismissed him.

Ivanovich Chuckwuk returned our clothes—they were clean and pressed—and fed us. Ivanovich sat at one end of a long table, the grand duchess at the other. The soldiers,

Rickie and I were seated in between according to some order of rank we didn't understand. We ate chicken pot pies while Ivanovich carried on simultaneous conversations in English and Russian.

In English, Ivanovich said, "The generals bicker for pennies at me all the time. If I say a videotape machine should cost them to pay me two ounces of gold, they give me the narrow eyes and seem like I tried to steal their children. Whatever it is they always say I should take rubles instead. Rubles are worth nothing, I say, and mostly they agree. I always win because I'm the one with the videotape machine. Pass the Fritos Rickie, okay?"

As the Fritos made their way around the table, the soldier who had spoken before adjusted his mustache and made a comment in Russian under his breath. Ivanovich laughed, and then so did the other soldiers and maybe even the grand duchess. Her somber arrogance did not lend itself to levity, but I thought I saw a twinkle in her eyes and a quiver on her lips, although it could have been gas. Another soldier made another comment and the laughter pitched again. Ivanovich slapped his hand on the table and let some pot pie gravy dribble down his chin.

Then the grand duchess said something, but didn't move her lips. She didn't say it loudly, and it was only a Russian word or two, but the effect was chilling nonetheless. The soldiers swallowed their laughter, and our host changed the subject, or at least he changed languages.

Ivanovich wiped his chin with his fist and then licked the gravy off. His breath was short and his words were labored. The laughter had taken its toll.

"You Americans can do anything. You can sell anything anywhere is how come my Russian friends laugh into their food. They can't even get good blankets and here it is we're eating Fritos all because America is just over there across the water. The soldiers think it's funny how come they can't get blankets because they're only cold. I can get Fritos and chicken pot pies just because I like them and have American friends who like to smuggle to me. The captain wants to buy your shoes. Do you take rubles?"

The soldiers used a long rope and a sealskin sling to lift us through the slippery tunnel connecting the old smuggler's apartments with the outer chamber.

I don't remember the sky or the water or the dark outline of Little Diomede as we paddled back to America. But I do remember Rickie Saroff hunched into his work in the lead kayak, flailing his arms as he pulled us along by a rope. And I remember how the grand duchess was wedged in my lap. She smelled of dust and jasmine and held onto her canvas bag as if it was life itself. She was very heavy but she didn't weigh much, like an old memory that won't go away.

Chapter 20

WE WERE THE CAUSE OF A BIG CELEBRATION ON LITTLE Diomede. By the time we reached the beach, a large crowd had gathered. The Saroffs embraced Rickie and the Kropotkins embraced me. We all stood around the grand duchess, who seemed perfectly at ease in the presence of awestruck strangers. Uncle Fred was carried to the beach and composed a fable in honor of the occasion: something about Rickie returning from a watery grave. There was a lot of discussion as to what the moral should be. The children played baseball and everyone gorged themselves on whale blubber and red salmon. The women of the island chatted at the grand duchess, who didn't understand a word they said, but chatted back anyway.

The festival lasted for two days. Uncle Fred presided over a memorial service for the Old Believers who had been blown to smithereens. I said a prayer in English, the grand duchess said a prayer in Russian, and the villagers said a prayer with too many *n*s and *g*s.

The villagers know death too well to worry about it much. After the memorial service, there was a blanket toss in which the two families competed to see which could vault their youngest boy higher into the air. The men performed an ancient men's dance and the women performed an ancient women's dance. The children did the boogaloo. The grand duchess regarded all of this frivolity with a regal smile, but never let go of her canvas bag. I was asked to explain why her back had shriveled into such a painful posture and why she spoke neither English nor Eskimo.

I told them that she was a great lady from the other side and that her name was Natasha Romanov, although some believed her to be Anastasia.

I told them that the House of Romanov had ruled a great empire for three hundred years, and that the last of them were killed in the basement of a modest home in the city of Ekaterinburg in the place called Siberia beyond Big Diomede. I told them how some believed that the youngest girl of the royal family, a plump and impish girl named Anastasia, escaped execution in the arms of a soldier who loved her.

"This is a good story," Uncle Fred said. "It has many morals: Power kills, Love saves and Never go into the basement with a Communist."

The *Leapin' Lizard* rode in on a northeast wind. The people of Little Diomede unloaded her cargo and paid the pilot in cash. Gatlin was in good spirits. When I told him about the grand duchess, he laughed out loud and said "Yo."

He uttered an excited "yo" again when she paid him in advance with a gold coin stamped with a picture of a dead Romanov and inscribed with letters of the Russian alphabet. He responded with an uncertain "yo" when she gave him instructions in a language he didn't understand.

I told him what I thought she wanted and he said, "Baranov's about a thousand miles out of my way." He rubbed the coin between his fingers. "Think she can cough up another one of these?"

I pointed at the coin and held up two fingers, but she didn't comprehend me. But when Gatlin shook his head and tried to hand the one coin back, she dug another out of her bag and handed it over. The pilot said "Yo" and we were on our way.

The grand duchess sat in the copilot's seat and I strapped myself down in the cargo hold next to a large tin filled with smoked salmon and a duffle bag stuffed with sealskins. Gatlin cranked the *Leapin' Lizard* into a great confusion of noise and smoke. As we rolled down the runway, he hollered back at me, "*Liz* won't make it all the way to Baranov. We'll stop for fuel in Aniak."

*   *   *

Aniak is both an island and a village where the great low water of the Kuskokwim River splits off into branches. Its main employers are the school district, the airport and a small gravel pit. The gravel pit used to be the site of a White Alice communications station, which was supposed to warn the president that Soviet missiles were on the way. A legend inscribed above the front door of the high school proclaimed Aniak to be "The Home of the Halfbreeds."

The grand duchess and I ate Louburgers at the Aniak Lodge while Gatlin oversaw the refueling of the *Leapin' Lizard*. Lou was a big, round man with absolutely no sign of hair anywhere on his body, including the ridges where eyebrows usually grow. He dispensed advice and Louburgers to a half dozen Halfbreeds while the grand duchess and I supped.

The old woman attended to her Louburger as if it were the extravagant concoction of a French chef. First she dismantled the sandwich into its component parts—the bun to one part of her plate, the meat to another and the lettuce, tomato and onion onto a small saucer she'd separated from a coffee cup. Her posture was a perfect as it could be, considering the sad hump which her back had become, and she ate small bites slowly with the tines of her fork pointed down, in the style of a well-bred Englishwoman. While I wolfed my Louburger down in four or five ill-considered gulps, she relished every morsel and made several condescending gestures in the direction of our host. Lou chose to interpret these as compliments.

"She don't talk too much, which is pretty special in a woman," Lou said.

"She doesn't speak English," I said. I paused for a second, and then thought, What the hell. "Her name is Natasha, but some people say she's Anastasia Romanov."

Lou gave no indication that he'd ever heard of Anastasia before, or that he cared to hear any more. I almost saw a giggle light her eyes and I'm sure the flaccid skin under her chin quivered a bit. It must have been the Louburger taking effect.

She was still fussing with her meat when Gatlin came in and announced that the *Leapin' Lizard* was fit as could be, full of fuel and ready for the long haul to the Kenai Peninsula. He quickly inhaled two Louburgers before she could even start on the salad she had composed from the garden parts of her own sandwich. I excused myself and asked Lou for permission to place a collect call to Baranov. He said that would be okay.

"Law office."

"Lindy Sue Baker, please."

"Who's calling?"

"Pres Riordan."

She was impressed with my story. One time she even called me "You poor hon." I told her we'd be at the Baranov Airport in an hour or two.

"Now let's think about this for a second," she said. "That big plane'll cause a big commotion coming into Baranov. If word gets around, that motorcycle cowboy with the KGB would catch on right away. How about if you sneak her in the back door?"

I thought about it for a second. She'd made a lot of sense. "Okay, we'll do this. You get a hold of a fishing guide named Danny Sawyer. You can reach him at the borough public works department. Tell him to take his boat up to Cooper Landing and meet us there right away. He'll move a little faster if you tell him it'll make him a little coin."

The Cooper Landing airport was more like an old road that had been abandoned and left to deteriorate, but the *Leapin' Lizard* had landed on worse. Gatlin turned around and headed back to Kotzebue. The grand duchess and I walked over to Harrison's Place. I offered to carry her bag, but she only clutched it tighter.

Lindy Sue, Michael and the Big Beluga were waiting for us at the big curve in the bar at Harrison's Place, which was crowded with noisy sportsmen who'd already caught their limit for the day. My friends were so enchanted by the attorney that they didn't notice us at first. She looked more Texan than she'd ever looked before. The severe blue suit she'd worn in court had been replaced with tight blue jeans and a loose blouse that clung to her curves every now and then. Her black hair was still tied back, but loosely. It seemed ready to fall to her shoulders at a moment's notice. She had a big wad of gum in her mouth. When she snapped it it sounded like the report of a small pistol.

I introduced the grand duchess to my friends. Something

162

happened between the old woman and the fat man at the sound of his Russian last name—Michael Gudunov. Her face brightened into a smile. His jaw dropped open, as if he'd never seen a woman smile before. I would have thought they were falling in love were she not sixty years older and three hundred pounds lighter than he.

Lindy Sue eased the grand duchess toward a leather dining booth crowded with fishermen. "Let the lady have a seat, will you boys?" The fishermen started to complain, but the Texan silenced them by snapping her gum as loudly as she could and adjusting her hips in a disturbing way. The big, tough fishermen went away and the two women settled into the booth and started talking in some sort of sign language that only women understand. They made a mirror image of youth and age that made me think that fifty years from now Lindy Sue Baker and Rachel Morgan and all the beautiful women I've ever known will have humped backs and swollen knuckles, but they'll still be beautiful.

Michael interrupted my reverie. "So she's a real Russian queen, huh?"

"A grand duchess," I replied. "She was the daughter of a cousin of the royal family or something like that."

"Was that a long time ago?"

I counted the decades backwards, from 1987 to 1917—to a different world still ruled by kings. "Shit. That was seventy years ago."

"Well she's about the oldest crow I ever seen," the Big Beluga said. "She looks like The Mummy come to life without no bandages on. I'd say she's shrunk about a foot and her wrinkles got wrinkles."

"Watch it, Big," Michael said. "I don't want you talking like that. It ain't right."

The Big Beluga changed the subject. "That lawyer lady said something about some coin."

"Not some. One."

The Big Beluga stretched out his tall frame and looked down at me. "What're you talking about, 'One coin'? I don't do nothing for one coin. If she wants a river trip to Vyg, it'll cost her three hundred bucks. Right now, no bullshit."

I laughed, but the Big Beluga was not amused. He went over to the dining booth and leaned his elbows on the table. The women continued their pantomine conversation until the Big Beluga put his wallet on the table and pointed at the grand duchess. "Rubles. Kopecks. The Big Grazoo. We don't go anyplace until I get some money. That'll be four hundred bucks."

Lindy Sue flashed her hands in a way that the grand duchess understood. The grand duchess tilted her head up at an arrogant angle that must have hurt her crippled back and dug into her canvas bag. With an oath that only she understood, she laid a coin on the table.

At first, the Big Beluga was angry. "This don't look like four hundred bucks." When he picked up the coin, his anger changed color and became more like confusion. "What's this?"

"Romanov gold," I said. "An ounce or so, I guess. It's worth about five hundred dollars if you melt down and a lot more if you sell it to a coin dealer."

The Big Beluga turned it around and held it close to the light. He tapped it against the table, chomped it with his eyetooth and then said, "Well, it ain't four hundred dollars but under the circumstances I guess it'll have to do.

Michael volunteered to hitchhike back to Baranov after the Big Beluga started complaining out loud to Lindy Sue Baker that his girth might sink the boat. I said he should tell the authorities that a Soviet spy was in the vicinity, killing Old Believers as fast as he could.

"You don't mean I should tell Peek-A-Boo Pete?" he said in a voice that betrayed his contempt for authority in general and for Peek-A-Boo Pete in particular.

It did seem silly when he said it like that. "Yeah, I guess you better. And watch out for a federal man by the name of Jon Jones."

The grand duchess sat in the stern of the boat on a carton of SpaghettiOs the Big Beluga had taken in trade from a grocer. She made canned starch look like a throne and the Big Beluga's riverboat look like Cleopatra's barge. But this Cleopatra was shrinking and had been reduced to wearing a threadbare peasant dress, babushka and clodhoppers. But her eyes made up for everything. They were blue-green and clear and certain about everything they saw. They did not dart about but always looked straight ahead at whatever caught her attention. When a bald eagle dived to the water to catch a fish, she turned her body full around and looked the eagle right in the eyes. When a cow moose and her calf splashed in for a drink, she turned her body full square the other way so that they might have her full attention. When the Big Beluga broke out in a sea chanty, she looked at him and tapped her toes to what she imagined to be the beat:

> Hey ho, and up she's rising.
> Hey ho, and up she's rising.
> Hey ho, and up she's rising,
> Early in the morning.
> What do you do with a drunken sailor?
> What do you do with a drunken sailor?
> What do you do . . .

On and on. Her attention never flagged through a dozen verses, some of which were hundreds of years old and some of which the Big Beluga made up on the spot:

> I got a boat with no downpayment.
> I got a boat with no downpayment.
> I got a boat with no downpayment.
> Early in the morning.

Or:

> I got a thing for Texan women.
> I got a thing for Texan women.
> I got a thing for Texan women,
> Early in the morning.

This got a rise out of Lindy Sue, but it was hard to tell whether she was irritated or amused or embarrassed or what. She snapped her gum more loudly than usual and looked through the Big Beluga with her big black Texan eyes. She seemed part Mexican when she looked like that.

The grand duchess listened to each verse with the same serene expression and the same tapping toes until the Big Beluga had the temerity to chant a verse about her.

How much gold in the canvas bag-o?
How much gold in the canvas bag-o?
How much gold . . . in the canvas . . .

But before he could get out his last "bag-o", something incredible and totally unexpected happened. The grand duchess stopped tapping her toes and her serene face became severe. She dug into her canvas bag-o and pulled out a small derringer perfectly suited to her dainty hand. She pointed the weapon at the Big Beluga.

"You understand English," I said.

"That's right, Mr. Riordan." She had the soft, high tones of a woman of rank. "My mother was English. She learned her manners from Queen Victoria and taught me what she could before the Bolsheviks murdered her."

"Why didn't you tell us you speak English?" I asked.

She turned to me, but kept the derringer pointed at the Big Beluga, who was pretending that he wasn't impressed by her threats. "As a women of breeding, I am aware of the various deceptions employed by unlettered peasants such as yourself. I wished to hear your candid comments, which I'm certain would not have been nearly so candid had you known that I could understand them. Frankly, Mr. Riordan, I'm a little disappointed to learn that my fate is in the hands of a lowlife. You speak English like an Irish pig and probably drink too much. What is your trade, young man?"

"I'm a journalist—a writer," I said. You arrogant bitch, I added, but only to myself.

Lindy Sue seemed to think this was funny. The grand duchess thought it was a crime against language. She asked Lindy Sue to sit at her side so that she too might have the protection of the derringer. The grand duchess turned back to the Big Beluga. "And as for you, you hooligan. The contents of my bag are no concern of yours. You've been paid for your services. I suggest you perform them."

The Big Beluga said something into his beard that none of us could hear. Lindy Sue tried to persuade the grand duchess that the guide posed no real threat to her canvas bag, but the old lady refused to put her weapon away.

The derringer made her seem even more regal. Her haughty manner seemed pathetic dressed up in the heavy peasant dress and clodhopper shoes the Old Believers wore.

166

But the derringer lent her an air of indisputable authority. It had an ivory handle and a gold-plated barrel and carried two shots at the most: one for the Big Beluga, and one for me.

"Hey, Lowlife," the Big Beluga said to me, "If you can catch my Drift-O-Matic, how about if you mosey into the box under that high falutin' butt and fetch me a can of SpaghettiOs."

The Big Beluga's slang had befuddled the grand duchess. I stepped in her direction. She squeezed her bag as hard as she could and pointed her derringer at me. "Stay where you are, young man."

The Big Beluga made a sharp turn into the river's current. The boat tilted at a dangerous angle, spilling me, Lindy Sue and the grand duchess into a tumble on the deck. The old lady whacked me in the knee with one of her clodhoppers while one of Lindy Sue's ample Texas breasts squished my face.

The derringer clattered loose. The Big Beluga, who had kept his feet, picked it up. Then he picked up the grand duchess and walked her over to the box on which she'd been sitting. Lindy Sue and I were left to fend for ourselves. When I tried to help her up, she slapped me with her eyes.

"You did that on purpose, you scoundrel," she said to the Big Beluga. She hadn't let go of her canvas bag.

"That's right, ma'am. I'm hungry and you didn't seem very agreeable."

The Big Beluga ripped open the box and pulled out four cans of SpaghettiOs. He closed the box and then eased the old lady down on it. He handed her back the derringer and then grabbed the wheel just in time to avoid running into a log.

"Nothing like a can of cold SpaghettiOs," the Big Beluga announced, more to himself than to us. He pried open the top and began to shovel it in. Artificial tomato sauce clung to his mustache. He threw me a can of SpaghettiOs and then threw me the can opener. He offered the same to the women, but they preferred to starve.

We ate SpaghettiOs and made good time. The Big Beluga had regained the old woman's confidence by his gallant gesture of returning to her the very weapon she had used to threaten his life. For a while she pointed it at me, as if this would stop me from destroying the language her mother had taught her. But soon enough she tired of this and put the derringer back into her bag.

We made Sterling by nightfall and decided to camp on an island in the middle of the river, which was a favorite place of many species of birds. The Big Beluga thought we could reach Vygovskaia Pustyn by mid-afternoon of the next day.

"Weather holds up and we'll be all right," he said while scraping away the birdshit from a flat place where we intended to raise our tents.

But the weather didn't hold up. There were no stars that night and a big rain come. The grand duchess and Lindy Sue slept in one tent and talked until late of mystical female things. I shared another tent with the Big Beluga, who smelled of fish and fell into a noisy slumber as soon as his head hit the ground. I listened to the rising wind and counted the raindrops as they plopped against the plastic tent. The more I counted, the heavier and more numerous they became.

My feet were wet when I woke up. The rain had stopped but the river had risen and half the island had been submerged. The Big Beluga made a fire from some dry wood he kept in a waterproof bag and laid open cans of SpaghettiOs into the flames. He said they'd be ready when the cans were charred black.

"The river's mean today," the Big Beluga said. "The best thing is we should find a dry spot and stay there until the water settles down."

But the grand duchess would have none of that.

The Big Beluga pulled out a pliers and used it to lift a smoldering can from the fire. He placed it before the grand duchess and she started eating with no further ado, holding her spoon in a delicate way.

"How come?" the Big Beluga said. "It wouldn't have to do with all that gold you got."

"Mr. Beluga. It seems to me that despite your appearance you are an honorable man. I paid you good money to take me to Vygovskaia Pustyn. The honorable thing is for you to take me there as quickly as you can."

The Big Beluga showed me a lot just then. I'd always admired his way with women and fish, but I never thought he could stand up to the likes of the grand duchess Natasha, or Anastasia if you will. I'm pretty sure he'd never been called honorable before, but he held his ground against her. He told her the river was too flooded for travel and suggested we head for Sterling, where he knew a warm little hotel with a bar in front and hot showers in back.

Lindy Sue agreed with the Big Beluga and I agreed with Lindy Sue. When everyone had spoken, the grand duchess pulled out her derringer and pointed it at no one in particular. "Mr. Beluga. I appreciate your anxiety, although I suspect you worry more about my bag than about my person. However, I am worried about something else altogether. I'm an old woman, Mr. Beluga. I've spent most of my eighty-eight years helping other Old Believers escape to freedom. I'm afraid I've done some horrible things since the Bolsheviks took over. I've lied and gone to bed with Communists and given them some of the Romanov gold I gave to you. If God forgave me that, I'm sure He'll forgive my placing a bullet between your eyes. What do you say to that?"

The Big Beluga didn't say anything. He shoveled in a spoonful of SpaghettiOs and chewed on them a bit. The grand duchess put her derringer away and graced us with a tired smile.

Chapter 21

WE DIDN'T BREAK CAMP SO MUCH AS SLIDE IT INTO THE boat, which already contained a couple of inches of rainwater. The wet cardboard had peeled away from the box of SpaghettiOs, leaving a dozen or so cans standing free in brown goop. The Big Beluga handed Lindy Sue and me some empty cans he kept in his knapsack and told us to start bailing.

The river was like dirty bathwater hurrying down the drain. The heavy rain and the high water had torn mud from the banks that in turn made the water a thick brown color. Trees were uprooted and carried away by the fast current, their exposed roots waving good-bye. A snag near the Moose River flats had tangled some of the trees into a great pile of tree confusion, with dozens of trunks and hundreds of branches all akimbo. This logjam so impeded the progress of the river that we could see a trailer court on the southern bank that had become flooded. I saw a picture in my mind of a mobile home drifting downstream with unwashed children leaning out the windows, rowing.

The Big Beluga guided us around the logjam, and was careful not to disturb it. He said, "You can feel the trouble if you hold real still. River's like a waterpipe ready to burst. I would figure there's twenty or so logjams just like this between Cooper Landing and Vyg. When a jam-up breaks up what happens is that the water comes through, pushing the logs before it, so when it gets to the next jam-up it'll blast through, like a bullet shot at wet toilet paper. It builds up logjam for logjam until by the time the breaker gets to the

170

sea you got a wall of wood and water about as big as a little mountain coming at you going about thirty miles per hour, and the only thing to do is you better be going thirty-five if you don't want to get killed. Is that what you got in mind, Miss Romanov?"

She dismissed him with a nod and summoned Lindy Sue to her side. They talked about everything and nothing all at the same time, in that remarkable way of women that men admire but are powerless to duplicate.

"Tell me about Vygovskaia Pustyn, my dear."

To me it seemed that Lindy Sue told her about everything but the village. They talked about criminal justice, religious freedom and the bad behavior of grown-up boys. When they had exhausted the subject without ever touching it, Lindy Sue asked a question of her own. "Why won't Ivan Smolensk defend himself?"

And in her turn, the grand duchess answered the question by avoiding it. She talked about the first World War to End All Wars and the habit men have of slaughtering each other. "The thing is, my dear, men don't respect death because they don't truly understand life. It's quite sad really, and causes a lot of trouble. If I was granted one wish that could change the world, it would be that men would give birth too. Women understand life because it swells the tummy and hurts like the dickens. But a man? Fiddle faddle and he's done. Death is nothing to men because to them life comes so easily."

The Big Beluga tried to make some sense of this by asking the question again. He did better than Lindy Sue. He said, "What I don't understand is they won't talk."

The grand duchess took a moment to unscramble his words, put them in their proper places. "Talk kills in Russia, boy. I was converted to the Old Belief by the grandfather of Boris and Fedor Yermak. I was a young girl then who didn't understand the war around me, as the Germans killed us year after year. I was only sixteen, but dying was all there was. I was attracted to the Old Belief because the Old Believers always did their dying bravely, singing the praises of Our Lord like in the opera by Mussorgsky. I dare say, Mr. Beluga, something in your eyes tells me that if you were a Russian you would follow the Old Belief."

I tried to look at his eyes, but they were fastened on the

river ahead. I grabbed an old rag and used it to soak up a puddle of rain with Rachel's face in it.

"The two women ignored me again as I blotted and squeezed; they blathered with a rich intimacy that men rarely share even with their wives. The Big Beluga watched the river while we pretended not to listen.

The grand duchess told Lindy Sue about the Russian royal family and the pitiful end of the Romanovs after three hundred years of uninterrupted rule. "I remember the boy. He was a bleeder, you know. They could have killed him with a pinprick instead of a machine gun. The czarevich was a handsome child and brave in his way. His bleeding episodes were horribly painful, but he tried not to cry. But Alexis Romanov will live again, my dear. Just as his sister Anastasia lives again when loyal peasants think I am she."

Lindy Sue started to tell the grand duchess about the deaths of Boris and Fedor Yermac, and the stoic silence of Ivan Smolensk.

The old woman looked very sad when Lindy Sue told her these things. "The Yermac family has served my family for hundreds of years, since before the Time of Troubles, when the Rurik kings ruled my country. They are as loyal now as they were back then. I owe them my life, such as it is."

We had reached the place where the Kenai River branches into the Vyg. The Big Beluga asked us to be quiet.

"How come?" I whispered.

"I gotta concentrate. I'm trying to see the rocks. Trying to remember."

I looked at the river. I didn't see any rocks and told him so. He said, "Those're the rocks I'm looking for. The high water covers 'em up. But they're there, all right. Just down under and if we hit one wrong we're all gonna take a bath, though to me you could probably use one."

The old woman closed her eyes and started to pray. A few seconds later, Lindy Sue Baker joined her. This gave me the opportunity to look at them more closely than I would have had they been looking back at me. Lindy Sue was dirty and wet, her hair all tangled in knots. The grand duchess was a wild arrangement of contradictions. Her arrogance was softened by her brittle bones. The tattered condition of her peasant dress somehow made her claims to be a member of the dispossessed nobility seem more brave than pathetic,

172

more modest than silly. In her crippled hands, a derringer became an object of admiration, a canvas bag a thing of mystery. She had threatened me and condescended to me and not even given me some Romanov gold for my trouble. But I wanted to help her do whatever it was she was trying to do.

She stopped praying and opened her eyes. It was a few seconds before I realized she saw me seeing her, time enough for her to look right through me and know everything there was to know, right down to the hurt feelings about the gold coin. Her smile was a well-worn display of wrinkled satisfaction. She was used to seeing through men and used to manipulating them into making the right decisions.

"You remind me of Alexis, Mr. Riordan. He was a scribbler too, although his English was always proper. And he was crippled like you by the bleeding and wore a leg brace for many months. The czarevich would have made a good ruler. He suffered as much as any peasant and would have been kind, I believe."

I wanted to ask her to tell me all about the boy, but the Big Beluga told us to shut up. Lindy Sue had stopped praying and looked at me in a different way that I found very unsettling.

The Vyg was wider than it had been before, especially at Russian Bend, where a great chunk of muddy real estate had been carried away by the flood. The current was so fast there that the Big Beluga used his motor more for navigation than speed.

We headed for a patch of golden brown river under a break of blue in the overcast sky. When we got there, the grand duchess took off her babushka and tilted her face to the sun. It was a girlish gesture that drew me into a daydream in which the whole panorama of her youth was played out on the brown screen of the flooded river.

She looked like a teenage Rachel and they called her Anastasia, because people need their myths, and carry them along from day to day. It was 1917. Six million Russians had been slaughtered by the kaiser and still the war dragged on. Alexis was bleeding and Rasputin had been murdered and the famished mob was looting the Winter Palace. There was blood on the German front and blood in the streets of

Petrograd and her papa, the czar of all the Russias, was stranded somewhere in between. His cousin Kaiser Willie, who'd started the whole catastrophe, was sending Lenin to Russia in a sealed railroad car to destroy a way of life that had already been destroyed. Lenin wanted to kill the Romanovs who had killed his brother for trying to kill their grandfather. But one Romanov with a proud manner and a bag of old gold coins stood up against this sea change and was not washed away. Seventy years later, history's tide rolled back and left the grand duchess Anastasia/Natasha/Rachel Romanov behind. But by then, time had done its dirty work. A back that never bowed to Czar or Kaiser or Lenin had shriveled into a state of permanent prostration. Hands that were once marvels of delicate charm became swollen claws. She consumed herself until she was no more, and the only thing left to fear was dying at the end of an unlived life.

The Big Beluga changed course and I snapped back into present time. I was startled to see that the fear I had seen in the old woman's face was real and had nothing to do with time or osteoporosis. Lindy Sue stood up and pointed at something behind us.

"What's up?" I said.

The Big Beluga leaned on the steering wheel and we veered to the left of an invisible rock. "We got company," he said.

"It's Vladimir Chen," the grand duchess announced.

It took me a second to place the name. By then Chen, who stood with another man on a flat-bottom riverboat, had mounted a tube on his shoulder and was pointing it at us. The tube spat out an orange flame and the Big Beluga made a sharp turn that knocked Lindy Sue down. A fireball exploded into the bank of the river. Some trees and a chunk of land became red-hot stuff that looked like lava and sizzled as it leaked into the river. The grand duchess made the sign of the cross in the two-fingered style of the Old Believers and whispered a silent prayer.

"Fuckin' A!" the Big Beluga said.

"What'll we do?" I replied.

The grand duchess pulled the derringer out of her canvas bag and pointed it at our pursuers. But before she could fire, the Big Beluga hit the gas and knocked her off balance too.

174

"Where we going?" I shouted at the guide.

The Big Beluga examined the river for submerged rocks. "The Vyg Rapids, and real quick. We got a shot if I can lead them onto a rock.

We skimmed over the flooded river, bouncing up and flopping down as if one of Fernando Valenzuela Kropotkin's skipping stones had been shot out of a cannon. The riverbanks raced by. When we added our speed to that of the river, we were traveling more than sixty miles an hour, which is safe enough in a car, but not safe at all in a flat-bottom riverboat.

"Keep your eyes open!" the Big Beluga said.

Chen was closing in. His companion wore a ski mask and held a steady wheel while he plugged something into the back of the tube.

"Get ready," I said. "We're gonna get another shot."

The grand duchess fired her derringer to no effect. Lindy Sue and I peeked over the stern and saw Chen lift the tube to his shoulder and take aim. The lawyer said "Now!" a second before I did. The Big Beluga cut the wheel hard right. The boat tipped up on its side and the three of us tumbled around on the deck. The missile sounded like a train and made a hot breeze as it split the air not more than five feet from the Big Beluga's head. This time a stretch of river up ahead exploded into a cauldron of bubbles and steam through which we dashed a few seconds later.

We bumped along and seemed to be widening the gap as Chen fussed with another missile. The Big Beluga watched the river and I watched him. Suddenly, he eased up a bit on the gas and said, "Oh shit. I was afraid of that."

"What's the matter, Mr. Beluga?" the grand duchess said.

"The rocks are all under water too. I was hoping the flood hadn't got that high yet. The banks have shifted and I can't quite tell where my river marks are."

The old woman made another sign of the cross. "Then perhaps you should trust in the Lord."

In one great sweep of his eyes, the Big Beluga looked at the river, me, Lindy Sue, the grand duchess and our pursuers. Vladimir Chen was again hoisting the tube to his shoulder. "Right," the Big Beluga said, punching the accelerator to the floor.

I don't pray much because I'm a little pissed off at God

about the polio and some other things. But I prayed then, because we needed it and because in prayer I could close my eyes without seeming to be afraid.

"He's gonna take another shot," Lindy Sue announced.

The prayer was over. I opened my eyes. The Big Beluga looked like he was in trouble and the grand duchess looked like she was in a trance. Lindy Sue looked over the back of the boat, and tapped her fingers in a slow rhythm against the deck, as if the act of firing a missile was like the Texas Two-Step. I wanted to scream "Now!" a second before she did. I was about to do so when the boat chasing us bumped into one of the submerged rocks that made up the Vyg rapids. There was a loud cracking sound, and it split in two. The loaded tube flew into the air and detonated when it crashed down into the water. The missile flew over the trees, in the general direction of Nikiski, where it couldn't do any damage.

We celebrated this miracle for about two seconds before we heard another loud crack. My whole body stung like your hands sting when you hit a fastball with a broken baseball bat. The boat teetered on its side for a bit, and then dumped us into the river. I heard a scream. It could have been mine.

I've always wondered if my brace could float. It's mostly made of metal. It didn't. It was all I could do to keep my head above water. Just as the damn thing was about to pull me under, a big log bore down on me, roots first, all twisted and knobby, like the severed hand of an old witch with arthritis and too many fingers. The roots scooped me up like a bag of fish and started to carry me away. I hauled myself up on the log and straddled it like a horse.

Upriver I saw the Big Beluga swimming for the bank with a soggy grand duchess wrapped around his shoulders like a cheap fox fur. I imagined I heard her scream, "No please. You must leave me be. You must get my bag first. That's the important thing. Leave me be and go fetch my bag. Those are my instructions, you filthy peasant."

Chen had already made it to the riverbank, and was running to meet the Big Beluga and his disagreeable baggage. I tried to warn them, but he couldn't hear me because the grand duchess was screaming in his ear: "Mr. Beluga, I want you to let me go right now and fetch that canvas bag! Those are my instructions.''

I saw Chen pull them from the river. He tore them apart and threw the Grand Duchess to the ground. She lay still in an awkward heap. His assistant with the ski mask stepped out of nowhere to help him pin the Big Beluga down. I didn't see what happened next, because the tree carried me around a bend and out of sight.

Chapter 22

LINDY SUE BAKER HAD FOUND HER OWN LOG AND USED A piece of wood to row it through the wood chips and the uprooted bushes and the rest of the flotsam and jetsam made by the flood and our collision with the Vyg Rapids. She tried to paddle toward me, but the current was too strong and her paddle too flimsy to accomplish much.

My own attempt at navigation was almost a disaster. I wanted to make for the right bank, which was across from where the others had landed, and on the same side of the river as Vyg Village. But the log to which I clung did not lend itself to much direction. I kicked the water with my good left foot, but instead of heading for the right bank, the log turned into the first half of an Eskimo roll, leaving me hanging underwater, upside down, like an opossum in need of an aqualung. My crippled leg slipped off and flopped around like a fishing lure. I hung on, but couldn't feel my hands. My lungs started to complain for air.

The mind works quickly when the body's in trouble. I thought about letting go and bobbing to the surface for a great gulp of air. Then I thought about my brace, and how it would drag me down to the river bottom. I thought about climbing back on top of the log, but feared it would keep rolling as I kept climbing, until I couldn't climb anymore. I thought about warm beds and sunny beaches and Rachel Morgan, with someone who was a little like me and a little like her growing in her belly. Just about when I couldn't take it any more and I was running out of air to think with, I thought about the roots of the tree and remembered how they had served me so well before.

I squeezed my lungs as hard as I could and sent all sorts of urgent messages to my hands, but since they were frozen numb by the glacier-fed river water, I couldn't tell if the messages had been received. Move ahead. Crawl ahead. Scratch ahead. Get us out of here or we're all going to die. I bet it wouldn't hurt so much if I just stopped squeezing my chest and sucked in a big lungful of water. My head bumped into something. My shoulder bumped into something else. I hoped they were roots, but couldn't tell for sure. If not, I'd have to let go and take my chances with the brace. I dug in deep with the fingers of my right hand and pushed off with the fingers of my left. The log rolled down and I rolled up. I saw light and felt heat and took a big swig of air that tasted stronger than Dago Red. I coughed out some water and took another swig. And another and another until I was drunk on the stuff. My right hand was bleeding. Slivers of wood stuck out from under my fingernails.

Lindy Sue had been paddling furiously to rescue me. She'd closed the gap between us, but not by much. "Are you okay?" she screamed.

I nodded and coughed some more. Then Lindy Sue said "Holy Moly! Look at that!" and I saw something that made me think there might be something to this praying business after all. All my rolling about had brought to the surface roots which had been under the water before. Hanging from one like an old homemade Christmas ornament gone to seed was the canvas bag which the grand duchess had carried over from Siberia. In it was something more precious to her than life itself.

I couldn't grab at it for fear of knocking it loose or capsizing again. So I hung on and waited for something good to happen. The waters of the Vyg took us where they wanted us to go. Lindy Sue gave up the paddling, and instead clung tightly to her own log. I thought about a mountain of wood and water rolling downriver at thirty-five miles an hour.

Lindy Sue looked like a nature girl, all wet and scruffy with her bandy Texas legs wrapped around that log. I must have been giddy from lack of oxygen or too much oxygen because I yelled to be heard over the rush of the current:

"Do you ever worry about dying at the end of an unlived life?"

She almost smiled, pointed her left one at me and yelled back: "Are you makin' love to me?"

"No. I mean yes. I mean not right here. Don't take it personal, okay?"

Making land was easy enough after all, although not without its harrowing moments. The river pushed us past Vyg Village and a couple of hundred yards out into Cook Inlet. We waved at the village but nobody saw us, or at least nobody paid any attention. The Old Believers had already built another onion-domed church. This one had three domes supporting three of the orthodox crosses. The biggest of the domes was blue with white stripes, very colorful like the *Pugachev*.

The prevailing current carried us southward, in the general direction of Homer. We lost hope, but not our balance, as Vyg Village receded in the distance. I started to sniffle and Lindy Sue started to sneeze and we both decided that if we stayed out all night we would freeze or drown or both. But as the sun began to set, the tide began to drift landward again. It eventually deposited us in the embrace of a setnet marked by a half-dozen red buoys.

I grabbed the old lady's canvas bag and we started wading through waist-deep water toward some lights on the beach. It was dark by then and hard to tell just how far we had to go. The water was so cold I couldn't feel my feet, but they did their duty anyway and carried me to safety

It seemed like the most natural thing in the world.

Our clothes were soaked and our hands shivered from the chill as we collected dry driftwood and applied to it the flame of a Bic lighter she produced from her skintight back pocket.

We held each other tightly to conserve heat. Bit by bit we took off our clothes and stretched them near the fire to dry. Nothing too exciting, at first. We started with our socks. But then I pulled off my pants, which were really soaked, and she took off her blouse, which was dripping wet. Then my shirt and her pants. My leg brace and her undies. After that we had to hold each other even more tightly to conserve warmth because we were half frozen and buck naked.

Lindy Sue turned to me and said, "That stuff you said out there in the water—about dying at the end of an unlived life . . . what did you mean by that?"

What happened next need not be described here, although I should point out that she didn't say "Yipee-Eyeoo" or "Ride 'Em Cowboy" or any of the other things I'd imagined that Texas women said when they'd been just a fever in my brain rather than a glorious warmth on the beach. What happened next has happened billions and trillions of times before in the long randy history of life on earth. With slight variations, it will happen billions and trillions of times more, although never with the consequences which this particular indiscretion was to have for me.

Our exhausted slumber was interrupted by the insistent bleating of a horn. We saw two headlights bobbing along the beach, and scrambled into our clothes just before the lights saw us. From behind the beams came a sourdough voice that sounded like it had been smeared with glue and sprinkled with sand. "Whatcha doin' on my beach, ya goddamn boneheads?"

But before we could answer, the sourdough pointed the headlights at his setnet and uttered a curse that sounded like the grinding of gears. He coughed up something wet and spat it on the beach. He lifted his eyes to heaven and said, "Whadya do to my net?"

I squinted and leaned forward. At first, it was hard to see much. But when my eyes adjusted to the shades of black and gray illuminated by the scarce beams of the headlights, I could see that the sourdough's setnet had caught the biggest collection of uprooted trees I had ever seen. The mountain of water and wood the Big Beluga had warned about had followed us to the sourdough's beach.

His name was Ernest McGrew. We got our first good look at him when he opened the door of his pickup truck and the hood light flickered on. He was about thirty years younger than his voice sounded. He wore a Fu Manchu mustache and a navy blue baseball cap on which was inscribed: USS Juneau, LPD 10. He was scrawny in the same way a junkyard dog is scrawny—underfed and overmean. He had four front teeth wedged between two black gaps. He chewed on a plug of tobacco as big as a billiard ball and squirted the juice into an empty can of Budweiser.

He extended a hard hand. I shook it. He said, "Who you?"

Lindy Sue and I introduced ourselves. We threw some more driftwood on the fire. Ernest fetched some water and a few raw potatoes from his truck. We put the potatoes in the fire and sat down to tell stories and wait for the tide to go out. Lindy Sue told him about faith and death and Vygovskaia Pustyn. I told him about baseball and death and the Diomede Islands.

Ernest McGrew was impressed. "Why, you're but a pair of hot-air liars if there ever was one. I think you been soakin' on that log too long. Now me, I'm the bastard boy of Dangerous Dan McGrew and the lady what's known as Lou."

Dangerous Dan and Lady Lou were the featured characters in a poem by Robert W. Service, the Bard of the Yukon. Ernest was convinced that he was their descendent. "And what I do when I'm not fishing, which is most of the time, is I write the sort of poems that Bobby Service would write if he weren't dead, which he is."

"Bullshit," Lindy Sue said, getting into the spirit of things.

"Well it's true and I'll prove ya."

Ernest McGrew's idea of proof was to pull out a worm-eaten notebook from an inside pocket of his lumberjack coat. He occasionally glanced at the book to refresh his memory as he chanted to us with practiced accents and intonations a poem he called "The Wreck of the Exxon Valdez."

> Let's go kill some animals.
> Let's go spill some crude.
> Let's raise the price of gasoline.
> Let's be downright rude.
> We are the crew of a big oil tanker.
> Our heads are made from blocks.
> Our skipper got drunk this afternoon
> He likes it on the rocks.

I laughed but Lindy Sue didn't. Ernest McGrew tucked his notebook back in his coat pocket. "Now it's yer turn," he said to us.

Lindy Sue told him about one of her Texan clients who had chopped his family into little pieces and served them in tacos from a pushcart in San Antonio. I told him a yarn about how I'd saved the Toyukuk River from the depredations of an environmental criminal while running the Iditarod dogsled race and winning the love of a beautiful girl.

Ernest McGrew pulled a potato from the fire and peeled back the skin. Satisfied that it was cooked, he retrieved the other two. He tossed one in Lindy Sue's lap and the other in mine. I never thought a plain potato could taste so good.

"Ja marry her?" he asked.

"Not exactly," I replied.

"Good. Show you ain't a total fool." He put his potato back in the fire and took out his book again. "Now you two eat up and dream up some more stories while I read some more. Then I'll eat my food and you can talk some more bullshit at me. No taco stories while I'm eating, okay?"

I told them about my domestic difficulties and the sinister influence which unborn children have on aging females. Lindy Sue was fascinated. Ernest mumbled into his potato. "What's that?" he asked.

His stubble-covered chin pointed at the canvas bag, which I had dropped on the beach and then forgot about in my hurry to get warm. He almost swallowed his potato whole when I turned the bag upside down and dumped onto the sand five gold coins and a heavy metal box.

Ernest picked up one of the coins and began to caress it as if it was alive. "Can I have one?" he asked.

I told him I didn't know, that the coins belonged to the grand duchess.

We examined the metal box. It was old and rusty, closed with a flimsy padlock and about the size of a shoebox. Ernest licked his lips as if the metal box contained the first meal he'd seen in a very long time. He gave it a little shake and peeked into a tiny black hole near one of the hinges. If it had been made of something softer, I'm sure he would have taken a bite. "I bet she's full of more gold," he said. "I got a hammer and chisel in the truck that we can use to rip her open."

"No. That's wrong," Lindy Sue said. I reluctantly agreed, and set my mind to concocting various excuses for doing the wrong thing. Ernest started to twitch about, as if his curiosity was trying to escape through the pores of his skin.

The twitching soon escalated into a full-blown spastic episode; his chin quivered one way, his elbow another; his feet did a sand dance. We watched the tide go out and the sun come up.

I said to Lindy Sue, "I bet whatever's in the box will get your client out of jail."

I had no reason to think so, but it sounded pretty good. The various parts of Ernest McGrew became very still. Lindy Sue seemed uncertain now, so I piled on as many excuses as I could as quickly as I could: maybe the contents were damaged by the salt water; or maybe she would want us to carry on; or maybe the box contained a secret map to a secret hiding place where Vladimir Chen and his partner had taken the grand duchess.

Lindy Sue hesitated just long enough for Ernest to fetch his hammer and chisel and apply them to the padlock. When his tools were in place, we both looked at Lindy Sue for some sign of approval. She looked away. That was sign enough. I nodded and Ernest McGrew smacked the chisel with a short but powerful stroke. The padlock flew off and the box popped open.

Lindy Sue made some sort of squeaking noise. I stroked my chin, as if I had a beard. The box smelled of yesterday and was stuffed with hundreds of loose sheets of paper of all odd sizes and shapes. Many were yellow with age and crumbling into dust. Each page save one was filled with faded handwriting in the Russian alphabet. The one exception was on top of the rest and contained a brief note in English written in a childish hand:

To the people of America, U.S.A.

Thanks a lot for the Buffalo Bill Wild West show, which came over here to Russia before the Big War and everybody started to kill each other. This diary isn't anywhere near as neat as Buffalo Bill, but nothing is. It's all I got to give anymore, so it'll have to do.

Your friend,
Alexis

"Who's that?" Ernest McGrew said.

"I'm not sure," I replied.

Lindy Sue wasn't sure either, so Ernest McGrew started to commit the note to memory and make up a fable about what it might mean. The tide started to retreat. Ernest McGrew said he'd drive us into Baranov if we'd help him untangle his setnet from the forest of uprooted trees it had captured.

Chapter 23

ERNEST TOOK LINDY SUE TO HER LAW OFFICE AND dropped me off on K-Beach Road, about 200 yards from my destination. I wanted to sneak up on Peek-a-Boo Pete, who was at his usual hiding place: behind the wheel of his squad car in a cranny behind K-Beach Hamburger Heaven.

I felt bad about disturbing him with news that the grand duchess and the Big Beluga were dead or dying or worse. Late summer is Peek's favorite time of year. The roads are clear of Winnebagos and the cannery workers are too busy sliming the last of the commercial catch to cause much trouble. In a week or so school would resume, removing the last disturbance to his tranquility. Once again he'd have nothing much to do and plenty of time to do it. With a little luck summer would linger for a couple of more weeks. He could fish a bit and take long drives to Homer on official trooper business that wasn't very urgent or important.

But there were disturbing signs of an early winter. Some termination dust had been spotted on the mountains near Seward. This first evidence of snow reminded us of the heavier snows which would start falling on the flatlands soon enough. The cannery workers and other migratory species seemed to be in a bit of a hurry and Walton's Full-Service Department Store had already put a lumpy snowsuit in one of the front display windows. Ernest McGrew had said some moose were already drifting down to feed on the tender bushes in front of Baranov's statue, and Peek-A-Boo Pete's snoring had so fogged up the windows of his squad car that only those familiar with the trooper's habits could tell who was inside.

I banged hard on the door, excited by urgency but not sure what to do. The state trooper wiped a bit of window clear and peeked through. He mouthed what could have been a curse and cracked the window open. Body steam leaked out the crack. "What do you want, Riordan?"

"Hey Peek. We need to talk."

"Well, as you can see, I'm working right now."

"This is work. And it really can't wait."

The lawman squared his shoulders and waved me into the passenger's seat. Inside the squad were all the comforts of home: the crumbs of lunch from K-Beach Hamburger Heaven, a dirty magazine opened to a blonde, a transistor radio playing a twangy country hit, a half-pack of cigarettes and an ashtray full of butts. He turned off the radio and said, "This better not be more horseshit about Ivan Smolensk. He's a convicted killer. Case closed."

I told him all about Big Diomede, Little Diomede, the grand duchess and the Big Beluga, last seen on the banks of the Vyg River in a whole bunch of trouble.

"Now what's this lady's name, this grand duchess?" He slurred the last two words in an effort to diminish the threat they posed to his late-summer tranquility. "Grand douchess," he said, like the feminine hygiene product.

"Natasha Romanov, although some of the Old Believers think she's really . . ." All of a sudden I realized how desperate the situation was. Michael was right. If Peek was our only hope, then there was no hope. " . . . Oh, shit, never mind."

The trooper shifted his haunches onto a mustard-stained hamburger wrapper. "I think you should go to the station and file a missing persons report. Put it all down on paper and we'll get right on it."

Peek-A-Boo Pete had no intention of letting Vladimir Chen ruin his favorite time of year. But I pressed on, with little hope.

"What about the Big Beluga?"

"What about him?"

"And what about the KGB?"

"The what?"

I told him that I didn't believe what Jon Jones had said

187

about Vladimir Chen, that he wasn't really an agent with the Soviet border patrol. "When we were on the island, the old woman said that spies will be spies. She said that spies need secrets or they wouldn't have anything to do. I think that Russian manuscript is some kind of state secret and that Vladimir Chen is with the KGB."

Peek-A-Boo Pete swelled up like a state trooper balloon in the Christmas Parade. Between guffaws, he said, "Well, call . . . the fuck- . . . in' . . . CI . . . A."

The house was empty, but Rachel was home from the Bristol Bay fishery. She had left a note for me: "Took Chena and Natty Bumppo for a run along the beach. We have a serious problem and we need to talk about it if you ever do come home."

The place still smelled of red salmon gone bad, the lingering aftereffects of the power outage. I called work and asked for Jack.

"Everything's quiet as can be. The American Legion wants to know if we'll do a big story about them, and there's a little problem with a story one of your reporters wrote, but that's no news. The main thing is, where've you been? You know, Pres, you've been gone a little longer than the deal we had."

I apologized for the delay. We scheduled a meeting for the first tee at the crack of dawn. I hung up the phone and looked for some food.

The refrigerator was still full of vegetables and multiple vitamins. The pictures were still on the wall and the kitchen table was still cluttered with my notes and Rachel's lesson plans and junk mail she couldn't throw away, just in case one of those glorious promises turned out to be true. But now these things no longer made me feel comfortable and a little bit lazy. Something was wrong. Something had changed.

A red blush heated my cheeks and made my skin all tight and prickly when I realized what it must be: Rachel would find out about Lindy Sue and me. Could she already know?

It could happen in a dozen different ways. Baranov is a very small town. Somebody who knew somebody would hear something and one of the fundamentalist preachers would denounce me from his pulpit. The Baranov Assembly of God would start rolling on the floor and the town would start to talk. Or maybe Rachel and Lindy Sue would meet at the horseback riding club or the Kenai Recreation Center or the Alaska All-Night Video Store and get to talking about Boneheads I Have Known.

"I'm living with one," Rachel might have said. "And he won't let me have a baby." To which Lindy Sue could have replied: "I just had one on the beach. He said he was cold but I know better. A cute little guy with a crippled leg. Works for the local paper."

My blood was pumping hard and fast. It would be all over if she ever found out from anyone but me. I read her note again and this time it was alien too. The words were stiff and formal, with a subtle tension between them, as if she already suspected something. The snotty way she put it: "If you ever do come home." And, more important, there were no cartoons of the sort she usually used to illustrate her messages: a stickman Pres walks Chena; a stickwoman Rachel buys groceries; a stickman Pres fucks the defense attorney in a murder case, and comes running home when he's finished. And what was this serious problem she wanted to talk about? I was in deep shit. That was the problem.

I tried to sit down, but my legs wouldn't bend. Primal instincts that are hundreds of millions of years older than me told me to run away and hide in the darkest tavern I could find. I grabbed my coat and was about to do just that when I heard Natty Bumppo trotting up the driveway. Moments later, the front door clicked. Rachel and Chena came inside.

I can't remember now if she was smiling or scowling or doing something else with her face because I didn't have the courage to look her in the eye. Chena gave me a perfunctory sniff. She checked her dog dish to see if I had put anything interesting in it. Finding I had not, she limped off to one of her favorite sleeping places and started to snooze. Rachel said "hello" and we hugged each other. But the hug was tentative, as if neither of us was sure that the other was hugging back. She patted me on the shoulder, which is what women do before saying, "Let's just be friends, okay?"

We let go and looked at each other. She looked at my eyes. I looked at her shoes. I pointed at the kitchen table

189

and made a lame attempt to lead our conversation in a safe direction. "I guess you're getting ready for school, huh?"

She was quiet but not unhappy, calm and more sure of herself than I had ever seen her before. Maybe if I played it right, she'd give me another chance. "Pres, we've got to talk."

I made a blubbering sound and dropped to my knees to bury my face in that soft, warm, wonderful place where her legs and belly met. "I'm sorry, Rachel. Please forgive me. I don't know what came over me. I'll never do anything like it again."

She couldn't hear me, because my apology was muffled by her soft form. Or maybe she could hear me, but did not believe her ears. She pushed me away and lifted me up by the chin. "What did you say?"

My tongue was thick and my eyes were wet. "I'm sorry."

The calmness that I had seen before was replaced by something else. "What are you sorry about?"

But somehow she already knew. She listened without saying a word and became very sad. I listened closely to my own words, as if someone else was speaking them, as if some other fool had been driven mad by the notion of Texan women.

When I was done, she said, "You don't even care enough to lie. Aren't you even ashamed? First you cheat on me, and now you want me to be the one that feels bad about it."

I mumbled another inane apology as she walked out of the room. Moments later, she came back with an armful of camping gear. She threw the stuff at my feet. "Get out."

"But can't we work this out?"

"I don't know. Maybe later. Not right now. I've got someone else to worry about."

"Like who?"

"Get out."

Chena followed me out the door and into the cab of my big red monster pickup truck. There was a big wind outside. It was a long time before I figured out who that someone else was, and a longer time before I ever saw Rachel Morgan again.

The Baranov gravel pit used to be called Kenaitze Hill, until they carried it away to make a road to Nikiski, where

190

the oil comes from. In the winter, the gravel pit was a desolate gash in the wilderness and an embarrassment to the community. In the summer, it was a festive tent city, the temporary home of dozens of cannery workers and an embarrassment to the community.

All the good camping spots had been taken by the time Chena and I arrived. Some cannery workers had pitched their tents on the natural high spots or had built their own high spots from slag too rough for the building of roads. A clothesline was strung between the frame of an old shack and a steel ring that had been pounded into the side of the pit for some forgotten purpose. The place smelled of body odor and salmon, a combination which Chena found particularly appealing.

I pitched our tent on the only clear spot left, an incline which angled into a puddle left behind by the storm. Chena loved our new home. She drank from the puddle and quickly became a gravel pit celebrity. Most of the campers were at the cannery, but the few who stayed behind gave her scraps of food and scratched her behind the ears. She took a liking to a tramp family and decided to nap on a pile of their dirty laundry.

For a while I killed time, hoping to think of some magical plan that would save the grand duchess and the Big Beluga and return me to the embrace of my beloved. No plan came to me. I made small talk with a young Norwegian couple, but they didn't say much. They were sliming their way across Alaska. Last year Ketchikan, this year Baranov. Next year maybe they would slime red salmon at Dillingham, a fishing port on Bristol Bay.

"Ya too late here to work now, you see. The shape-up is over and the work's all gone until tomorrow," said the woman. She was tall and strong-looking. I wondered if she'd ever been to Texas.

The tramp family were annual visitors to the gravel pit, and knew the ins and outs of cannery life. I'd seen them taking free showers at the Baranov Recreation Center and watching TV at the Wash and Dry while doing their laundry one load at a time to stretch out their stay. Every summer they worked in the Davidson Cannery, and every winter they went someplace else.

Chena's slumber was interrupted when one of the tramp

191

family tents spat out a wild gang of children, who started throwing slag chips at Chena and at one another. They were tended by a young mother who'd lost some of her teeth. She cooked salmon over an open fire and talked to the children in a low, uneasy way. She looked at me every now and then, and seemed disturbed by my presence.

Their campfire got brighter as the sky became dim. Chena stretched her legs and took another nap on a clutch of weeds that had fought their way up through the gravel. The other tent dwellers were starting to return from the cannery, tired and cold, their clothes smeared with fish guts and fish blood. I zipped up my tent and tossed my valuables in the truck. I tried to lure Chena into the cab, but she was too busy enjoying the attention of an exhausted coed. I grabbed the grand duchess's bag and headed toward Kenai. Perhaps a plan would occur to me there.

My destination was Kenai Joe's, where I expected to find Michael and maybe some news about the grand duchess and the Big Beluga. On the way, I stopped by the *Beacon* to pick up editions of the paper published during my absence. Jack would quiz me in the morning. I planned to read them over enough beer to make me forget my troubles.

The volume of the music and the level of excitement at Kenai Joe's had already been turned down a notch. Like the squirrels and rabbits, the people of the Kenai Peninsula slow down as winter nears. Drilling and other work in the oil and gas industry drop to the maintenance level and fishing of both the commercial and sports varieties comes to a halt. The children are busy with school and their parents hurry from one warm spot to another. Only the moose become more active when the temperature cools as they wander in from the wilderness in search of food.

The jukebox played a sad cowboy song as I stepped into the place. A blast of cool air coming in behind me made a little wood flurry of the sawdust on the floor. "Hey, Shorter-Than-I!" said Michael, who hovered near the dartboard looking lonely and forlorn.

I plopped my newspapers down on the bar and ordered a pitcher of beer. Michael Gudunov put his glass down in front of me, so that I'd be sure to see that it was empty. "So what about the Big Beluga and the Grand Lady too? I heard some talk around town."

It is impossible to keep any kind of secret in Baranov. People don't have enough to do, so they talk everything to death. In the few short hours since I'd banged on Peek-A-Boo Pete's squad car, the story of our journey down the Vyg had been inflated and distorted beyond recognition. The grand duchess had become an eighteen-year-old beauty and her canvas bag was now full of jewels and state secrets. Our tormentor and his masked assistant were now an entire army of godless Communists bent on destroying our way of life.

"But Michael," I said. "You saw her yourself. She hasn't been eighteen in almost a hundred years."

My friend looked at the bottom of his glass, tipped it up and made a big noise sucking down the last drop. "I thought she mighta had some kinda wrinkle disguise like I seen one time on a TV horror show." He offered me his glass and I filled it again. "Too bad about that," he said. "She looked at me so nice, she had to be older than old. Young girls never look at me at all 'cause they'll always be afraid that I'll look back. We got to find her, Pres. Tell me what happened, okay?"

I told him about our trip down the river, and about the calamity that befell us at the Vyg Rapids and about the heroism of the Big Beluga. First we worried about the grand duchess. Then we worried about the Big Beluga. We figured that our friend could take care of himself, but the grand duchess was another story. Michael looked worried. He said, "A spill like that'd be pretty rough, you know. Old bones like she's got can't be too strong. What're we going to do?"

I said I didn't know. "Peek says I should file a report."

Michael rolled his eyes and slapped a big hand on the top of the bar. This made both the bar and his great fat tits jiggle a bit.

"Calm down Mike or you're out of here again," the bartender said.

Michael whispered, "That asshole Peek couldn't find snow in January, and he don't care besides because if you're right then he's wrong and he put the wrong man in jail. What're we going to do?"

Again I said I didn't know.

193

"Well what does that lady lawyer say? Or Rachel, better yet? She always knows what to do."

I sank a little deeper at the mention of Rachel's name. Michael kept talking but I stopped listening. I tried to persuade myself that she was wrong instead of me. I replayed our good-bye, and the way she said there was someone else. Like who? Barney with the mermaid muscle? That didn't make any sense, but women never did. I mean, Lindy Sue was a big mistake, of course, but . . .

Michael he poked me with a chubby elbow. "Don't ya think?"

"What?"

He looked at me as if I was the stupidest person he'd ever met, and had just said the stupidest thing he'd ever heard. "You listening to me? I'm talking about the two moose calves that got gunned down over by Nikiski, like it says right there in your own paper. I figure the black leather man is living on the run and he probably did it. It's all right there, don't you know? I mean, don't you always read the news before it gets in the paper?"

"Right," I said, wanting neither to confess my ignorance nor explain it. All I wanted was for Michael to leave so I could look for the story he was talking about. He helped himself to a glass of beer and swallowed it in one big gulp. "So?"

I was starting to get annoyed, but couldn't tell whether it was with Michael, or Rachel, or Lindy Sue, or myself or the general condition of mankind. "So what?"

Michael seemed to enjoy my annoyance, as if he knew I was trying to fool him. "So, are we going to start with the moose or what?"

I thought about five things at once. "Either that or the Old Believers. First I need to talk to Father Nick. That's if he wants to talk to me . . . I'll bet you a pitcher of beer you can't hit thirty bull's-eyes in a row."

Michael nodded, took out his chromium-tipped darts and headed for the dartboard. I rifled through the newspapers and found the baby moose story splattered all over the front page of a Monday edition.

Michael called over his shoulder, "You watching?"

"I'm watching. I'm watching. Thirty in a row."

I heard the dull, steady thump of his darts as I examined

the page. Wrapped around a muddy picture of what I suppose was the carcass of a moose calf was a story that read as follows:

TROOPERS BAFFLED BY HUNTING VIOLATIONS
By Byron Schiller

Alaska State Troopers are investigating a series of illegal moose hunts which have already claimed the lives of two calves in Nikiski.

Troopers say the moose were gunned down in two separate shootings with an automatic weapon of unknown manufacture. The poachers only took enough meat for a couple of meals. The rest was left to rot, officials said.

One carcass was discovered by a motorist on the North Road who saw several eagles hovering over a clearing near the Swanson River flats, which are home to . . .

Michael sat down on a weary barstool. He gently laid his chromium-tipped darts in their case, then pushed the empty pitcher toward me.

"I'll throw if you go," I said.

Michael nodded as I handed him a five-dollar bill. While he was gone, I read some more:

. . . the world's largest moose, including a 320-point bull downed last year by Orin Michaels of Clam Gulch. The second carcass was set upon by a pack of dogs known to frequent the Nikiski area. Troopers believe the second calf was also the victim of an illegal hunt.

The hunters violated a number of Alaska game laws, including: hunting out of season; hunting immature moose; and leaving meat to rot. Troopers say this last violation indicates the hunters may be transients.

"Any of the usual suspects I come across would have eaten some of the evidence and put the rest in their freezer," said Trooper Commander Peter Roberts. "We're going to take a look over by tent city and talk to some of the cannery workers who might have had their fill of eating fish all the time."

The most baffling aspect of . . .

Michael coughed. I looked up. He had a grin as wide as his belly. He'd been watching me for some time—time enough to toss down almost half of the pitcher of beer. "What's the story, man? Don't you read your own newspaper?"

> . . . the case is the hundreds of rounds of heavy ammunition found near the scenes of the two crimes. Roberts said the bullets were unlike any he had ever seen. He said the number and size indicate they came from some sort of military assault weapon.
> "Those bullets were made to kill people, not moose," Roberts said . . .

The jukebox played a good-night song. Michael walked me to my pickup truck and I drove him to the rectory. He was going to sleep in the churchyard tonight and help Father Nick in the morning. We sat in the yard with the motor running and the radio playing and talked about tomorrow. The stars were bright and the air was crisp. The sky beyond the bluff where the tides came from seemed like nothing and everything both at the same time. We could hear the water crash against the riprap, and feel the tide tug at the earth beneath our feet.

"The Grand Lady can't last in the woods too long no way," Michael said. "They can't move around in the woods too much, so if she's still alive I figure maybe they got a place where they stay most of the time. I say maybe if we go to the place where the moose got killed then maybe we can start to try to find out where that is."

Chapter 24

AT FOUR A.M., THE CANNERY FOREMAN CAME INTO THE gravel pit and banged two metal pots together. "All awake now. Wake up! We got a boatful of reds just in this morning. Slimers do your duty."

Chena, being at least 130 dog-years old and deaf as she could be, slumbered on. She stirred a little when I moved my feet, which had been tucked under her belly for warmth. The tent smelled of man and dog. I poked my head outside and saw a crew of sleepy slimers file into the old school bus which would take them to the cannery.

I went to the Baranov Recreation Center for a free shower. I then went to the Wash and Dry and watched a little TV over a breakfast of Fritos and a candy bar. The bachelor's life.

Jack's the best partner I've ever had. He's the only partner I've ever had. He never worries about angry letters to the editor and he loves the *Beacon* like a mother loves a backward child—not expecting too much and applauding our most modest accomplishments. His ambitions were well within the paper's limits. He wanted to make money and friends and elect Republicans whenever possible so long as they were deserving. Beyond this, he wanted only to make sure that the Baranov Public Works Department kept the road to the golf course clear of all obstructions.

The publisher pressed his tee into the grass. "What did you find on Diomede?" he said, mispronouncing the name of the islands—"Die-oh-meedie"—to emphasize their obscurity.

"I don't know. I found something, but I'm not sure what it is."

"Well, I'm glad I didn't pay for it."

I asked him if I could take a couple of days' vacation starting tomorrow.

He smiled a bit, then smacked his golf ball right down the middle of the fairway. "I heard you live over in the tent city now. I won't ask you how you got there if you don't ask me over for dinner, okay?"

I found Father Nick over by the bluff giving hand signals to my friend Michael, who was behind the wheel of the St. Alexander Nevsky pickup truck. The back of the truck was filled with odd chunks of broken concrete—some more riprap for their never-ending struggle against the tides.

"Hey, Shorter-Than-I!" Michael said as I approached.

"Attend to your business, son," the archpriest said.

Michael backed the truck to the edge of the bluff, to a spot where the carefully-tended grass gave way to naked soil. Small trees leaned over the precipice, waiting for a big wind to blow them away.

The truck's shock absorbers groaned when Michael dismounted. "Why don't you give us a hand over here, Short Man? Then we'll head out for Nikiski."

The archpriest gave his handyman a solemn look, but only said, "Small chunks first."

The concrete had been donated to the church by the work crew which was laying a new parking lot in front of Baranov High School. The task of moving it was designed for weak minds and strong bodies, not a fat man, a holy man and a crippled man. Michael shot-put the smaller pieces, while the archpriest and I bowled larger ones over the edge. The archpriest pushed one chunk too hard and might have followed it down to the beach had not Michael snatched the hem of his cassock and held him steady.

Some of the concrete landed on a rusty old Ford which had been stripped of all its moving parts and donated to the cause. The biggest chunk required all our strength. With a "One-Two-Three" we dropped it from the truck and rolled it over the bluff. It took a bush and a piece of earth down with it.

"How many more loads we got?" the archpriest said.

Michael looked at his feet and shuffled them a bit. "But Father, the Short Man and me are supposed to go out to Nikiski on this big news story he's working on. Ain't that right, Short Man?"

I shrugged my shoulders and nodded.

"I heard about what happened," the archpriest said. He cradled a football-size chunk of concrete in his arms. "I don't need you to find any more trouble for Michael. He finds enough on his own."

"I need to talk to you, Father," I said.

The archpriest dropped the concrete over the side and turned to his handyman. "How many more loads are left?"

"Five or six, Father—not counting Andy's refrigerator."

The archpriest nodded. His beard wiggled and he set his jaw in place. Whether it was five or six loads or fifty or sixty, he and Michael would move as much riprap as it would take to protect God's church from God's tides.

"Can you talk and work at the same time, Mr. Riordan?"

Although I'd rather not, I said I probably could. The archpriest drove. I sat next to him and Michael sat on the flatbed of the truck like a mountain of riprap Jell-O. I showed the archpriest the contents of the canvas bag and told him how they had come into my possession.

He'd already heard most of the story from Michael and the rumor mill. He picked his questions carefully: "And she calls herself Natasha? The grand duchess Natasha?"

"That's right. But other people say she's really Anastasia. That would make her the czar's daughter."

"That was very long ago. How old does she seem?"

"It's hard to tell for sure, but she sure looks old enough to me."

Andy Sacramentov was one of only two people left on earth who spoke the Kenaitze Indian language. The other was his sister Jessica, and she was fading fast. They lived at the end of a long dirt road and had just purchased a new refrigerator. Their old one was a solid Admiral with faulty wiring which they wanted to donate to the cause.

The Sacramentovs and the Kalifornskys had gotten their

names in a curious way, or so the legend goes. Many years ago, when Russian traders still ruled Alaska and parts of California, their ancestors joined the circus and toured the brand new cities of the West Coast as "Great Hunters of the Frozen North," or the Russian translation thereof. A few years later they came home with Russian wives and California names, which they passed on to their children and lent to Sacramentov Road, Kalifornsky Beach, K-Beach Hamburger Heaven, two schools and a half-dozen lesser landmarks.

The Sacramentov refrigerator was a foot taller than its owner, who was quite proud of it. "What you need to do Father is you pack it with dirt and stones. That'll make it heavy so the tide won't carry it away."

Father Nick complimented Andy on his contribution. They talked about church affairs while Michael and I wrestled the appliance onto the back of the truck.

"Have you notified the authorities?" the archpriest asked me when we were back in the truck and on our way.

I nodded. "But I don't think Peek is going to be a lot of help. There's also this Jon Jones guy, but I don't know about him . . ." My voice trailed off into an uncertain whisper.

"What's wrong, Pres?"

"I don't trust him, Father. All he wants is the canvas bag. He doesn't care about the grand duchess or anybody else. I don't know what to do."

"Welcome to the club," the archpriest said. "But I think that you should do something. But something else is on your mind. You seem very troubled, my friend."

I look out the back window. Michael was using his great bulk to hold the refrigerator steady. I looked back at the archpriest and answered him this way. "Michael says we should start with the baby moose that were killed. He thinks the men who took the grand duchess may have killed the moose for food. I can't see that, but I don't have any better ideas."

Our next stop was the schoolyard. It was a busy place. The old concrete had been broken up and scraped away and piled on the east side of the school. On the north side, workmen poured new concrete between fences made of string. Children with a basketball watched forlornly, the last few days of their vacation spoiled by this ill-timed construction project. The archpriest organized them into a work crew to assist us.

The biggest chunk of all had a basketball pole and backboard sticking out of it. It weighed more than the rest put together.

"It's too heavy, Father," Michael complained.

But the archpriest was determined to enlist the basketball goal into his battle with the tides. He gathered us around it and described how the backboard would catch some of the eroding soil and perhaps build a little buffer for a while. We heaved against the concrete without any result. The children tried to help us, but only got in the way.

"How come we don't take that one over there?" said Michael, pointing to a scrawny bit of playground without so much as a wire sticking out.

The archpriest closed his eyes for a second to pray, or think, or both. After opening them, he dismissed the children and marched off in the direction of the construction crew. Moments later he returned, followed by a front-end loader. The operator was a member of Father Nick's congregation. The cleric lectured him about more regular attendance at the marathon church services held every Sunday. The operator warned the archpriest that the heavy piece of concrete might do irreparable damage to the St. Alexander Nevsky pickup truck.

"I'll drive slowly," the archpriest said. "And Michael will have to walk."

The muffler of the St. Alexander Nevsky pickup truck didn't survive the ride back to the bluff. It scratched the road for a mile or two, and was scraped off altogether when we hit a pothole on the Kenai River bridge. We sounded like a war on wheels after that. Peek spotted us on the outskirts of Old Town, and followed us for a block. He backed off when he saw us turn into the church parking lot.

The tide had come in while we were gone. The rusty old Ford and the rest of the riprap were already under water. The archpriest said, "I can't tell you too much. The Old Believers do not believe as I believe. They would never confide in me. But I must act like their confessor anyway.

Anything Ivan Smolensk told me about the murder of Boris Yermak is a secret until I die."

We stopped talking and went to work. The archpriest jumped onto the flatbed and began handing me pieces of playground. I tossed the riprap over the edge, and watched it splash into the sea. When only Andy Sacramentov's refrigerator and the great piece of basketball playground remained, we sat down to wait for Michael and watched the fishing boats ease into the small port which had been built where the river spills into the sea.

I kicked a small pebble over the edge, and watched it disappear into the water below. Father Nyuknuvuk scowled at the assistance I had given to the tides. I thought he was going to scold me, but he decided to let it pass. I said, "What else do you know? What can you tell me?"

"Just legends and rumors. Nothing of substance."

"So tell me the rumors, if that's all you've got."

We watched an old fishing boat drift in with the tide. It made a great cloud of black smoke and was decorated with bright red setnet buoys, as if all gussied up for a night on the town. The archpriest picked up a lump of dirt and crushed it into dust. Wind carried the dust away.

"Now this is just talk, you understand, but there's not many Old Believers left anymore. After the World War—the First World War—they ran away from Stalin. They didn't mind the Communists, because they weren't any worse than the Romanovs. But Stalin was another Antichrist only with bigger hands and a longer reach. That's when the Old Believers started to wander, looking for a quiet place to be. They went to South America and Oregon—places where there was a lot of room and not many people. Then they found Alaska and they thought it was the Promised Land, because it used to be Russian many years ago, before the Americans took over.

"Back in Russia, Old Belief started to die away. So the Old Believers made an underground railroad—a secret path to freedom just like your black American slaves did a hundred years ago. The Diomede Islands are their point of entry, and the fishing boat called the *Pugachev* would carry the refugees here every summer when the red salmon run for the last thirty years or so. The grand duchess was their protector and benefactor. She bribed the Communists with

Romanov gold so they would let her people go. Now she's old and there's no more Old Believers left any more. She is the last refugee. Now it's her turn to be free."

Father Nick let out a big sigh and added, "That's the rumor, anyway. Peasants like to talk because they have no television, and Russian people love their legends. They are always coming up with phony Anastasias and Pretenders to the Throne. It's a traditional way of avoiding work. If every Russian who said he was a Romanov really was one, there wouldn't be anybody left to persecute."

I tried to think of a question, but I didn't know where to begin. The story was like a calliope in my brain, a great spinning wonder of noise and light and steam. I was about to ask another question when Michael lumbered up with a half-dozen barflies in tow. They wanted to know what happened to the Big Beluga. When I said I didn't know, they started to worry about something else.

The archpriest and I watched as they lifted the big chunk of playground out of the truck and tossed it into the sea. It made a great splash in the water below. They next made for Andy Sacramentov's refrigerator, but Father Nick said it wasn't ready yet.

"We'll have to fill it with sand and stuff, so the tide won't take it away."

The barflies lingered for a few minutes, hoping for some payment. Father Nick paid them with a blessing. They drifted back to Kenai Joe's.

It took us the rest of the morning to move four more loads of chopped-up playground, but the hardest part of the job was done.

Michael said, "If you want, Father, I'll go get some sand and stuff to stick in the refrigerator."

The archpriest shook his head and moved over to the bluff. We stood near the edge and looked down at the result of our labors. The tide was retreating, and the backboard of the basketball goal was sticking out of the water. The water was already starting to wear it down.

As Michael and I piled into my big red monster pickup truck, the archpriest said, "Leave her gold and the book with me, Pres. I'll keep them safe until you find a home, and maybe I can translate some of the Russian if I have the time."

Chapter 25

THUNDER ROAD IS A SMOOTH, FAST, SERIOUS ROAD MOCKED by its own destination. Nikiski is everything north of Kenai, which is not much of anything by the usual standards. It has few laws and obeys even fewer. Any order found there is imposed by oil companies and motorcycle enthusiasts. In Nikiski you can get stoned, drunk, robbed or killed and nobody will disturb you. It is a haven for the outcasts of society, for survivalists and other people who don't like people. The people of Nikiski take pride in being different and accept everything but the normal. They don't mind if you're crippled like me, or fat like Michael, or a homicidal maniac like Vladimir Chen of the KGB. It's a place with no borders and plenty of elbow room—Alaska as it used to be, the Great Alone.

Michael and I talked about women on the road to Nikiski. He'd never had one that he didn't have to pay for, an indignity he bore with great courage. I, of course, had had one too many, a crime which had been committed many times on Michael's favorite soap opera.

"The best thing to do on TV with women is to act like you don't care," he said. "That's what they do in the afternoon show I watch where they make a lot of sucking noises every time they kiss. On this show, the ones that don't care always get all the girls and the ones that do care either get the heave-ho or never even make it to the heave. So the best thing you can do is you don't care. I mean look at me. I care a lot and I always gotta get my girl from the Boom-Boom Cabaret."

One noisy blur going our way almost blew us off the road, while another noisy blur going the other way almost creamed us on a curve. The State of Alaska had built the road with gravel from the pit in which I had taken up residence. They named it North Road because they couldn't think of anything better. Some of the people who live there call it Nikiski Road but just about everybody else calls it Thunder Road because Peek-A-Boo Pete stays away and because some of the best marijuana in Alaska can be found growing on some of the more remote acres. The farmers call it Nikiski Thunderfuck and it's the biggest cash crop in Alaska.

Thunder Road starts out from Kenai like it knows where it's going. On the left is Bookie's, a hamburger joint, and on the right is Little 'Skimo's, another hamburger joint. Thunder Road picks up speed at a country bar and breaks the sound barrier at a rock n' roll joint called Biker's. It slows down a little at the Flatlands Boom-Boom Cabaret, where even if you look like Michael you can get a beer with a head on it and a dance with a girl with no clothes on. Thunder Road picks up speed again as it goes by a half-dozen oilfield service companies, where big men and big machines are hired for big jobs. It hits light speed where the oil is refined. That's where Nikiski starts.

The air smelled like metal and was gray, tasting like unwashed socks dipped in a batter of cod-liver oil and lead shavings. To our left was Cook Inlet, where an oil tanker bellied up to a pipeline. To our right was the Omnicorp Natural Gas Refinery, which had some smokestacks belching smoke and others belching golden fire. A sign said: NO TRESPASSING. PLEASE PARK OUTSIDE THE GATE.

We pulled into the Nikiski Full Service Eating Place and ate a greasy lunch with a bunch of greasy men who talked like they'd come from Texas, just like Lindy Sue Baker and her oil-slick husband.

Michael ate half the menu and some of my french fries. He chewed like a guilty man and didn't want to talk. He refused to look me square on, and cradled plates of food between a curled arm and his big fat tits. He swallowed big gulps quickly, as if worried that someone might come along and take his food away. He washed it all down with a Diet Pepsi.

I tried to talk about Old Believers and murder and the

other things we'd been talking about for weeks, but my friend was too busy shoveling food into his face to talk back at me. When I mentioned the grand duchess, he squeezed down a mouthful of unchewed food and said something I could understand.

"She so small and real old and looked at me so nice. We gotta find her, Pres. She's counting on me."

Thunder Road is a pleasant drive north of the refinery. Few people go that far, and the air clears up after a mile or so. It follows the shore for forty miles and stops at a place where you can either get out and walk or turn around and head back to Kenai. We parked by a sign that said No Thru Street and headed for the banks of the Swanson River, home of the world's biggest moose.

As we walked through the tall bushes, Michael told me about the biggest moose and the biggest salmon. "I mean, why would they come to Kenai?" I said. "There's nothing happening here."

At first I thought he didn't hear me, but he was only thinking about his answer. "Well, the Big Beluga says it's the water and Andy Sacramentov says it's the Kenaitze Indians. Big's a white man, so he always takes the scientific approach. He says the moose and the king salmon got so big because of the glacier water coming down from Kenai Lake. Thing is, Big says, glacier water is clear and clean and strong and there's so many rivers and lakes around here that the strongest moose and the biggest kings make the Kenai home because it's gotta be the best place in the world for an animal to be."

He said all this over his shoulder. He led and I followed, because he knew where we were going and because his great bulk made a path through the underbrush that an elephant could follow. He continued: "Now Andy Sacramentov says it ain't that way, because he's a Native guy. He says the biggest moose and the biggest fish live on the Kenai because of the Kenaitze Indian tribe. He's a Kenaitze just like me, and he's also part Russian, too. The Kenaitze love the kings and the moose and have a rule where they never piss in the river. Andy says the animals appreciate this, and that's how come the biggest ones of all come to live here, although that doesn't show how come they didn't all move away when the white Russians and Americans came. I wouldn't be surprised if Andy was right and the only reason they didn't move away is that right now the white man is everyplace. All the white men are pretty powerful—for right now anyway, although maybe another time will come for us Kenaitze Indians to be pretty powerful, too."

The same flood which had carried Lindy Sue and me into the embrace of sin and Ernest McGrew's setnet had made a mess of the Swanson River basin. The underbrush was a big tangle and some of the scrawny trees showed roots. In other places mud had washed away, leaving slabs of naked rock behind.

Michael said the flats stretched for miles and had been made by a big forest fire which raged across the northern part of the Kenai Peninsula about twenty years ago. Thousands of acres with thousands of trees had been burned into stumps and ash.

"That's another thing that Andy says, and he should know since he's an Indian and all, just like me. Right after the burn the little trees start to grown again real quick and the baby branches and the baby leaves are just about the best thing a real big moose could ever want to eat, which is another reason how come the biggest moose ever would wanna be here."

After that, we didn't talk very much. It took us almost an hour to hike the mile or so between Thunder Road and the site of the first illegal kill. Michael's fat-man lungs couldn't get enough air and I had all I could do to keep my bad leg from getting tangled in the vigorous new growth. The afternoon sun began to burn away the frost which had covered everything when we started out, and it looked like it still might be a beautiful late summer day. One time when Michael stopped on some high ground to catch his breath, I turned back and saw Cook Inlet sparkling like a diamond sea and beyond that Redoubt Volcano venting puffs of steam. I might have felt like the king of the world if my leg didn't hurt so much.

The killing place looked like the First World War. The state troopers had cleaned up the carcass, but left a blood-stain on the ground. There were other clues that a crime had been committed. Michael found a scattering of eagle feathers where the scavengers had gorged themselves on the remains, and maybe argued over a morsel. Evergreens had been cut

207

up and chewed by errant shots. One young tree which had been mowed down spat green wood splinters onto the ground.

"Look here at this," Michael said. He was down on all fours, poking his nose at a clutter of smashed weeds. He tugged on a leaf to produce a few strands of wirey hair.

"Here's where it fell," Michael said. "He must have led him with the shots that knocked down the tree and the dumb thing just run into the line of fire. It looks like there was a goddamn army. Check this out over here."

He led me to one of the mangled trees that had taken a shot square in the trunk. There was a hole the size of a nickel where the bullet went in, and a hole the size of a manhole cover where it had come out. We hunched down a little and started to skulk around, as if realizing that maybe we didn't want to be there after all.

"You should have seen them on the river," I said. I described in detail the bazookalike weapon and the missile-like projectiles which had almost blown us to pieces.

Michael surveyed the scene. He peeked through the hole in the evergreen tree, and used his thumb to mark an imaginary line from the hole to the blood to a place in the distance that only he could see. "It's over there. Come on over this way."

He plunged into the shrubbery, flattening a path with his great blubbery stride. Michael could move quickly when he had someplace to go. I started to lag behind. I kept one eye on my friend, and another eye on the ground, but tripped a couple of times anyway. After one spill, I bounced back up as quickly as I could only to discover that Michael had dropped out of sight. I listened for his elephantine steps, but couldn't hear any. I started to run, or at least I started to hop-skip-lunge, which is my fastest gear. I was certain my friend's heart had finally given out. I rushed to help him but instead fell into a hard clump of brush and came up with a mess of bleeding scratches.

Still no sign of Michael. I hopped-skipped-lunged up the flat path he had made, and tried to remember something about cardioplumonary resuscitation. I'd seen it performed once. It had to do with blowing air into a dying woman's mouth and pressing hard against her chest. The woman had died anyway, and she didn't weigh more than four hundred pounds and hadn't collapsed in the middle of the Swanson River basin. I tripped again and hopped-skipped-lunged into a small clearing where my friend was sitting on a rock that was much too small for his fat behind.

"Hey, what's happenin', Shorter-Than-I? Where you been so long? You look like somebody used your face for a dartboard."

I passed my hand over my cheek, smearing it with blood. Michael was breathing hard and sweating. So was I. I wiped my face and arms off with my shirt.

"Michael," I said. I didn't say anything more, because I didn't have enough air. That's just as well, since anything I might have said would have sounded pretty stupid. Michael said, "I don't believe this shit. I mean, look at this."

I looked around the clearing, but didn't see too much—just weeds and shrubs and evergreen needles flattened into a brown mush by the rain and the moose and Michael Gudunov. "Look at what?" I asked.

Michael made a fist of his right hand and held it up to me, like angry children do when flashing the "fuck you" finger. But instead of the finger, in the place where the finger would be, there slowly arose from the crease between the other two fingers a small sort of tube that could have been the finger were it not so thin and short and had it not caught the light in a funny way—not quite gold and not quite a sparkle, the dull yellow-brown of a brass shell casing.

I looked at the clearing again and this time saw dozens of bits of dull yellow-brown just like the one Michael had produced in his upraised fist. He said, "If I don't croak for a hundred years, I'll never see an asshole bigger than Peek-A-Boo Pete. He didn't even check to see where the shots came from."

Michael supervised while I collected the spent casings. "I say they were here for a day or two," he said. "Waiting on the moose or some caribou or whatever come along first. Hiding too, I guess, even though with Peek on the case they could open up a goddamn hardware store and the troopers'd probably buy their spark plugs there."

I collected thirty-seven bits of dull yellow-brown and handed them to my friend. He examined them one by one, then stuffed them into various pockets. "There's more than this by about twelve, I bet, but this is enough for us." He

209

rolled up onto his feet, stuck his hands in his pockets and started jangling the casings. He walked back and forth, looking at the ground and sounding like a tambourine. He stopped and made an X in the dirt with the toe of his boot, then stepped back a little so that he could look over his belly at the mark he had made. "I say they made two fires right here. Maybe three."

The spot was lower than the rest of the clearing and the dirt a darker shade of gray. I dropped to my knees and prepared to start digging, but Michael touched my shoulder and said, "I think you better let me."

He plopped down on his stomach and took a close look at the area. Then, with a twig of evergreen needles, he began to brush away the dirt until it gave way to black ash and a few chunks of blackened wood. He picked up a piece of this wood and sniffed it. He squeezed and it crumbled in his hand.

"Okay, that's number one. Driftwood from Captain Cook Beach is my guess. The spruce around here don't burn too good unless it's been on the ground for more than a year.

Now he brushed away the ashes to reach another layer of gray dirt not so dark as the first. "Hey, Short Man. You just looking or you wanna help too?"

I nodded. He said, "Okay, then find me another broom. This one's about done in."

By the time I'd returned with a new spruce twig, Michael had uncovered another layer of ash. "That's two. More driftwood . . . and . . . and . . ." He raked the ashes with his fingers and came up with a blackened fish head. "This is before they bagged their moose. They had a king for dinner. I bet they sat around the fire and bitched about the food. Too much salmon can make you crazy and you start dreaming about mooseburgers all the time. Gimme that."

I handed him the spruce twig and he applied it to the ashes until he came up with a third layer of dirt. "Okay, Short Man. We're going for three. That's how long they had her, right? Ever since Tuesday. Three's the charm, like Father Nick says, only he calls it the Holy Trinity. Andy Sacramentov says something like that too, only he says it in Kenaitze Indian language so nobody but his sister can understand him."

Gently, slowly, he brushed away the dirt. He looked as if

210

he were painting a Kenaitze masterpiece, a woodlands tale about how the big animals came to Kenai. Gently, slowly, the dirt turned to ash again. Michael was about to congratulate himself, when something caught his eye. Most of his face froze, but his jaw dropped open.

"Jeeeezuuuuus . . ." He brushed away some ash and found a little chain. He picked up the chain and pulled it from the soot. A dirty gold coin swung in front of our astonished faces. There was Russian writing on the coin, and a picture of Czar Michael, a Romanov king who died long ago.

The tides came in and the sun fell into the sea. I don't remember the ride back to town, except that we talked about the coin and what it might mean. "It's like a medal, right? I mean what else could it be?"

I nodded, and said it was like the coins I'd found in the canvas bag and given to Father Nick for safekeeping.

"Father Nick would know. He knows a lot about Russian stuff. So what do you think?"

"I think they either killed her and took the medal for a souvenir and then threw it away . . ."

Michael finished the thought. ". . . which don't make any sense at all. Or the grand lady left it there as a signal that she's still alive and we should come get her. She's no bullshit woman at all, Pres. We got to find her. She's countin' on me."

Chapter 26

NEITHER FATHER NICK, NOR THE GOLD COINS, NOR THE manuscript were anywhere to be found. The archpriest's wife was near hysteria. She said, "So the man comes over and says he wants to take the tour in the church, and Nick says, 'That's okay, you gotta dollar?' "

"What did he look like?"

"He was blond all over. A thin man but strong. He smiled too much, like a liar."

"So then what happened?"

"So I went over to the Wash and Dry with a bunch of clothes and when I came back Nick was gone."

Michael was puffed up like a water balloon. One more drop of trouble and I thought he might explode. He said, "What about the altar?"

Tatiana shook her head. "I didn't. I couldn't. I mean, I don't know."

Michael said, "Well, then we better go see."

We walked down the short cobblestone path which connected the rectory to the church. The door was locked. Tatiana and I shared an uncomfortable moment while Michael fetched the key. I looked up at the onion church domes and their Russian double crosses while she looked right through me. Then I looked over at the bluff. The St. Alexander Nevsky pickup truck and the refrigerator it had contained were both gone. I wondered where they were.

Michael came back with the key and a quiet file of young children in tow. They jostled for position as the handyman unlocked the door.

St. Alexander Nevsky Church was about as big as a rich man's closet. It had wooden floors, the faint smell of incense and plywood walls dotted with icons. The simple style of the church itself made the icons seem even more rich and beautiful. A silver Mary cradled a silver Jesus. A golden Jesus carried a golden cross. In the sacred place where the archpriest and his altar boys stood, was the Corpus, or image of Christ, and next to it the most magnificent icon of them all: St. Alexander Nevsky, with Russian peasants at his side and vanquished Germans at their feet.

I didn't know it then, so I looked it up later. St. Alexander Nevsky was the first of the great Russian heros, which meant that everybody could agree on him—the Romanovs, the peasants, the boyars and the church. The Communists even made a movie about how he destroyed the Teutonic Knights in 1242. Adolf Hitler was knocking at their door and Mother Russia was about to take another heavy hit. The peasants made him a hero. The clergy made him a saint. The Communists made him a movie star and the half-breed Natives of Baranov, Alaska, made him an icon and nailed him to the wall.

"Can I go look and see beneath the altar?" Michael asked of the archpriest's wife.

The children had slipped inside. They huddled in a corner under an icon of Jesus wearing a sunburst for a crown. Tatiana gave an almost imperceptible nod, the sort of nod a politician gives when he might want to deny it later.

Michael tiptoed over to the altar and got down on his hands and knees. Tatiana and I tiptoed after him, and the children tiptoed after us. We all held our breath as the handyman dropped to his knees, stuck his finger into a knothole and pulled back one of the floorboards. Tatiana closed her eyes and whispered a Russian prayer. Michael reached under the floor and pulled out a strongbox, two manila folders, a plain white envelope, a sable cossack hat stored in a large Tupperware tray, a coffee can full of things that rattled and a soft leather pouch in which was wrapped a single gold coin.

We compared this gold coin with the one we'd found in the third layer of soot and ash made by the baby moose killers. They were the same size and weight and had the same Russian writing and the face of the same Romanov who'd died a long time ago. The only difference was one was dirty, and had a tiny hole with a chain strung through.

"This is all the stuff that Father Nick ever had," Michael explained. "He said we should look here if anything ever happened to him and sell the hat to pay for his funeral."

We filed out of the church. Tatiana herded her children indoors. Michael walked over to the bluff and looked down at the beach. The tide was out and the scrap heap glistened in the setting sun, a graveyard of American dreams that had been buried at sea.

Father Nick's dreams had been added to the pile. Andy Sacramentov's refrigerator had landed first, and the truck on top of it. They had done a somersault during their fall from the bluff, and landed with a crunch. I tried to imagine Baranov without its shabby priest doing battle with the tides. Michael and I watched the tide roll in, swamping the riprap barricade that had been Father Nick's mission in life.

Chapter 27

MICHAEL AND I WENT TO SEE PEEK-A-BOO PETE EARLY the next morning. "Father Nick isn't missing," the trooper said. I looked at Michael. Michael looked at Peek. Peek looked out the window. "He's dead."

A seller of spare truck parts had climbed down to the riprap barricade in search of spare tires, a carburator and any other parts the St. Alexander Nevsky pickup truck didn't need anymore. He found Father Nick upside down, behind the wheel. The body was bloated and looked like a nightmare. His neck was broken, his face smashed in. There was no sign of the canvas bag or the old manuscript or the five gold coins I had given to him for safekeeping.

Peek said it looked like another murder. I thought he was going to blame it all on Ivan Smolensk, but instead he said, "We're investigating, of course."

"You fuckin' asshole," Michael said.

Peek said, "Now Michael . . . we need to fill out a report. When was the last time you saw Father Nick?"

The Baranov Motel 6 is where Georgievsk Redoubt used to be. In the 1790s, Georgievsk Redoubt was an outpost for gang of Russian *promyshlennik,* or mountain men, who terrorized the Kenaitze Indians by murdering their men, raping their wives and stealing their furs. The ringleaders were a man named Grigor Konovlov and his sidekick Amos Balushin. They had learned how to terrorize Natives in Siberia before their kind depleted the place of furs.

Konovalov and Balushin waged a fur war against Baranov

until a group of Kenaitze Indians ambushed a party of promyshlennik. The Russians were tortured, mutilated and crucified, the last being a new trick the Kenaitze picked up from the Russian Orthodox missionaries. Baranov came to power then, and ruled the territory with marriage, not terror, by encouraging his men to take Native wives. Their children tore down Georgievsk Redoubt, which remained an empty field until Wallace Dunwitty built the Baranov Motel 6.

Wallace was a jovial man from Kansas with solid Midwestern views. He let me look at his guest book. There were four guests listed.

Wallace was glad to help us because he was a good friend of the archpriest who donated all of his hard metal junk to the struggle against the tides, although he considered the Russian church to be mostly mystic mumbo jumbo. He said, "Three of them are in here from the Outside. ARCO's paying their bill, so I'd say they're here on account of this natural gas they wanna sell to Japan. The other guy . . . well, about him I don't know. Sam Smith is his name. He paid cash advance with no bullshit, but he didn't want to talk too much. He's in there now if you wanna say hello."

Michael said, "We don't want to say hello, and keep it to yourself, okay?"

We hid behind a "Welcome to Baranov" sign that gave us a clear view of the parking lot in front of the Motel 6. "You better let me drive," Michael had said. "I know the back roads best, if that's where we have to go."

I handed over the keys to my big red monster pickup truck and slid over to the passenger's seat. For three hours we drank black coffee and talked about what had happened, and what might have happened and what hadn't happened yet. There were three cars in the parking lot: Dunwitty's Plymouth, something from Hertz and a Mercedes roadster with California plates.

"We can't follow that thing," I said. "Not if he hits the pedal."

Michael smiled, and drummed his fingers on the steering wheel of my most valuable possession. "No problem. He gets in that car and I'll be up his ass like a doctor's thumb."

Sunglasses, a bulky coat and floppy hat with the brim pulled down could not disguise the fact that Sam Smith was also Jon Jones, supposedly of Customs and Immigration, possibly of the CIA or some such agency with an agenda all its own. He jumped into the Mercedes roadster and pulled out of the parking lot. Michael gave him about a hundred yards, then clicked my big red monster pickup truck in gear.

A word about my pickup truck. It rides high on big tires and is mounted rather than entered.

I've always wanted a big red monster pickup because I'm short and always have been. That's why Michael calls me Shorter-Than-I. My first car was a Volkswagen, my second a Chevette. I spent my formative years smelling the exhaust of other vehicles and trembling at the passage of big trucks traveling at high speeds that could crush me like a bug if I made a mistake or they did.

When Rachel and I moved to Baranov and started having more money than we needed, I purchased a heavy Chevy with big wheels, The Mud-Gobbler, The Bug-Crusher, the kind of truck that climbs all over lesser vehicles on Sunday! Sunday! Sunday!

It was my pride and joy, my top-heavy reason to be. Michael drummed his fingers on the steering wheel.

We followed the Mercedes roadster at an easy pace to Kenai, where Sam Smith/Jon Jones purchased something at the 7-Eleven while we idled behind an eighteen-wheeler. Then he went to the Rig Café for a bite to eat and then to the Rainbow for something to drink.

The sun started to go down. It was getting cold, and all the coffee we'd drunk outside of the motel was making me nervous and Michael sweaty. "This sucks," he said after an hour or so. "Gimme some money."

"What for?"

"I'm gonna go in and see what's goin' on. Maybe he spotted us and snuck out the back, or something else like that. I need some money 'cause the guy who owns the 'Bow won't let me sit down if I don't have a drink. It's a long story, and, you can't go because he knows you, right?"

"Just sit tight," I said.

Michael sat tight for about thirty seconds. "Or it could be he's having some kind of secret meeting. Did you ever think of the secret meeting angle?"

I saw a mind picture of Michael getting drunk on my money and then smashing up my truck. I looked for singles or a five, but could only find a ten. Five minutes after Michael went in, Smith/Jones came out and hustled into the Mercedes. A few moments after that, Michael ran clutching a bottle of beer and made a running plop into the driver's seat. He handed me the bottle. There was one swig left, so I took it. We burned rubber and followed our suspect to the Kenai River bridge.

"So how was the secret meeting?" I asked.

Smith/Jones seemed to be going back to Baranov, but at the other end of the bridge he made a quick U-turn and headed back the other way. He beeped and waved as he passed us by, then turned on the speed.

Michael leaned over the steering wheel. His U-turn wasn't as tight, and it took us longer to break the speed limit. But when the Mercedes turned left onto Thunder Road, my friend pounded the dashboard, screamed "Yeah! Yeah! Yeah!" and let out a cackling laugh that sounded truly insane. The best I could do was say, "Oh shit!"

The Mercedes made time on the straightaways. We made time on the curves. North Kenai and the oil patch were a flash of color and a whiff of smoke, although Michael did slow down a bit at the Flatlands Boom-Boom Cabaret. "We got him, goddamnit," Michael said. "Where does he think he's going? There ain't no place to go."

I squeezed the beer bottle hard. "What are we going to do when we get him?"

Nikiski was dark, and for forty-five frightening miles, all we could see were the taillights of the Mercedes. A big wind blew through a little crack in the window, and my truck seemed on the verge of rattling into pieces. But then the taillights of the Mercedes started to flash, and got bigger very quickly. Michael hit the brights, and we saw the Mercedes come to a dead stop at the place where Thunder Road ends in a sign that says "No Thru Street." I braced myself so I'd be ready when Michael hit the brakes. But he never really hit them. He just touched them a little, so that we wouldn't be launched into outer space when my big red monster pickup truck with the oversize tires rolled onto the Mercedes and crushed the hood just like they do on Sunday! Sunday! Sunday!

We rolled back down and came to a stop. I peeled my face from the windshield. My nose felt like the inside of a rotten tomato, but everything else seemed to work okay. The Mercedes looked like it had been stepped on by Godzilla. Michael started to laugh but stopped when he saw in the rearview mirror the hot red flashes of a trooper's party lights.

Smith/Jones had apparently called for help on his cellular car phone. Michael and I were handcuffed together and locked in the back of the squad car while the Baranov Fire Department used a big can opener to separate the man from his Mercedes. He was unharmed, pissed off and full of impressive credentials, which he waved in Peek-A-Boo Pete's face.

"Officer, my name is Jon Jones and I'm an agent with the U.S. Customs office. I have reason to believe that these two men are smuggling Russian artifacts into the United States."

Peek gave us the once-over. He seemed torn between glee at our catastrophe and confusion over the strange accusation made by the stranger. "Well, artifacts is a federal matter, Mr. Jones, and that's outside my authority."

"Bullshit, Peek," Michael said. "I bet he's the one we told you about. You ask Tatiana and she'll say he's the one that saw Father Nick before he turned up dead. You just ask her."

The trooper adopted a more coplike countenance. He turned to the stranger and pointed at Michael. "I know these men, Mr. Jones. The fat one thinks I'm a fuck- . . . ing . . . ass- . . . hole."

Chapter 28

WE PASSED THE BREATHALYZER TESTS, BUT PEEK WOULD not be denied. Michael was arrested for driving without a valid license, assault with a deadly Chevy, and crushing an expensive German automobile. I was arrested for letting him use my truck.

Our cells were around a corner from each other. His was by the door, mine was by the window. We could hear but not see each other. "Did you see me cream him, Shorter-Than-I? I mean, did you see his face?"

"Yeah, and look where it got us. What's the big idea? I mean, what were you trying to do?"

"I figured we could squish him and then make him tell us what happened to Father Nick. I didn't figure on a car phone, or that asshole Peek. Sorry about your truck, but we gotta find the old woman."

Each of us was allowed one phone call. I tried to call Rachel. I let the phone ring thirty times, but still there was no answer. Michael called Andy Sacramentov and was out within the hour. He asked him to post bail for me, too, but Andy refused to do so because his son kept showing up in my newspaper's police report.

"Don't worry, Short Man. I'll get the money for sure and you'll be out right away."

I wondered how long it would take Michael to borrow $250 in quarters from the drunks at Kenai Joe's. I settled down for a long wait, and eventually fell asleep.

I dreamed I was a bleeder about 13 years of age, with four older sisters and royal parents who loved me dearly. We

220

used to rule one-sixth of the world. Now the Mob ruled Russia and the clockmaker was going to get us.

At night, Mama would lead us in prayer. We prayed for freedom and for the other Romanovs, whom the Mob hunted like dogs. We prayed for Mother Russia, and for the new American Army which had just entered the Great War against our Cousin Willy the kaiser. We prayed that the Lord would forgive them, for they know not what they do. But mostly we prayed for freedom, until that early morning when the clockmaker came into our cells, smelling not of vodka and tobacco, but of strong perfume. In a honey voice that sounded like Hank Williams' guitar, she said . . .

"Wake up, Pres . . . Prester . . . Prester John Riordan . . . Wake up, now."

The clockmaker was played by Lindy Sue Baker. Her hair was bigger than before. She wore a sticky black dress and too much makeup. Her left breast had squeezed between the bars of my cell, and she seemed pretty amused by the whole situation. "I've got to say, hon, that you look like a real mess. When I saw your name on the list, I knew I had to laugh. So how you doin'?"

"Lindy Sue . . . what's . . . I mean, why . . . I mean . . ."

"I'm your lawyer, hon. Don't you remember? The public defender."

A female state trooper who wore sunglasses indoors stood outside the interview room while we went over the details of my case. I was charged with several traffic violations, and wanted for questioning by the U.S. Marshal in connection with the investigation of a smuggling ring. Lindy Sue wanted to hear about the smuggling ring.

"We'll get the charges dropped as soon as we can find a sober judge."

I noticed that her Texan drawl seemed to become more pronounced when she talked about love, and more subdued when she talked about the law. She moved freely between the two topics.

"Judge Holiday's in Homer, right now, and won't be back until tomorrow. You're stuck until then if you can't post bail. What about that sweetie of yours, that Rachel that you couldn't ever stop thinking about even when you're making love to me?"

I'd had enough of confessions. I'd rather spend the rest of

my life in jail than to ever again confess to any woman any of the incredibly stupid things I've done. "What's the latest word on Ivan Smolensk?"

Ivan Smolensk was still in jail and Lindy Sue was still his attorney. She was working on an appeal, but without much hope. "He still won't speak up. I don't have a case if he won't speak up."

"You've got a case. Just get me out of here and I'll go make it for you."

"I will. I'll call Rachel right away, and if she can't make bail I will. She works at the school if I remember right. I'll call her there."

I wanted to say no, but the no would require an explanation, would be as humiliating as the yes and be less likely to get me out of jail.

"Whatever it takes. Just get me out of here."

Apparently it took some sort of dark, moist female conspiracy. Three hours later Lindy Sue came back and bailed me out of jail. When I asked her where she'd gotten the money, she said she couldn't say. "What do you mean you can't say?"

"I mean just that. The person who bailed you out of jail did so on the condition that you must not know her identity." She leaned over the interview table. I got a good view of her cleavage as she pinched my cheek—the sort of thing grandmothers inflict on their progeny. I was as unenthusiastic as any grandson. Lindy Sue added, "But I can say that you're luckier than you think you are. Very lucky, as a matter of fact."

The sign on the front lawn where I used to live said my house was "For sale." I called the school and was informed that Miss Rachel Morgan had canceled her contract for the upcoming school year, and no, she didn't say where she was going. I called home again, but this time the phone was disconnected.

Chapter 29

A TENT IS NOT THE WORLD'S SAFEST PLACE, AS EVENTS soon made clear. It's nothing but a Ziploc plastic bag painted green, perfectly suited for hermetic storage and transportation. Sitting in a tent feeling sorry for yourself is like sticking your head in the sand: There's a world out there, but you can't see it. But the world can sure see you, especially if you've happened to pitch your tent in the middle of an abandoned gravel pit.

I crawled into my pastic bag and Ziploc-ed myself in. I heard the wind kick up dust, and watched it agitate the fabric. The sun and the flimsy plastic membrane made a strange light together. Everything is simple when seen from a tent, and can be put into one of two categories: inside and outside. Inside were me, some clothes, a book and an empty peanut butter jar I used for a chamber pot. Outside were Chena, the wind, the noise, the light, a soft green essence from everywhere. This, I thought, is how it all began: a single glob of flabby green stuff noticed the light and then there was life. Soon after that, the hunt began for some more green stuff to squish around with. Beware of Texan protoplasm.

For many minutes or a couple of hours, I thought about Rachel and mindless green goo that was looking for love.

Then I stopped thinking and dozed a bit until my plastic tent collapsed in on me. An unknown number of thick strong arms dismantled the tent with me still in it, squeezed out all the excess air and tied me into a bundle with my own bungee cords, which I'd conveniently left outside the tent. I kicked

223

and struggled as best I could, and started to chew on the piece of tent that had been shoved into my face. My idea was to make a peephole so that I could see who was accosting me. The book—it was *The Prince and the Pauper*, as I recall—pressed against my spine. The peanut butter jar became lodged under my chin. I didn't struggle after that, fearing that if the jar broke I could slit my throat with pee-tainted glass.

But I kept on chewing. By the time I ate my way to a spot of light, I had been lashed face down to the back of a large motorcycle. I had a clear view of Thunder Road as it raced by at an unimaginable speed. The center lines were hot yellow flashes on the black tar. The blood rushed to my head and the vibrations of the angry bike made my whole body tingle. I smelled the engine and the road and tasted melting rubber.

The hot yellow flashes faded away and the bike slowed down. The smooth highway was replaced by a rough dirt road, which pelted my crumpled Baggie with small pebbles and sprayed a mouthful of dust through my peephole. We slowed to a halt in front of a log cabin. Hairy arms untied me. They belonged to Vladimir Chen.

He was built like any Asian thingamabob, with Mongol eyes and wide, Slavic cheeks. He had a profusion of curly black hair and thick cossack legs bowed to fit a horse or a motorcycle. He was dressed mostly in black leather studded with metal, but wore wool hunting gloves which kept the first two knuckles of his fingers free. He carried a heavy handgun and pointed it at me.

"Where is it?" His English was without accent or inflection, as functional as his gun.

"Where is she? . . . The grand duchess?"

He wagged his gun at the cabin. "Citizen Romanov is inside. Would you like to see her?"

I made the mistake of saying "Yes." He pushed me through the cabin door and locked it behind me.

224

Chapter 30

It was a big dark in a small room. The windows were boarded up and painted over, and the bigger knotholes had been plugged with globs of plastic wood. The air was thick and smelled of jasmine and death. The place was full of flies.

In her delirium the grand duchess drifted in and out of time and place. For a while she talked in Russian about things that almost made her smile. She saw me through the gauze of memory and thought I was someone else. Then she said in a voice that was frail but somehow sure of itself, "You must speak English, my dear. Russian is a barbaric language. It has no word for crumpet. Refined thoughts must be expressed in a refined language. That is what English is for, you know. My great-aunt was English. Her name was Queen Victoria and she had the gene that made our poor Alexis bleed."

After that, she mostly spoke to me in English. One time she thought I was her chambermaid, so we talked about civil war in Siberia and famine on the Georgian steppes. Another time she thought I was an agent of the secret police. She wanted to spit on my shoes, but didn't have the juice.

Her mind ran wild in the dark, to the house of special purpose in the city of Ekaterinburg, a railroad town in Russian Siberia. She had memorized the diary her cousin Alexis had given her, just in case the manuscript was lost at sea or stolen by the Reds. She read to me for hours on end from pages printed on her heart. After that we slept for a bit, and I think I dreamed that the pages were printed on my heart too, and that I was a bleeder named Alexis.

My name is Alexis Romanov. I'm thirteen years old and a bleeder, the heir to the Russian throne. You can bet right now that's not as great as it sounds. The worst part is, I have four older sisters, which is like having five mothers, which is too many. Before, sometimes, when Mama and the girls would drive us crazy, Papa and I would go outside and chop wood if I wasn't bleeding or in a fever. But now the Bolsheviks lock us in a room. There's nothing to do but wait and see what the clockmaker will do with us.

The clockmaker draws some dirty pictures in the water closet. Now, I have nothing against dirty pictures. Me and my cousin Felix Yusupov used to look at French postcards all the time. But these dirty pictures are not the same as French postcards. Every time I take a pee I have to look at Rasputin feeding the sausage to Mama and Anastasia. Papa demands that they erase the pictures, but the clockmaker just laughs at him. Papa used to be their czar. Now they laugh at him. Figure that. The Anastasia picture gets erased anyway because one of the Bolsheviks loves her. He must be crazy. Everybody must be crazy, I think.

The Czech Brigade is coming to rescue us, so the clockmaker wakes us up at 3 A.M. and takes us to the basement. Papa has to carry me because my knee joints are bleeding since I jumped down some stairs and I hurt like hell.

"Where are we going?" Mama says.

The clockmaker smiles. He's a real asshole. "You're going to die, you Romanov bitch."

The Bolsheviks start blasting away. Anastasia ducks. Mama screams. Papa takes it right in the chest, like a man. My three older sisters die right away. I get a bellyful, but it's not enough. Imagine that. I'm a goddamn sissy bleeder who has to be carried to the killing room and when the smoke clears I'm the only one that's still alive, except maybe for Anastasia, depending on how much you want to believe.

The clockmaker pulls a pistol from his blouse, sets the hammer, pulls the trigger. My skull explodes and my brains leak out. My dog Joy comes into the room and starts to cry for me.

Joy is still crying as they load our bodies into a farmer's cart, so they kill her too. The Czech Brigade is on the march, and the clockmaker is afraid of them. He takes us to the Four Brothers coal mine. No one will suspect. They chop us into little bits, set the bits on fire, soak our bones in acid and toss what's left to the bottom of the mine. But they're still afraid of me seventy years later because before I die I write it all down and give the manuscript to my cousin Natasha. She says she'll translate my English words into Russian, because Russian is sacred and English is profane. Natasha is an Old Believer. It must be nice to believe in something, even if it is very old. Natasha's friends will protect her. I'm pretty sure of that.

The door banged open. Light filled the room and burned my eyes. Tears put out the fire. "Bring her outside," said Vladimir Chen.

She weighed less than I thought possible and her hips were made of broken glass. Her dress was soiled and her eyes were as unfocused as those of a newborn baby. I set her down on the ground and washed her with soap and water. The fresh air helped. Her eyes cleared up a little.

"You mustn't play so rough, Alexis. You're not like other boys."

Vladimir Chen handed me a bowl of food—moose meat, mostly, with mashed bits of this and that thrown in to make a stew of sorts. I spoonfed the grand duchess, but she wasn't very hungry.

"I don't know what your problem is, but blood's no answer," I said to Chen.

"You're very wrong, I'm afraid," Chen said. "Blood is the only answer if a new world is to be made, because blood must be purged with blood, Mr. Riordan, starting with the Romanovs. That is what the Founding Fathers wrote and that is how it must be."

"The Founding Fathers?" I inquired, thinking of Franklin, Washington and Jefferson.

Chen corrected me. "Marx and Lenin and Papa Joe Stalin, the Man of Steel. Stalin was a spy himself, you know. He was an agent in the secret police before the Revolution. You see, I'm not ashamed of being a spy because I spy for the proletariat. I am a true believer, you see."

"Just like the Yermaks you've been slaughtering. They're true believers too. They believe in God and you believe in . . . what? What is it you believe in?"

"Class struggle, of course. I'm a real Communist, not one of those fat toadies from the Politburo you see on television. I believe in violent revolution and the imperatives of history, and there's lots of others like me, especially in the KGB. We believe that a new society can only be achieved by the destruction of the old one, and that includes foolish books written by rich little Romanov bastards. Especially the book that the old hag here smuggled out of the country. That book will make Russians feel sorry for the very ghosts that haunt us. We can't allow it to be published. It has counterrevolutionary tendencies and must be purged from the body politic."

He had been speaking as if in a dream, chanting the ancient verities. Then he added, as an afterthought, "I'm sorry about the Yermaks, but it had to be that way. They wouldn't tell me what I needed to know—the when and the where and the why of that old hag coming to America. I wouldn't have taken such extreme measures if they had told me what I needed to know. They are very misguided people, I'm afraid. It's a shame that all their courage is wasted on God and autocrats. They'd be a lot better off if they believed in Marx. Now where's that book of hers?"

"What about your American partner? Jon Jones. What does he believe in?"

Vladimir Chen smiled. "Why he believes in money, of course. All he wants is the Romanov gold. He is an American after all. And now I think that this conversation has lost its usefulness. Where is the boy's diary, Mr. Riordan? I'll give you the same deal I gave all those Yermaks. Tell where it is and I'll let you go free. You and the woman too if you feel like hauling away that old bag of Romanov bones. If you don't tell me, I'll kill you too."

"Alexis! Alexis!" the grand duchess said. "Don't trust Rasputin. He's a filthy peasant with only one thing on his mind. Cousin Felix says he's a German spy. Watch out for spies, especially our own. They love dirty secrets and grow in the dark like poison mushrooms."

228

"Is that true?" I said to Vladimir Chen. "Are you a spy? Do you love dirty secrets?"

Our captor smiled. "The truth isn't dirty, Mr. Riordan. And it's not clean either. It's just the truth, and the truth is this Romanov book will upset the balance of things. The balance of things is very important. Our missiles balance your missiles and our spies balance yours."

"And our books balance yours," I offered. "Why does a book make you so afraid?"

His dark eyes clouded darker, as if he didn't know. "That book is full of Romanov tears. We don't need tears about criminals who got what they deserved seventy years ago. That book will embarrass the Soviet government, or at least the part that I'm working for. Where is it?"

I said I didn't know. He smiled. It was a strange smile. He walked over to his motorcycle and came back with a heavy leather thing that rattled when he walked. He rattled it in front of my nose.

"Do you know what this is?"

I did, but I didn't say.

"It's a knout. Do you know what it is for?"

Before I could answer, he stepped up to a spruce tree and started to flog it. Within seconds it was stripped of bark and bleeding sap, just like the tree near Boris Yermak's body. "It's your turn next if you don't talk. I'll give you some time to think about it."

This time it was a bigger dark in a smaller room. Through experience I'd learned how to tell day from night. The night was colder, and darker, and the flies were more at ease. The day was warmer and had a stronger stench and if I looked long enough I could see dozens of little starbursts where the light leaked through tiny holes in the roof. But the surest sign of day was that the flies became lively and hungry, spoiling for a fight. A day passed and then a night. The old woman's delirium carried her to another time and place. She knew she was going to die, and thought I was a priest. She read to me from pages printed on her soul.

My name is Natasha Alexandrovna Romanov, but some people think I'm Anastasia. We look alike, but I'm younger and she is more silly. We have nothing in

229

common, really. She makes faces at dignitaries and does a marvelous imitation of Kaiser Wilhelm. I make the sign of the cross with two fingers and follow the Old Belief. She falls in love with a Czech soldier who rushes to her rescue. I hide in the suburbs of Petrograd, and hope that the Bolsheviks don't find me. She is dead. I am alive.

Her brother Alexis gives me a book he wrote and a boxful of Romanov gold. The book is in English, a profane tongue. I will translate the words into Russian, the language of the saints. Alexis has asked me to deliver his message to the Americans, because he loves their Buffalo Bill cowboy show and thinks it will do them some good. I promise to do this, but don't know how I can. He is dead. I am alive.

I run away to Siberia. The Bolsheviks run after me. We fight in the forest and the hills and the Americans come to Arkhangelsk and fight at our side for a while. But their will is weak and they want to go home and enjoy their Roaring Twenties with their flapper sluts and their bathtub gin.

I become a captain's whore. He's a strong soldier in the Red Army. He loves me and protects me. I love him, but I can't protect him. When Stalin cracks down on the innocent, my captain stands in the way. He is dead. I am alive.

I'm a Romanov and a dead captain's whore. But I make the sign of the cross with two fingers and follow the Old Belief. I run to them. They pray for me. I buy their freedom with Romanov gold from my dead captain's friends. His friends are all colonels and generals now, and wiser than they used to be. They think twenty million dead Russians is more than enough and don't want a third World War. The younger soldiers aren't so sure. They know they want something, but they don't know what it is.

The Old Believers believe in me. They think I'm Anastasia, and I don't mind, really. I'm old now and will die soon. My hands hurt all the time and my back is as bent and weary as that of a peasant who worked in the fields. I'm running out of gold and have nothing left in life except to do what I promised I'd do seventy years ago: deliver Alexis' book to the Americans, who put on a great cowboy show. The silly boy thinks it will do some good. He's wrong, of course, but a promise is a promise. The Communists won't like it much. They've had their fill of Romanovs dead or alive, I'm afraid.

The door banged open and the light burned my eyes. Tears put the fire out. I braced myself for a flogging, but the flogging never came. Vladimir Chen was in handcuffs. Michael Gudunov said, "Hey in there, Shorter-Than-I. Where's the Grand Lady? Are you okay?"

Chapter 31

THE THING IS, MY FEET SMELL. ACTUALLY, THE THING IS, my left foot smells. That's the good one. The bad one, the one with polio and the cold foot syndrome, spends most of its time flopping around to no good use and feeling sorry for itself while everybody thinks, "Aw, poor thing, you are brave." It doesn't work hard enough to build up a proper sweat. Meanwhile my left foot—my good smelly foot—is slaving away: doing the work of two good feet; carrying around all that beer and all those chili cheese dogs from the 7-Eleven; dragging the polio celebrity around; working hard with neither applause nor sympathy while old noodle toes gets all the attention. My left foot is the hardworking foot-toiler of all time. Sometimes, as it does the work of two, it works up a smelly sweat that is disgusting to everyone but:

Chena, my faithful dog.

Chena loves my left foot. She loves dead fish, other dogs' assholes and my left foot. She licks it when I let her because it smells so bad. As far as we can figure, when I was grabbed by Vladimir Chen she followed its smell for seventeen miles, stopping for a rest every now and then.

"That's about the oldest dog I ever seen," Michael Gudunov said. "She'd sniff the trail until she couldn't sniff no more and then take a long nap. We'd wait all day and then she'd get up, take a pee and go sniff some more."

Peek-A-Boo Pete put the knout into a big plastic evidence bag and locked Vladimir Chen in jail. The grand duchess was rushed to Baranov Municipal Hospital, where she was loaded with drugs and fed through a tube. A doctor was flown down from Anchorage to look at the bag of broken glass that used to be her hip. A state trooper waited outside her room to arrest her when she was well enough.

I was held for questioning. Peek took the old gold coins I had hidden in my shoe and laid them on his desk.

Jon Jones was polite. Peek picked up the coins and clinked them together, an accusation of sorts. He managed the neat trick of being apologetic and obnoxious at the same time. "Now I'm not saying that we won't take another look at the murders—maybe Mr. Smolensk didn't do it after all and, if so, we'll reconsider. But there're some other issues here and if we don't get some answers, you're going to do a little cage time yourself. That about what you had in mind, Mr. Jones?"

The federal man nodded. "Where's the book, Mr. Riordan?"

Peek adjusted his desk lamp so the light shined in my face. He was trying to impress his fellow lawman with how many old movies he'd seen.

"I don't understand something here," I said. "Why do you care? She's an old woman. She'll be dead soon. Let her die in peace." I turned to Peek and added, "Doesn't it bother you that this guy is making such a big deal about an old lady with a broken hip?"

"No. Answer the question."

"I'll answer his if he'll answer mine."

The federal man spoke up. "That's all right, Commander. I'll answer his question and then he'll answer mine."

He circled around my chair and didn't speak again until he was directly behind me. I had to twist around to see him. The federal man looked mean in a tidy sort of way. He would have made a good bank branch manager.

"We don't care very much about Miss Romanov. We care about the book. It's illegal contraband and it belongs to the Soviet government. I don't approve of their methods, of course, but it belongs to them and I'm going to see that it is returned. This is a delicate situation—a diplomatic thing."

"But how much harm can one book do? He was just a boy and now he's dead. How can he harm anyone?"

The federal man circled some more and stopped in front of me. I thought I saw some worry in his face. "What boy?"

"Alexis Romanov. He wrote the book. You know that."

233

"And how did you know?"

I could have told him the truth, or some variation: that there was one page in English scribbled in a childish hand that mostly thanked America for the Buffalo Bill Wild West Show; that the grand duchess had told me sad and terrible things in her delirious rantings from seventy years ago; that I had figured it out for myself because I'm a great newsman, even if I'm only the editor and part-owner of the *Baranov Beacon*.

Instead I told him a lie so outrageous that he never suspected the truth, or any of its subtle variations: "I know Russian. I can't speak it very well. But I read it okay." To prove it, I rattled off some jibberish that sounded like the growling of an angry bear.

This made Peek pretty mad. "What are you, some kind of Communist?" he asked.

I ignored him. So did the federal man. "What does the book say?" Jones asked.

"It says watch out for spies, especially when the spies say they're on your side. Spies only care about other spies. That's what the book said. He was pretty smart for a little boy, even if he was a bleeder."

"Where's the book?" the federal man said.

"At the bottom of the river, I guess. Your friend Vladimir Chen put it there when he tried to blow us up."

"You're a goddamn liar," Jones said. "Where is it?"

I said I didn't know.

They asked me the same question in many different ways. Where'd you get the gold coins? What were you doing on Little Diomede? Who did you say wrote that book again? How come the one coin's got a hole in it? How come the other one's all dirty and burned? What about the Native priest, this Father Nick? The light gave me a headache and the chair hurt my back, but I still said I didn't know. After a couple of hours they decided that if I did know I wasn't going to say.

The official charge was accessory to a crime, although they weren't too clear on what the crime was—smuggling gold coins, I suppose. I called Rachel but our phone was disconnected. I called Lindy Sue. A sleepy man answered.

He sounded like an oil slick when he said she was indisposed.

"Tell her Pres Riordan is in the state trooper lockup again."

They put me in a cell across from Vladimir Chen. He looked good behind bars, like the star of a carnival freak show. He walked around his cage just as a lion would do—close to the walls and the bars, making his space as big as possible.

He ignored me for a while, so I laid down on my cot and looked at the ceiling, waiting for something to happen—waiting for Lindy Sue and hoping her husband had delivered my message. I pushed Rachel into the back closet of my mind where I hide all my other mistakes.

"You got the time?" Chen said. His voice was still, even and unaffected, as if jail was just a bad cold.

I said, "It's after eleven, but before midnight. You can hear the church bell every hour if you listen carefully."

He circled his cage some more. I said, "Aren't you going to a lot of trouble for nothing?"

He stopped in his tracks and looked at me. I wondered if the world looked different through angry Mongol eyes. "What do you mean by that?"

I told him that an old book and a dead boy couldn't do much harm to anyone. "He was just a sick kid who liked a cowboy circus. So what's the problem here?"

He answered but kept on circling his cage. "You're a journalist, aren't you?"

"That's right."

"Well, like most journalists you have a naive and simple-minded picture of the world. You see right and you see wrong and you see nothing in between. The fact is, that book could be very dangerous. The clockmaker killed all those pathetic Romanovs because Lenin told him to. Reading that book is like picking at a wound that's almost healed."

I let him circle some more before I asked the trickiest question of them all. "I can understand that. Maybe I don't even blame you. But why is Jones helping you? I always thought you people were on opposite sides of the fence—bitter enemies in a secret war and all that stuff."

I think he was going to answer me, but before he could we heard some distant music in the night. The bells of St. Cletus Catholic Church announced midnight with twelve muffled bongs.

Everything becomes interesting when you're trapped in a cage, everything deserves your undivided attention. At the sound of three, Chen stopped pacing and I drifted into that back closet of my mind where I stored all my mistakes.

I'd left the closet door open. All my old mistakes started to escape: Lindy Sue in the sand; leaving my mother alone and never looking for my father. If these mistakes ever escaped, they would torment me for the rest of my life. I'd better slam the closet door shut.

While I'd been thinking about old mistakes, Vladimir Chen had produced two thin wires and wrapped them around the top and the bottom of a section of bars. He put a spark to the wires. They smoked and flared like sparklers on the Fourth of July.

As the bells bonged twelve, he dived to the floor and rolled under the cot. The bong echoed for a while, then exploded into heat and light, then dark and quiet.

When I came to my senses, two members of the Baranov Fire Department were loading me onto a stretcher. My head hurt. They carried me through the rubble and smoke—past the neat hole Vladimir Chen had blown in his cage and past two paramedics who attended without much hope to the crumpled form of a state trooper spitting blood through a smile in her neck.

The firemen set me down in the parking lot at the feet of another state trooper who was more worried about his fallen friend than about me. Uniformed men and women rushed in and out of the station. I saw Byron Schiller and Ronda drive up in her station wagon. She took pictures while he interviewed witnesses for the lead story in the next day's edition of the *Beacon*. I hid my face in my sleeve so they wouldn't try to interview me. The trooper who was guarding me asked them for news. The news wasn't good. Stable but critical. Her brain wasn't getting any blood.

He had regained his composure by the time Lindy Sue Baker stomped up with a lot of hip and plenty of noise, her spike heels clacking against the pavement. She had mussed-up hair, a man's T-shirt on inside out and a piece of paper signed by the watch commander that said I should be released into her custody.

Chapter 32

MICHAEL AND CHENA WERE WAITING IN MY BIG RED monster pickup truck. They'd kept the engine running. Michael said, "Hey, Shorter-Than-I." Chena lay crumpled on the floor, dreaming of old dog heaven, as Lindy Sue and I climbed into the cab. The dog thought my bad foot was a rabbit, and scratched it with her paw. Lindy Sue rubbed her belly and Chena barked some sleepy thanks.

It was a clear, clean night with a big blue moon and a threat of winter in the wind. Michael kept a lookout for trooper squad cars as we drove toward Baranov. The moon followed us over the Kenai River bridge. Michael said, "Mumble garble hubba hubba?"

My ears were still ringing from the explosion. "What did you say?"

He repeated himself in a louder voice: "I said, what was all the trouble with the troopers about?"

I told him what had happened at the jail, that Vladimir Chen had blown a hole in his cell and slit the throat of a state trooper. Michael pushed a little harder on the gas. "We better get to the hospital, then. He'll go right after the Grand Lady."

When we turned right and headed for downtown Baranov, the moon hid behind some trees. Some more light came from the headlights of a car behind us.

"Slow down, Michael," I said.

Michael complained and then slowed down. So did the car behind us. Michael said, "I went to see the Grand Lady, but

238

the doctors wouldn't let me in. That asshole Peek's got a guard on her, like she's gonna run away, though she's almost dead already, I heard.''

The parking lot of Baranov Municipal Hospital was filled with dozens of Old Believers. Old babushkas and their bearded husbands and their strong children and their young grandchildren were keeping a silent vigil beneath the window where the grand duchess was recovering from surgery. Some of the men held torches. Others whispered among themselves or bowed their heads in prayer. One young woman who was as wide as she was tall knelt on the gravel and made the sign of the cross in the Old Believer way. Standing in their midst like Jesus Himself arisen from the dead was the Big Beluga. He waved at us, but we didn't stop to ask him how was he still alive. There'd be time enough for tall tales later.

We caused a commotion as we filed through the crowd to the hospital door. The praying stopped and the whispering got louder. One old man walked up to me and lowered his torch to illuminate our faces. It was the same man who had been in the bucket brigade when we fought the fire at Vygovskaia Pustyn. He said something that sounded like the growling of a bear: a thanks or a warning or a blessing or a curse or something else altogether. I couldn't tell by the look on his face, which was intense but otherwise inscrutable.

Some official types were gathered in the lobby—three doctors, four nurses, the borough mayor and Peek-A-Boo Pete. We heard them discussing the grand duchess and the crowd she had drawn to the hospital parking lot.

The mayor said, "Well, what do they want? Why don't you send them home?"

Peek answered, "I don't know. With the breakout and all I need more men if what you want is that I should . . . " He stopped in mid-excuse. I'd caught his eye. "Excuse me, Mr. Mayor, but I've got an asshole problem here. What do you want, Riordan?"

"I want to see her."

A tall doctor said that was impossible. She's in no condition to receive visitors.''

"But she wants to see me. I bet she's been calling for Alexis, right? Well that's me."

Peek said, "You're not Alexis." He turned to the mayor. "He's not Alexis. His name is Prester John Asshole Riordan."

"I know who he is," the mayor said. He should know. My newspaper had been impugning his motives on the issue of oil taxes. Byron Schiller said he'd kissed so much oil industry ass his breath smelled like gasoline.

I said, "But she thinks I'm her cousin Alexis. I don't know why. I think it's the polio. Her cousin used to limp sometimes."

Peek and the mayor and the doctors huddled in a corner. When they were done, Peek said, "Okay. You got five minutes. But I'll be right there with you. Miss Baker and the Fat Boy had better stay down here."

Her room smelled of flowers and antiseptic death. One tube went into her groin, another into her arm and a third into her nose. A machine made low beeps and a green glow. Her every breath sounded like her last, but she managed to take another.

"Alexis? Is that you? I'm sorry about the dirtball. I was aiming for Derevenko . . . but he ducked. . . . I didn't mean to make . . . you bleed. You bleed . . . so much. I'm sorry, Alexis. Alexis? Is that you?"

Peek said, "What was that? What did she say?"

I leaned over and touched her face. It looked like leather, but felt like pastry. I said, "I'm right here, Natasha. Can you hear me?"

She looked but didn't see. My mother said that if I cried too much as a child, I'd have no tears left for when I really needed them. Natasha reminded me of this. For almost ninety years, through two revolutions and two World Wars, through a civil war and the death of her captain lover, through famine and purges and Five-Year Plans, she had managed to save a single tear. Her parched eyes cried it now for Alexis and for me and for all the fucked-up children of the world.

"Give me . . . your book, Alexis. The Old Believers . . . will protect it. . . . My captain will . . . the Old Believers . . . I have some . . . gold . . . to get away. Bring the book to me

240

. . . bring me . . . Alexis? Is that you? The Americans will print . . . it . . . they print . . . everything because they never . . . "

Her voice trailed off into a scratchy wheeze. "What was that?" Peek asked. "What did she say?"

I said, "I don't know. She was talking in Russian."

Chapter 33

THE MOON MADE A HEAVY SHADOW OF REDOUBT VOLCANO while we waited for the tide to go out and listened to the water splash against the riprap barricade Father Nick had made from the trash that is our society's most enduring product.

Lindy Sue said, "They say it takes a billion years to turn the carton for a Big Mac back into something useful."

Michael said, "Oh, yeah?"

"Yeah. There's something about Styrofoam that nature doesn't like. It's not biodegradable."

Michael said, "I'm gonna do what Father Nick always did and the church won't have to pay me either. I'll collect lots of old stuff from all the Kenaitze Indians who believe in God the Russian way and throw it on the beach just like he did so the church won't wash into the sea."

The moon disappeared and the stars came out. Millions and billions and trillions of stars, each with a story to tell. I wondered if they all had as many good stories as our star had, if they all had estranged lovers and troubled fathers and angry brothers and would-be mothers and Texan lawyers and fat Natives and young princes who bleed too much and then get murdered by a clockmaker.

Michael said he didn't know, but figured things would get out of hand if every star was as crazy as ours. "I wouldn't mind seeing their TV, though. Cop shows with little green crooks and all. . . . Listen."

We listened but didn't hear anything. Michael said,

"That's what I mean. The tide's gone out or we could hear it splash around. Are you sure you want to do this?"

I said I was sure, but I wasn't. I was pretty sure. I think it happened like this: Father Nick is working by the bluff when Jon Jones comes along. The government man wants the book. He'll kill to get it. He beats Father Nick, but the archpriest won't talk and then he's dead. The government man puts the body in the driver's seat of the St. Alexander Nevsky pickup truck and sends it over the bluff. It crashes onto the beach. Andy Sacramentov's refrigerator is still in the back, so it crashes too. The tide rolls in and hides the crime for a while. The government man looks around but he can't find the book because when Father Nick saw the government man coming, he hid it in a special place. You can't find the hiding place unless you know Father Nick and remember the things that were important to him, remember that to Father Nick an old refrigerator was a valuable soldier in his never-ending battle with the never-ending tide.

Michael fetched rope and a flashlight from my big red monster pickup truck. He wrapped the rope around my waist and handed me the flashlight.

He said, "I mostly don't mind, but right now I wish I wasn't so fat. That's way I could climb down and you could pull me up. But now it'd be like you were trying to lift up a house, or something like that, if I went down there."

"Don't worry about it, okay?" I hate it when people worry about my polio leg. It gets all the sympathy.

"I mean it's not right that you two should climb down because you're crippled and she's a woman, but if anything goes wrong just holler or give me three flashes of the flashlight and I'll pull you both right back up."

I imagined Michael trying to pull me up the bluff with a rusty refrigerator door lodged under my chin. "But don't pull if we don't yell or flash the light, okay?"

It was a lot like fishing and we were the bait. I went first. Michael let out the line. The first few yards were hard and dry. Every time I banged against the bluff, some dirt and stones shook loose and tumbled onto the beach. The next few yards were wet and gooey. Every time I plopped against the bluff, some bluff stuck to me. This was the part the tides had touched.

The last few yards were slick and sharp. I landed in the

243

riprap, on a stove wedged between an old oil drum and a Ford convertible with fins that Wallace Dunwitty had donated to the cause. I pointed the light at the upholstery. It was peeled down to the rusty springs.

Michael reeled in the rope and tied it around Lindy Sue's waist. I scanned the rubble with the flashlight while he lowered her onto the beach. Old stoves, tired engines, broken bits of this and that. Anything that was too heavy to float away had been used in the construction of the barricade. The archpriest had sawed some telephone poles in half and driven them into the sand to make a rough picket fence to contain the stuff. Five or six little gullies had been made where, pebble by pebble, bit by bit, the salt water washed away the land Baranov was built on. Lindy Sue landed with a gentle grunt.

There's an art to everything. The art to walking/crawling/climbing over a riprap barricade made of Rust-Art America is to never take a step you can't take back. I learned this on my second step, which was made on a seemingly solid bit of stove. My crippled foot made a jagged hole in the stove and my leg brace followed it through.

"Oh you poor dear," Lindy Sue said. "Are you okay?"

If this had been my good leg, it would have gotten all cut up by the shards of rusty metal. As it was, my brace just scraped metal against rusty metal and I didn't even get a scratch. But there was no reason to tell Lindy Sue that. "I'm all right, really," I said, with some strain in my voice, as if I really weren't all right but brave as hell about it.

After that, I never took a step I couldn't take back. I advised Lindy Sue to do the same, and we soon perfected a sort of spider crawl designed to evenly distribute our weight over all four limbs. In this way we inched over a garbage can and around a length of chicken wire fence, slowly following the bobbing beam of the flashlight to the spot where the truck and the refrigerator had landed.

Michael screamed at the top of his lungs. "Hey, Shorter-Than-I! Are you okay?"

Lindy Sue screamed back in her shrillest yawl: "We're okay! We're okay! Don't pull on the rope until we tell you to, okay?"

Michael screamed okay. We moved in a crazy zigzag, over

the engine of a Cessna Wildcat and a dentist's chair that Dr. Ellis Franklin had donated to the church.

I flashed the light and we crawled on, around this, over that. I slipped a couple of times and a couple of times Lindy Sue's progress was impeded when the rope around her waist became snagged on bits of old junk.

Lindy Sue said, "Hey Pres, let's sit down for a second, okay? I need to talk to you."

I tested an old filing cabinet for strength while she wrapped her legs around a piece of heavy equipment—an oil drilling bit, I think it was. I shined the light on a patch of sand that had been stained red by the rusting metal.

"Look, I don't want to say this with Michael around, but your girl came to see me yesterday. I'm her lawyer now."

I wanted to make some smart remarks, but didn't. Lindy Sue continued: "I'm supposed to take care of selling the house and things like that. She gave me a letter to give to you. I took it to your office because I couldn't find a mailbox over by the gravel pit."

"And why is she talking to you? I mean, I would think you're the last person she wants to talk to, except for me, of course."

She thought about this for a while. "I don't know. Maybe she was curious. You really blew it. I told her there was nothing going on with us and at first she didn't believe me, but now I think she does. I think she's worried about you. She wants you to be okay."

"How was she? How did she seem?"

"Well, she's got the look."

"The look? What look is that?"

She didn't answer me. I shined the light in Lindy Sue's face. She turned her eyes away from me. "You don't know then, do you?"

"Know what? I don't know shit. If I knew anything, it wouldn't have happened. What are you talking about?"

She hemmed and hawed for about five minutes about how women are special and hate to grow old. When I asked her again about Rachel and "the look" she had, she tried to pin it on me. "You screwed up pretty bad."

"What're you saying? It's Barney, right? She's going to run off with Barney and have a bunch of children that smell like fish and wear tattoos."

"No, that's not it."

But before she could tell me what was it, Michael hollered down from the bluff. "Hey, Shorter-Than-I! Are you okay?"

Lindy Sue jumped at the chance to end our conversation. "We're okay. We're okay. I think we can see it now."

She dismounted the oil drilling bit and grabbed the sleeve of my shirt. "We better get going. Those goons are bound to figure out we're here if they didn't follow us from the hospital."

Andy Sacramentov's refrigerator reminded me of those old commercials: the luggage that gets thrown around by a gorilla; the watch that takes a licking and keeps on ticking; the twenty-five-year-old refrigerator that falls thirty feet with a truck on its back onto a scrap heap and then gets drenched with salt water. The truck had done half of a somersault, enough to turn all topsy-turvy, with the truck on topsy and the refrigerator turvy. The impact had crushed the cab of the truck and snapped its frame. The only marks on the refrigerator were a couple of dents and a loose piece of rubber molding that flapped in the wind.

"Hey, Short Man! Are you okay?"

The weak beam of the flashlight crawled along the bluff and found Michael's broad shadow. The shadow waved and shouted. "You better hurry up."

I tugged on the handle. The door popped open and let loose an avalanche of small stones which the archpriest had used for ballast so that the refrigerator wouldn't float away on the first outgoing tide.

Lindy Sue opened the freezer compartment and there it was: Father Nick had put the goods in a Tupperware tray made for leftover cake or leftover lasagna or leftover something that was square and flat and needed to be hermetically sealed.

I peeled back the airtight cover and rubbed the pages and counted the coins. The pages were intact and the coins were all there and at that's when it sunk in that Father Nick really was dead and impossible to replace. Who else but Father Nick would dare to battle the tides? Who else would think of using Tupperware?

Maybe Michael would. He was learning fast. He bellowed from above. "Hey! Shorter-Than-I! Are you okay? Are you okay?"

We were okay. I followed Lindy Sue and Lindy Sue followed the rope back to the spot where Michael had let us down. I held onto the Tupperware while Michael hauled her up. Then it was my turn. The first few yards were wet and sloppy. The next few were hard and crumbly. The last few were the toughest, because the tides had carved under a big overhang that I didn't notice on the way down. It stuck out like a fat lower lip. My feet dangled over nothing and I could hear Michael and Lindy Sue huff and puff as they pulled me up the last few yards. When I was safely up on solid ground, I hugged the earth and clutched the Tupperware and listened to Michael and Lindy Sue huff and puff some more. I huffed and puffed, too, until the starry night exploded into blinding light.

We were paralyzed for a moment, as happens to raccoons and groundhogs when they wander onto the highway late at night. The light came from the high beams of a car parked in the churchyard. A voice broke the spell. It was Vladimir Chen's. "Put it down at your feet and then walk away."

I was so confused that at first I didn't know what he was talking about. My first instinct was to step back. I almost stepped back over the bluff, but Michael caught me by the collar and said "Don't do it, Pres. Remember what the Grand Lady said."

I tried to remember what the grand duchess had said. She had said I should bring the book to her.

Another voice came out of the light. Jon Jones said in his lockjaw accent, "If you don't surrender that contraband, I'm going to have to kill you, Mr. Riordan. All in the line of duty, of course."

Michael stepped in his way. I looked around for Lindy Sue, but she had moved out of the light. I don't think they noticed she was gone. I said, "What duty is that, Mr. Jones? Who are you, anyway?"

I thought I heard him whisper, but it could have been the wind. All of a sudden, Chen charged out of the light. Michael leaned low and braced himself, but the Russian agent with the Mongol eyes faked right and moved left. Michael tackled air and tumbled into a blubbery fall.

I held onto the Tupperware as tightly as I could, but dropped it when Chen stunned me with a precise kick to the midsection that knocked the wind out of me. I rolled on the ground, gasping for air. My lungs felt as if they had been turned inside out. Chen picked up the Tupperware and waved it at the light. I heard him say, "Kill them now and let's get out—"

He choked on the "out—" His eyes popped wide and his mouth froze open. He was shocked and hurt and surprised and stunned. I didn't know why until I saw that a chromium-tipped dart had been planted deep in his ear, right up to the plastic feathers, which quickly became drenched with brain blood. Perfect shot. Bull's-eye. You're dead. It was the dart throw Michael had been working toward all his life, as easy as hustling cannery workers out of their paychecks. Like an elephant giving birth to a mosquito. Chen started to fall. I think he was dead before he hit the ground. The Tupperware slipped from his hands, bounced once and then tumbled over the bluff.

There was a long quiet, a second that seemed like an hour. The government man stepped into the light. His shotgun was drooping a bit, and his lockjaw seemed to slacken. He looked at Chen's body. At Michael. At the beach. He had two problems too many and he didn't know what to do. When I caught my breath, I gave him another problem to worry about.

"Where's the woman, Jones? Where do you think she went?"

I don't know what he thought about, but he thought about it quickly. He said to no one in particular, perhaps to his dead partner, "What'll happen now? Does Tupperware float?"

I said it did. Michael said it didn't. Jones jumped in his car and rushed away.

Lindy Sue arrived a few minutes later with a handful of state troopers, a busload of Old Believers and the Big Beluga. The river guide was wearing a peasant shirt. He made the sign of the cross with two fingers.

The toopers asked a lot of questions and made an outline of Vladimir Chen's body with some sort of white powder that reminded me of the batter's box at Wrigley Field. The Big Beluga and the Old Believers waited half of the day for the tide to go out, and spent the other half looking for the

Tupperware in the countless nooks and crannies of Father Nick's riprap barricade. They gave up the search when the tide came in.

I faked it. Lindy Sue said it would be okay.

"Alexis? Is that you?" the grand duchess said.

I said it was me. When she asked me to give her the book, I gave her a Tupperware box stuffed with loose sheets of nothing. She rubbed a page or two and smiled. "Whash aboo zee goo?" she said.

I didn't understand her, so I put my ear to her lips and asked her to say it again. Her breath was as thin as a shadow. "What about the gold?" she asked.

"I gave it to Michael. He's very poor."

I think she almost smiled. "You're a good boy, Alexis. When you are czar you must always remember the poor. They are Russia's . . ."

Russia's what?

She didn't say. She fell into a fitful sleep and died within the hour.

Chapter 34

WINTER BLEW DOWN FROM THE CHUGACH MOUNTAINS TO the flatlands by the sea. The dark came first. The days were gone in a blink. The first snow of the season was only an inch or so, but it covered everything: Thunder Road, the Kenai River Flats, and the bluff beneath St. Alexander Nevsky Church. It covered the gravel pit where Chena and I shivered in our lonely, snow-covered tent while waiting for something to happen and wondering what we should do if it didn't. I wrote it all down and showed it to Jack. He said, "I don't think so."

"Don't say that, Jack. It's a great story. It'll win you a Pulitzer prize."

Some publishers can be talked into a Pulitzer prize. Jack wasn't one of them. He said, "Let's go golfing and talk about it."

The first snow of the season had also covered the Baranov Municipal Golf Course, but Jack didn't seem to mind. We wore lots of layers and used red golf balls. Tee time was at sunrise, about 10:45 A.M., so we'd have enough time to finish our game before sunset, which happens right away in the winter.

Jack's tee shot was a hot bolt of red-hot matter roaring into the whiteness of space, mine an errant marble. My senior partner outlined his views while I thumbed through a Par Three in eight strokes. I was worried about the water traps, which were iced over and covered in snow, just like everything else.

"We can't afford a lawsuit, Pres. We used up our legal budget getting sued by that Old Believer with the Texan lawyer."

I had no hope that the decision would go my way, but labored through the motions anyway, like a punch-drunk fighter boxing with his past. "But what about Ivan Smolensk? He's in jail for a murder he didn't commit."

Jack thought about it while two-putting the first green. "I'll talk to the governor. He owes me one. I'm sure he'll grant some kind of pardon since it seems pretty clear that Ivan didn't kill anybody. They'll pin it on that dead biker from Nikiski and the case'll be closed. You can write a story about that if you want. But I don't want to hear anything about secret agents or shit like that. Peek-A-Boo Pete says what you wrote never happened, and I think he should know because that's his job."

The words "Dead Biker From Nikiski" had become a sort of prayer ever since Peek turned his flashlight on Vladimir Chen's ear and saw Michael's dart buried in it up to the wings. The first thing Peek said was "Helluva shot, Michael." The second was "Looks like a biker. He must be from Nikiski."

The second hole was a Par Four dogleg, but I couldn't tell. It all looked like winter to me. I said, "What about the *Pugachev?* You can't let that go by."

Jack said, "Peek says there's no evidence and he says that nobody filed a complaint about a missing person or a dead person or a boat that blew up or anything else. The Old Believers aren't talking and if they don't talk there is no criminal case which means there is no story because we can't afford to get sued. You want to know what Peek said?"

I tried to crush my golf ball but sliced it instead, right at Myrtle's cabin, from which billowed a cozy cloud of woodstove smoke. I started after it. Jack said, "I wouldn't do that if I were you. Myrtle might think you're a moose and shoot you for freezer meat."

"Tell me what Peek said."

I walked slowly, so he'd have time to do so. "Peek doesn't know where the biker came from because he doesn't have papers and his prints aren't in the FBI files. All he had with him that made sense was an old gold coin made in Russia engraved with the picture of some dead czar. Peek figures

251

the stories are right about how the Old Believers have a mountain of gold somewhere—coins like this and other valuable stuff. Peek figures that this Dead Biker From Nikiski found out about it and tried to make them give up the gold by killing all these Yermaks—Boris and Fedor—and the people in the *Pugachev*, if you still insist there ever was a boat like that. Peek figures the Yermaks can't file a criminal complaint about the murders or anything else because they're smuggling gold into the country, just like the customs man said, and they know they'd go to jail if they ever told the truth. Those people must be pretty tough if they'd rather be dead than poor.''

He stopped at an invisible line where the golf course ended and Myrtle Sheppard's homestead began. I skipped over the invisible line and kept on walking. Maybe Myrtle would get out her shotgun and put me out of my misery. Her dog barked a lot, and she watched from her window as I took a five iron to my red Tru-Flite. Three strokes later I was back on the fairway. "Okay, Jack, there is no story. Nothing ever happened, but I want out. I can't spend the winter in a gravel pit, and I can't see staying here now that Rachel's gone.''

Rachel's letter was buried in the mess that had collected on my desk since I went to Little Diomede. She'd typed it on our home computer.

Dear Pres,

I'm sorry I left, but I had to. I love you and it wouldn't be fair. I'm going to have a baby. You are too, if you want one. Remember when we were driving to Homer that day and I said I was going to have a baby? What I should have said is, *I'm going to have a baby* because I went off the pill about four months ago. I shouldn't have done that without asking you, but you're a real asshole for what you did to me and mostly for what you didn't do, which was agree with me on the baby situation.

Anyway, you're off the hook, like the biggest fish that ever got away. If you want to get on the hook again, you'll have to come and find me but don't wait forever because I'm starting to get old. The reason I'm going away like this is because that's the only way I'll ever know for sure how you really feel about me and the baby.

Love, Rachel

Jack made it easy for me. He bought all my stock for $40,000 and threw in a two-month's severance bonus. With my share of the money from the sale of the house and a small loan from the Alaska Industrial Development Administration, it was enough money for me to buy a big part of a little radio station in the Matannska Valley. I would do my penance there and then go look for Rachel, which is another story altogether. In the meantime I try to imagine what the tides that Father Nick labored against are doing to a Tupperware box. I imagine it washing up on a hot summer beach where dark-brown white people gather to play, people who have never heard of Alexis Romanov and couldn't care less that he lived and died seventy years ago and thought enough about it to write it all down. Tupperware floats, you know.